WATCH DOGS®
STARS & STRIPES

"After a dangerous high-speed chase late last night, authorities are reporting that Aiden Pearce, better known as Chicago's Vigilante, is dead today after police cornered the notorious hacker and domestic terrorist. More on this later…"

The screen returned to black glass.

"What's it like being dead, Aiden?"

He blinked at the woman's digital eyes. "Same way it's felt the last two decades."

"This can be a fresh start for you. No more running and hiding. Don't you want a chance at a normal life – keep all your freedoms and avoid a jail sentence? Retire in peace."

"Everyone already thought I was dead, so your little piece won't make any kind of waves where it matters. You've got nothing to offer me. All I have to do is figure a way out of this current problem. Then, I'll be a ghost. You won't get a second chance at me."

ALSO AVAILABLE

ASSASSIN'S CREED®
The Ming Storm by Yan Leisheng

ASSASSIN'S CREED® VALHALLA
Geirmund's Saga by Matthew J Kirby
Sword of the White Horse by Elsa Sjunneson

TOM CLANCY'S THE DIVISION®
Recruited by Thomas Parrott

TOM CLANCY'S SPLINTER CELL®
Firewall by James Swallow

WATCH DOGS® LEGION
Day Zero by James Swallow & Josh Reynolds

BASED ON A UBISOFT CREATION

WATCH DOGS®

STARS & STRIPES

Sean Grigsby &
Stewart Hotston

ACONYTE

First published by Aconyte Books in 2022

ISBN 978 1 83908 126 2

Ebook ISBN 978 1 83908 127 9

Cover art by Martín M Barbudo

Distributed in North America by Simon & Schuster Inc, New York, USA

Printed in the United States of America

9 8 7 6 5 4 3 2 1

ACONYTE BOOKS

An imprint of Asmodee Entertainment Ltd

Mercury House, Shipstones Business Centre

North Gate, Nottingham NG7 7FN, UK

aconytebooks.com // twitter.com/aconytebooks

CHAPTER ONE

Baltimore.

The forty-fifth floor of a new skyscraper, dubbed the Peppercorn Building.

CTO Trevor Erins stood outside his corner office. He was on the phone, talking in the kind of voice meant for everyone to hear him, so they could ascertain just how important he was, and how they should shut the fuck up and listen while he changed the world. After all, thought Trevor, it might make their lives more interesting.

"I'm telling you, Karen, it's a win-win. It would help if you picked up my call. You're supposed to be available *at all hours*." The Optik at his ear automatically sent a signal to his office door, opening it as if an invisible servant stood on the other side, and Trevor charged through without even noticing. New tech from London of all places. Trevor liked being the only one to have something like it on this side of the pond.

It was dark and lonely on the forty-fifth floor, but Trevor liked it that way. It didn't stop the way he talked. He got more done at night when the bumbling morons who thought they ran the company were at home in bed or jerking off to porn while their partners slept. The day was for managing them, keeping them focused, but the night was for real work. A quick bump of high-grade sugar and Trevor was blasting off till four or five in the morning, then he'd catch a few blinks before becoming Daytime Trevor.

Boring, Public Trevor.

A narrow band of light lit up the office where he walked, and then blinked dark as he passed. He liked it that way, too. He wondered if Karen was on the other line in some brightly lit restaurant in Chicago, ignoring him. Then he remembered he hadn't cared enough to ask since they last spoke. Most likely, she'd be moaning about him to the CFO, but neither of them would do anything because without him they'd be toast and they all knew it.

"Call me in the morning when you have the right answer," Trevor said. "I'll be up."

A dark, buzzing shape sped across the floor, catching Trevor's foot the moment he ended his call and sending him head over heels, mind whirling and arms flailing. He hit his head on the edge of the desk. A flash of light exploded in his eyes, and he dropped onto the dark mahogany floor.

I've only just had that installed from Chile, he thought blurrily. The incredible cost of importing it, the thing he was most proud of, blinked through his mind. Had he damaged it?

He hoped he wasn't bleeding. It would be a nightmare to have the floor cleaned – the carpenters hadn't had a chance to seal it yet, and blood would soak right in like coffee or grease.

His vision was foggy, but the office lights brightened in response to his presence and movement. Soon, the room came into focus. As Trevor got to his hands and knees, breathing in short gulps, small lines of warmth ran from his recently restored hairline down into his eye.

Trevor wiped it away with his fingers, only just stopping from rubbing it onto the floor at the last moment.

Sure enough. Blood. He cursed whatever had tripped him. There was always something trying to make his life harder than it should be. This felt like a Daytime Trevor problem, not something Nighttime Trevor should have to deal with.

His Haum robot vacuum was bumping into the far corner by the windows like an angry bull, damaging the new paintwork. Glossy and black, the sheen reflected the office lights like a beetle shell. He realized he'd been assaulted by the stupidest member of the office.

"What the hell?" he murmured.

What on earth was it doing? Who knew it could move as fast as his Papavero sports car parked downstairs? Fucking technology, he thought, finding the humor in what had happened.

If it could go wrong, it would. There was a law about it. He was reminded all over again that being CTO of Peppercorn Unlimited didn't mean he was immune to the vagaries of technology, just that he had people who were supposed to insulate him from such bullshit.

"We are going to sue the living fuck out of Haum," Trevor growled as he placed a hand to the still bleeding gash in his head. It stung, but he managed a laugh as he took a selfie to record the injury for the lawyers. "Almost worth it."

He grabbed the edge of his desk and staggered as he got to his feet. "Samantha, call my lawyer," he commanded.

"I'm afraid I can't do that, Trevor."

Samantha was his smart device, a glorified speaker mostly used for food delivery and to remind him of unavoidable appointments. Her voice was feminine and cold. It sounded that way because he liked the clinical inflection. He'd set it to never use his name, though. Maybe the whole network was acting up?

"What… Samantha, open settings." Trevor's head throbbed. Maybe the fall had been worse than he'd thought. It felt like a spike had been buried in his temple. His knees felt weak, and he kept his hands on his desk to stay upright. "Restore to factory." He started to sidle around the edge of the desk to get to his seat.

"You're not leaving this room," Samantha said.

His office door swung shut. The lock clicked into place with the deep bass of powerful electromagnets coming online. Panicked, Trevor stumbled across the room and grabbed the handle, but it wouldn't budge. Pulling off his suit jacket, he wadded it up and used it to protect his hands as he jerked and shoved at the handle. He put all his weight into it and succeeded in moving it precisely nowhere.

The lights in the room, from those in the ceiling to the low energy bulbs screwed into the Edison lamp on his desk, brightened further, until he felt the sun was in the room. Trevor let go of the door and turned to gawk at the supernova blooming in his office. He raised a hand to shield his eyes from the light, wincing in confusion.

Every bulb exploded.

Trevor threw himself to the floor. Glass shattered into every corner of the room. The only light came from the streets far below, a soft glow of white and yellow doing nothing more than highlighting the blackened shapes of his furniture.

I locked it down, he thought. I always lock it down. Any time he left his office – even for a quick piss or to watch the apartment windows next door with his binoculars – he always set his devices to lock when his face wasn't there to be continually scanned.

Someone was fucking with him. It was the only explanation. The robot, his office door shutting on its own, the lights, and now his digital assistant.

It's all connected, he thought.

Trevor got to his feet, the door at his back. He was dizzy but shook the glass from his arms, legs, and back. Picked at the shards in his hair.

Then he yelped as his earpiece screeched at a head-splitting pitch, the VR covering his vision with green and white static. He ripped the Optik from his head and tossed it against the window.

"All right, you slimy pricks," Trevor snarled at the empty room. He wanted to hit something, someone. He knew what this was. He was being hacked. Their head of security would find they'd never work again by the time he was done with them.

"What the fuck do you want from me? I know a fixer when I see one! You think you can fuck with me? You have no idea."

"But you can't see me from over there, Trevor." Not Samantha speaking this time. It was a man's voice. "Come on over and let's have a conversation."

Trevor blinked in the gloom.

Who did this sonofabitch think he was? Trevor could have a dozen fixers bag and tag this guy before sunrise. He just had to get out of the office, had to get somewhere he could trust the communications and the network.

Rather than head toward the window, Trevor took a step toward his desk.

"But be careful," the voice said. "You might stumble in the dark."

The thought was scary enough to enrage Trevor. He ran through the dark and swung around to the other side of his desk. He bent over to shove his face into the screens, which hung there in empty space, the tiny projectors embedded in his desk. He had just the man in mind to make this one suffer.

"Here I am, you ugly mother…"

Trevor Erins stumbled backwards and fell into his chair when he saw the face staring back at him.

"Go on, Trevor. I'd love to hear the rest of that sentence." The man staring back at him wore a dark baseball cap with some crisscross triangular symbol. Everything below his eyes was covered by a mask with yet another symbol. It didn't matter. Trevor knew exactly who he was looking at. After all, he'd hired the Fox a month before, just before Christmas to catch a whistleblower, who thought they could steal company secrets and try to blackmail Trevor with them.

He couldn't remember the exact details. The moment he'd hired the face in front of him he'd done his best to forget it. There was no forgetting Aiden Pearce. The broker who'd introduced them also called him the Vigilante. Trevor had worried it meant the man had a conscience, but the broker assured him that wasn't the case, that it was a nickname earned a long time ago in Chicago. Trevor hadn't cared – as long as the fixer did what he was told.

They'd never met, just talked like this, those eyes measuring him.

Those same disturbing green eyes peered out at him from between the cap and the mask.

"You? What do you want?" Trevor felt simultaneously cold and hot. Frying and sweating and bleeding, but somehow still chilled to bone. "I paid you for the work you did," he spluttered defensively.

"Yes, you did," Pearce said. "Paid in full." It sounded to Trevor as if Pearce cared for money as much as Trevor cared for other people. It stopped him from offering the man more to go away and leave him alone. It made him angry. Why couldn't people be relied upon? Why weren't their prices clear?

Pearce's masked face filled the other screens. The wrinkles at his eyes told a story of age and violence. A seasoned predator. The Vigilante could have been talking to him from anywhere in the world right then, and the distance wouldn't have stopped Pearce from getting to Trevor.

Worse yet, he could be waiting there on the forty-fifth floor of the Peppercorn Building.

"Honestly," Pearce said, "I was thankful for the job. It was a nice break, not having to kill anybody. But like you said: that contract is old news even if it was bogus."

This is something new, thought Trevor, curiosity picking at the edges of his fear.

"You're pulling a double-cross, huh? Didn't deal with my whistleblower at all. You lied to me." Trevor tried to sound calm, defiant, though his hands shook, and he'd long forgotten to wipe away the blood leaking into his eyes. Trevor pulled himself forward in the wheeled chair, pedaling his feet along the floor. "Is that it, Pearce? Pretend to work for me then turn around and join up with my enemies? Smart business sense.

Can't blame you. Not one bit. But I never did shit to you, man. Don't you have any honor?"

Pearce's wrinkles deepened. His cheeks under the mask lifted a bit. Was he smiling?

"Honor is a fluid thing," Pearce said casually. "Every person on the planet has their own version of it. Believe me. I've listened in. Honor changes with the wind. I don't go in for it. The whole concept seems too much like a set of rules designed to let me do what I want, especially when said rules can change on a whim, and you know what? I decided a long time ago to do what I want without needing to explain myself to anyone.

"If this had been a few years ago, I wouldn't have wasted time talking to you. I would have had your vacuum finish you off. And then I'd burn down your office with your smart bulbs."

Trevor looked at the busted lamps, and then at the glowing green light on the Haum robot, still banging itself into the corner. No way in hell would he have let a goddamned appliance take him out. If he was going to be killed, he'd rather look his murderer in the face. At least… that's what he'd always told himself when he thought of his dealings south of the border.

Thing was, he was having a hard time looking at Pearce's eyes. His mouth was about as high as he could bring his gaze.

Trevor crawled out of the chair and stood, the better to argue with Pearce. The chair's wheels squeaked as it rolled away. The robot vacuum continued to bump into the corner. *Thunk, thunk, thunk.*

"And what's stopping you?"

"It would be too easy," Pearce said. "Too merciful."

Trevor laughed. He laughed all the way to the far corner of the room where he raised a foot and stomped on the vacuum as it bumped into the corner windows. Pieces of casing and wires and springs flew everywhere as its shell cracked open. Standing there, leaning on the wall gasping, he regretted wasting energy he could have put to better use even if it had felt good to remind Pearce who was in control.

"What do you want?" Trevor asked. Blood and sweat dripped from his face. He no longer cared about his Chilean floor.

Aiden Pearce spoke. "I check out any potential employer before I agree to accept a fix. No one's completely clean, but some people, some jobs, are far easier to swallow than others. Usually, when I don't like what I see I walk away. For you, though, I decided you needed schooling. So, I took your money and hid your whistleblower, and now I'm here for you."

"I'm cleaner than anyone," Trevor said, with too much pride.

"You only say that because you think you're brilliant at hiding what you've done." Pearce's face came closer to the camera. "But I'm meticulous at lifting the carpets and turning over the rocks others ignore. It's why you hired me in the first place."

The monitor screens changed. Instead of Pearce's death stare, they showed emails, files, and pictures. It went from one piece of incriminating evidence to another, slow enough to recognize, but fast enough to show the vast amount Pearce had been able to collect.

He had everything. Every morsel Trevor had believed was destroyed or hidden or safe. How had he done this?

Audio clips played in a mishmash of recorded phone calls and live recordings Trevor hadn't been aware of when he'd spoken the words. He recognized his own voice. But there were others, some voices that wouldn't speak again. He knew because he'd been there to see them silenced.

The screens went blank.

Aiden Pearce appeared again. "All of this is going to tell the feds a very clear story."

Now it was serious.

"Hold on, Pearce! This is–"

"Shut your mouth, Trevor," Aiden said calmly. "What I'm saying will help you decide what you're going to do next."

For the first time in his life, Trevor resisted the urge to speak over someone else.

"Good boy," Aiden said. "The story is this: aside from vanilla money laundering, the textbook corporate sabotage, the demented things you look at online between jaunts at whatever it is you call work… none of that gets you off like it used to, does it? Neither does the standard sleaze of your comfortable corporate gig. We both know where it gets sticky. You got into bed with the Mexican cartels. They pressured all those small towns into letting Peppercorn set up shop. Factories. Cheap labor. Saved your company a lot of money… that they kicked back to you. In return, you gave the cartels cloaking tech. Dodging the border patrol, that's impressive, a veritable arms race between the government and the cartels. Thanks to you, your friends can go back and forth with their drug mules anytime they want at a scale no one's begun to guess at. But it gets worse…"

"You don't have to go through all this," Trevor said. "I know what I've done. Just get to the damn point!"

"Every convict goes through a trial before sentencing," Pearce said. "What I never could understand was why you inserted yourself into these drug mules' lives. You obviously didn't care for their wellbeing. You said it was business. But why did you ask to call them? To speak with them? I think this was like a soap opera to you. A real-life VR experience."

Was that it? Trevor thought, trying not to grin at how mundane it all was. Who doesn't love an escape? He'd enjoyed talking to them, promising them something better, watching the hope in their eyes.

"You promised these people you'd personally see that they'd be given citizenship, housing, and even a job once they completed their work for the cartels. I'm sure most of them knew you were full of shit. Your Spanish is terrible. I don't think it mattered to you."

Trevor swallowed.

Pearce's gaze had him locked in place. "You lied to them. As soon as they were free of the cartels, asleep in a motel on this side of the line, you called ICE to round them up. You know, I followed up on one of the mules you betrayed. He was a kid. Thirteen years old. Died in custody. Asphyxiation. Have you ever been choked, Trevor?"

Trevor shook his head, slowly. He imagined Pearce's hands around his throat, and no matter how hard he tried, couldn't shake the image.

"The other victims were detained, abused, starved, and then deported, where your cartel friends grabbed them again and ensured they joined their families in unmarked holes in the ground. *That* is why I'm here."

Trevor walked to his chair, wheeled it over to his desk, and sat. "How much?"

"A long time," Pearce said.

Using the back of his sleeves, Trevor wiped away the blood in his eye. "Is the connection bad, Pearce? Did you not understand what I said? I asked how much money you wanted, you blackmailing sonofabitch." He knew it was a mistake, but it was the only road he knew how to travel.

"No, Trevor. You're the one who doesn't understand. I don't want your money." Pearce looked briefly to the side. "Although, your personal funds have been transferred to those who survived your interventions. At least, those of them I could find."

"You didn't!" Trevor grabbed the top of his desk.

"I absolutely did," Pearce said. "I'm going to let the government raid your company's holdings. And I do mean everything. Peppercorn is no more. And this way it'll be more public, more newsworthy. Everything I just played for you will be getting the shotgun treatment. It's going everywhere. Within twenty-four hours, you'll be arrested. Cameras, SUVs outside the office, the walk of shame. Then you'll be tried and found guilty, especially as the company won't have the money to pay for your normal set of lawyers. I hope you look better in orange than you do in that sweaty three-piece suit."

Trevor clasped his hands together, as if begging, as if in prayer. He leaned his head against the desk. This couldn't be happening. He'd been so careful, so quiet. Feelings of loathing swept over him. He'd fucked up, he'd let it become more than work. It had been a craving for something like the rush of the drugs he used to keep going, and once he'd had it, he just couldn't help it.

Even there, bleeding in his office, Trevor Erins thought sending those bastards back across the border, the hope guttering in their faces as they realized what was happening, was the only thing that'd ever made him smile.

Wait. Pearce had said something before, something he'd not paid attention to.

"Another option," Trevor said aloud. He looked back to the man on the screen. "You said 'a long time.' Pearce, I swear, if you let me go, I'll disappear. No one will ever hear from me again. Please. I'll take that option."

"Oh, you don't go free," said Pearce. As he spoke, the air conditioning units started to smoke. Air rushed around the room.

Pearce stared at Trevor.

"You can't be serious," Trevor said. The open window felt like a cocked and loaded revolver.

"You have a choice," Pearce said. "Face up to what you did, suffer the consequences, or you can try to escape. The building is on fire, in case you hadn't noticed. You've got about thirty seconds to decide before getting downstairs becomes… difficult."

The remaining screen went blank. Pearce was gone. But the momentary relief of being alone in his office was short-lived.

"Pearce?" Trevor called out, alone with his thoughts. Nothing. "Aiden! You can't. Pearce!"

The CTO's desperate scream didn't reach Aiden Pearce as he stood across from the Peppercorn Building. However, about a minute later the CTO stumbled from the building, face a mask of fear and body a marionette playing out motions his mind wasn't directing.

Satisfied Trevor wasn't about to make a bid for freedom, Aiden walked over.

"You're done, but you're alive. It's more than you gave your victims, Erins. In the years to come, when you think you're undeserving of your fate, remember they never got a chance to choose."

Aiden turned away and shoved his hands into his coat pockets as he walked down the street.

Trevor Erins wouldn't be needing his Papavero anymore. The car sat ready and rumbling on the block's corner. He pulled the mask from his face.

He reached for the Papavero's door handle but stopped when he heard several vehicles approaching from behind. They were moving fast. Breaking the law, chased by police.

Black SUVS. Four of them. They sped toward him down Charles Street. Aiden stood slack with surprise. Then he saw three more racing to meet him down the street to his left.

They weren't using sirens, and they were too early to be there for Trevor.

They're coming for me, he thought.

CHAPTER TWO

The Papavero hit sixty miles per hour in less than two seconds. Pressed into the seat, Aiden savored the thrill of it.

Turning hard at the next corner, the back end of the car tapped a traffic pole, and it was all he could do to stop it from spinning out. With both hands on the wheel, he corrected the jerking tires.

Pedestrians weren't a problem this late, but a man sleeping on a bench scrambled to his feet as Aiden zipped by. Aiden saw him in the rearview, arms raised, two fingers swinging in his direction. Silhouetted by the trailing SUVs, the man turned to give them the same message, but they ignored him too. They sped past, and while he wandered out into the street in their wake, the four SUVs split off, two to the right and two to the left.

Fixers? Aiden thought. Given how stupefied Trevor had been, it wasn't an ambush set up by the CTO. Other than him, Aiden wasn't sure what he'd done recently that might bring them out in such force. This felt different, and not just because they were trying to flank him.

A T-bone surprise, he realized. But at which intersection?

He grabbed at his earpiece, linked as it was to the phone in his front pants pocket.

There was a steam pipe buried under the street, just ahead at East Pratt and South President. It was the perfect stretch of road for the fixers to try to crunch him to a pulp. Aiden linked to the steam pipe, happy to turn the tables by blowing the pressure right under them.

He used the hand brake to slide left onto South President as two of the SUVs appeared on his right. One of the fixer vehicles behind Aiden couldn't turn in time. It continued forward and crashed through the glass frontage of a global coffee place. Ignoring a red light, the two failing to flank Aiden crossed into the other lane.

Aiden saw it through the rearview and tapped his finger against his earpiece.

The steam pipe burst, ripping through the asphalt and filling the intersection with a thick, boiling white cloud and chunks of concrete. One of the SUVs swerved to the left, crunching into a line of parked cars, while the other skidded, almost on the verge of rolling over, before landing back on its wheels and promptly smashing straight into a concrete post.

Which still left four of them: the two he could see behind him, and the two who'd disappeared earlier. That T-bone was still on the cards.

A bright spotlight from above slashed across his vision, followed by the whoop of a helicopter. He turned down the sunshade to keep from being dazzled.

"Just who did I piss off?" Aiden asked aloud. The timing with Erins was suspect, but it was clear they were after Aiden, not his previous target. Either way, the police would be on them soon. If he could draw this out until law enforcement arrived, he'd be fine. Sort of. The fixers would back off and he could make his escape, regroup, and figure out just what the hell was going on.

He turned again, missed the corner, and smashed through a restaurant's patio section, the back end of the Papavero swinging around, tires screeching, as he aimed for the road. Aiden hissed as he bumped up and down in his seat and told himself to concentrate.

The helicopter stayed right over him. He used his profiler to scan local police frequencies. They came up with empty static. The SUVs hadn't been using blue lights. They hadn't shot at him. They hadn't even tried communicating.

Not cops. Not fixers. The conclusion did not improve his mood.

The two missing SUVs appeared ahead, keeping pace with each other side by side, blocking Aiden from continuing straight on. With no choice, he readied to turn again, then noticed a large construction crane rising from a cordoned lot.

Aiden didn't turn. The SUV on his right wavered before returning to formation. The other driver accelerated. Aiden felt time slow, and for a second, considered the possibility he'd lose this game of chicken. The Papavero would crumple like paper if he collided with the SUVs, and both sides knew it.

But the crane, still holding a large metal container, swung out from the construction site, exactly how Aiden had told it to. It was a good thing the SUV had accelerated because Aiden's timing was off. The metal crate slammed into one of the SUVs, crashing it into the other, sweeping both cars from his path.

The helicopter highlighted the scene with its spotlight before turning to keep pace with him.

Aiden sent a disruption signal to the bird. Whoever was flying it had countermeasures at the ready. After a moment, its lights went out, but then the bird came back online, jerking upwards as the pilot wrestled to keep it under control. It was enough of a warning that the chopper pulled back into the sky, disappearing from view.

This kind of mayhem doesn't go unnoticed, he thought. Whoever was coming after him had to know they would be making headlines on the morning news.

Yet they didn't seem to care. Which meant it was government. Men in suits of the black ops variety.

Shit, he thought, checking his mirror again.

Two SUVs left. He knew he had to ditch them as soon as possible. As if reading his mind, they kept the distance between them to two car lengths.

He put a call out to the broker who'd found him this job in the first place. It went straight to messages.

"Damn it, Jordi. Pick up. Someone's after me." He tried another three times, but Jordi remained nothing more than a voice on an answering service. Jordi should have been on the other end of his phone waiting for Aiden to confirm the job was done – however it turned out. For him to be MIA stank of collusion with the feds on his tail. Had Jordi sold him out? Fucking likely. Aiden scowled. It was always a risk to trust Jordi Chin.

The two SUVs were no longer behind him when he checked the rearview. One appeared alongside the driver's side window. Its glass was tinted too dark to see inside. With a sudden jerk, the vehicle slammed into Aiden's Papavero, forcing him to turn right. The other SUV charged from the other side. Aiden turned once again, but this time to the left, edging ahead of the SUV and careening down Madison.

A public bus was stopped ahead, and the driver was outside, helping an elderly woman to her door. The destination board read "Out of Service."

Perfect, he thought.

Aiden tapped his smartphone, hacked into the bus, and sent it screeching in reverse, leaving the driver staring befuddled as his vehicle abandoned him on the sidewalk. As the SUVs chasing him swerved to avoid the bus, Aiden turned it sideways, and he squeezed around its front end at the last second. The drivers slammed on the brakes and the SUVs crunched up against the side of the bus, their hoods crumpling like soda cans and leaving them trapped on the wrong side of the wreckage.

Aiden slowed as he searched for a place to park and hide. Still no police. It was too good to be true. Regardless, he spotted a garage door at the base of an old factory building. He'd wait there until things were cool enough that he could get the hell out of Maryland.

What really bothered him was Jordi. Where the hell was he?

He remotely opened the garage and eased the Papavero through.

Before he could bring the door down behind him, the helicopter's spotlight illuminated the entrance and new SUVs skidded in behind him, pushing up against the back of the Papavero and forcing him deeper into the garage.

Aiden pulled his pistol from the glove compartment and

readied to get out when he saw the blue lights come on, one set for each SUV.

Someone spoke into a loudspeaker, a gruff, male voice. "Exit the vehicle."

Aiden went still. His beard itched, but he kept his hands where they were: one on his lap cradling the pistol and the other on the gear shift. It was hard to focus on anything besides the blue lights, but he scoped out what he could of the factory. There were chains and hooks and a conveyor belt ahead. Nothing he could use. He let his VR outline the edges of the space, showing the single exit at the far end of the room. The garage door was the only thing connected to the wider world. Everything else was old school. He had nothing to hack, no advantage to be wrung out of the situation. Which was fine – he'd normally shoot his way out. Except there he was, facing the wrong way with at least eight agents pointing guns at his back.

There's always a way out, he thought.

"You have ten seconds," came the voice.

His 1911 pistol itched in his hand. He'd slung the SMG in the trunk.

Without moving, he checked the rearview and confirmed the lack of the Baltimore Police Department seal. Not on their armor, not on their SUVs. Maybe they showed the blues only to have him calm the fuck down. As Aiden considered his options, the car jolted when one of the SUVs pushed him even further into the garage. The garage door closed behind them, sealing him in with whoever was trying to take him down.

"Aiden Pearce," the man at the loudspeaker said. "Don't make this easy for us."

Interesting way to put it. Aiden shifted the gear to park.

"Now get out of the car."

Aiden searched for the speaker. There were a lot of people pointing guns his way, and none of them had a microphone to their lips. Nothing he could pick up and use to his advantage. He opened the door slowly, not willing to give them any excuse to shoot.

"Turn the vehicle off first."

They were adding commands to the list. That never boded well.

Aiden killed the engine.

"Open your network."

Aiden hesitated.

"Now."

Aiden gave the command to connect to the public network and lowered most of his security protocols but deactivated his profiler – there was no way he was giving them access to his most precious piece of code. There was enough of an opening to give them the sense he was surrendering but not enough to allow them to barge into his safe space and ruin his life. Not yet, at least.

"Step out slowly with your hands above your head."

There were no more commands after that. Sure, Aiden could step out, wielding his pistol and do as much damage as possible before being riddled with assault fire, but after all this time, what a waste. So Aiden left the 1911 on the seat and did as they asked while his mind raced for a solution, a way to break through. But this wasn't a puzzle. He hadn't prepared for it. It was a trap. He realized it as he watched four people in heavy ceramic armor and masks approach and place his hands behind his back.

In his head he saw them access his network like red flies buzzing about his space before it was shut down and he was as electronically isolated as the day he'd been born.

They forced him to his knees, slapped the cap from his head, forced his coat from his shoulders, and emptied his coat pockets. When the handcuffs closed around his wrists Aiden knew it was over. There was no way out. Fatal error. 404. They'd nabbed him, and he'd let them do it.

"Put him in the back with the other asshole," someone said.

Two of them lifted Aiden to his feet by his armpits as the others got to work ripping open the Papavero. He shook his head. No way to treat a work of art.

The cop to Aiden's left kicked him in the calf just below his knee. Aiden stumbled, but the same guy held him up by the arm. "You killed friends of mine."

Aiden stood straight and glared at the man. His mouth filled with words. They'd still be alive if they hadn't gotten in his way. They could have just called him, asked him nicely. Instead, they'd gone straight to high-speed pursuit and assault rifles. Aiden turned to keep walking toward the SUV they'd intended to shove him into without saying anything.

"I was really rooting for you to escape," a familiar voice said. Jordi Chin stepped out from the left-side passenger seat. "But if they nabbed me, it was obvious they were going to get you too."

Jordi wore the same type of light gray suit he always did. But he'd changed the shirt from his beloved red to a deep blue with sharp collars. White streaks threaded through his goatee.

Aiden stopped walking. "What did you do, Jordi?"

"Buddy," Jordi said. He looked worried. Jordi never looked

worried. "Trust me, the next time I decide to screw you over, I won't use the United States government." He looked around at those detaining them. "Then again, maybe I will."

CHAPTER THREE

The last time they'd seen each other in the flesh, nearly seventeen years prior, Aiden had thrown Jordi over the railing of a lighthouse in Chicago. It could have ended there, or later with a bullet between Jordi's eyebrows. Hell, Jordi had had his chances to kill Aiden, and they both knew it. Somehow neither of them had taken the shot when given the chance.

Some people weave into your life no matter how much you distance yourself from them, Aiden thought. In his line of work, the same rats worked for the same cheese.

By the look of things, Jordi was better at navigating the maze. He rode shotgun, arms free, while Aiden sat in the backseat with his hands still handcuffed behind his back. A metal grate separated them.

"FBI?" Aiden asked.

"Not that I can tell," Jordi said.

"How do you not know?"

"Give me a break, Aiden. They picked me up three hours ago. I'm still learning what my new government contract is all about. But she's pretty smart this one, and, you know, angry all the time. Like a hornet got stuck down her bulletproof vest."

"Hey," the driver said. "Both of you shut up."

Jordi pivoted and rested his arm against the back of the driver's seat, very casual. "Why don't you keep driving and let the adults talk?"

The driver hunched his shoulders and kept his eyes on the road. Aiden wasn't sure what he was seeing – they were arrested, but the normal bags over heads, beatings, and silence-until-spoken-to weren't apparent. He did have to glumly watch as his phone and gun were thrown into the Patapsco River, though. Given the reaction of the driver to Jordi's bullshit, he felt like they were being taken to meet someone and they'd just used an entirely ham-fisted approach to bringing him in from the cold.

"You reek of rookie," Jordi told the man at the wheel. "I bet you drew the short straw to be the unlucky guy to drive us, too. Or are you one of those idiots who volunteers for this kind of thing?"

"Jordi," Aiden said. The fixer's mouth was going to make things worse.

"Don't worry about it, Aiden," Jordi said. "He's not going to do anything. He may not know it, but he's a plant."

The driver turned his head. "I'm not a–"

Jordi shushed him. "No talking. Just drive. No one likes a driver who takes their eyes off the road."

The driver turned back to the front, jaw clenched and knuckles white.

Back to Aiden, Jordi said, "He's a plant because the point of this ride is to let us get comfortable and chat it up. By telling us to shut our mouths, he's trying to make us think they don't want us to talk, but Aiden, they very much do. She's listening."

"You sound paranoid." Aiden looked out of the tinted window. Another SUV cruised alongside them. "And who's she?"

Jordi shrugged. "She calls herself Leech."

Sounded like a hacker name, thought Aiden. But the feds would never let Aiden's kind run things. Not normally.

"What does she want?" Aiden asked.

"You," Jordi said.

"And how the hell was she able to find me?" Aiden had a feeling he wouldn't like the answer, but best to have Jordi tell him the truth now rather than later.

A guilty look crossed Jordi's face. He showed his teeth and sucked in air, as if it stung. "Snitches get stitches and all that, but this Leech woman had a lot on me. Too much. You know they caught me coming out of a burrito place? Mouth full. Had to drop it on the street like a bum. Embarrassing."

"You led them to me."

Jordi didn't look *that* ashamed. "I had no choice, pal. I hope you can believe me. I never wanted to help these clowns, but Leech wanted you, and it was the only way I could bargain. Upside, we're both government contractors now. Good pay, good benefits. Don't say I'm not looking out for you."

Aiden sighed and leaned back against the seat. His hands were falling asleep.

Fool me once… Aiden thought.

He should have learned. Should have known. Working with Jordi, it always ended with Aiden losing something important.

You've got nothing left to lose, Aiden, he thought. Family gone or beyond reach, friends gone, together with any chance at aging gracefully. Fucking Jordi.

"Don't get too frustrated," Jordi said.

Aiden was beyond frustrated. "What does this Leech want with me?"

"I don't know," Jordi said, sounding irritated. "My job was to lead them to you and be a friendly face for this ride. Beyond that? It's up to you."

"They want me to work for them?" He'd taken Jordi's motor mouth as talking bullshit.

"It means these are the type of people who could have just killed you when they found you. And they didn't. Think that one through."

The city dwindled as the black SUVs rolled further out. Signs on the road said they were headed toward Frederick. Out west.

Maybe this Leech woman was going to lock him up but wanted a face-to-face first. Maybe there was some secret prison in DC for people like Aiden. Seemed unlikely. The US government never wasted an asset they could co-opt for their own schemes. He decided Jordi was probably right – there was an offer coming, and it was going to be hard to refuse.

"I guess it's fitting," Jordi said. "I've never paid a cent in taxes. Not in my whole life. This is my karma to pay back Uncle Sam. I had to be a good American at some point."

"Never took you for the patriotic type," said Aiden.

"Never took you for the beard type."

Aiden smiled because he couldn't do much else.

Jordi smiled back. "I'm not patriotic. Only losers, psychos, and assholes take government jobs. This is a no-choice, no-win situation, so that's why I'm hoping you can let this one slide, Aiden. We're both stuck."

"Doesn't look like we're stuck." Aiden nodded toward the window. "It looks like we're heading to DC."

"Well, you're wrong on that, too."

The driver turned the wheel. The motorcade took an exit that led to a two-lane road. Then another left. No more buildings and sidewalks. There were trees and large stretches of mud and grass outside the window and less of anything resembling civilization. A rural setting meant there was less to hack, not that it would have mattered with his access shut off.

Aiden felt like he'd been muzzled and had to fight the urge to grab for the door, simply roll out, and take his chances.

"I'm getting kind of worried here, Jordi."

"You and me both, buddy."

"You're not helping."

"Wasn't trying."

There's always a way out, Aiden thought. He remembered Clara and how she'd died in the cemetery. She hadn't had a way out. But again, that one was on him. She'd still be alive if he'd been faster. Age and time had allowed him to shave off the imperfections. Or so he thought. If this Leech woman wanted him, she'd get him and everything Aiden Pearce had to offer.

They turned down a dark gravel path, tightly lined with trees and brush. In the darkness, it looked more like they were digging through the earth than driving through the woods. The man at the wheel flipped on the high beams.

Jordi turned to the driver. "You do know where you're going, right?"

"Lay off me, man," the driver said.

"Maybe I should be more like my friend back there and assume y'all are going to bury us in the middle of nowhere."

"We're not the criminals here," the driver said testily.

"Tell that to anybody on the street," Jordi said. "They'd laugh in your face."

"I am so done with this." The driver pointed ahead. "That's where you both get out."

The path opened into a small field, where a double-wide trailer waited, lights on – a yellow bulb fixed just above the front door, encased in a glass tube. A crack ran up from the bottom. Aiden was reminded of the Liberty Bell. The trailer was the color of blue sky, and as the high beams found it, the driver shut the lights off. A black sedan was parked to the right of the trailer, churning steam out of its exhaust, its rear lights burning scarlet in the darkness.

"Out," the driver said, just before he slammed on the brakes, causing Aiden to slump forward and hit his head against the grated barrier.

"Fuck you, man," he said.

"She's waiting inside," said the driver.

The locks popped up. Smiling as always, Jordi shaped his fingers into a gun, pointed it at the driver, and made a *pew pew* noise as he fired an imaginary bullet. Jordi hopped out and held the back door open for Aiden.

"A little help?" Aiden asked.

Jordi raised his eyebrows. "Aiden, if I lean in there to help you, you're just going to headbutt me and run away."

Aiden didn't smile, but he couldn't help his eyes thinning in amusement. Jordi knew him too well.

"I know you're more than capable of exiting this vehicle without my help," Jordi said. "Besides, I would have dodged the headbutt and tripped you with a rolling leg lock." He fixed his shirt collar and walked toward the trailer's front door. He kept talking. "And even if you managed to run, they've got this entire area covered. Those theatrics in Baltimore? That was them trying to stay quiet and keep you alive."

"They could have just called," Aiden replied.

In the SUV, the driver turned to look at Aiden through the grate. "Does he ever shut up?"

"No," Aiden said, and scooted out the door. His feet landed on soft dirt. They must have airlifted the trailer in rather than get stuck in the mud.

Cursing to himself, the fed driver jumped out of his seat and stomped around the SUV's fender to shut the door Aiden had left open. "You could have shut it for me," he grumbled.

"And you could have watched how you handled those brakes," Aiden said. Though his legs felt stiff, Aiden trudged over to stand beside Jordi. "Let's just get this over with."

Nodding, Jordi lifted a fist to the door, but it swung inward before his knuckles made contact.

Through the open doorway Aiden saw a gray table standing in the middle of a gray room, with walls covered in dark glass. The lights were on, but dim, and more modern than he'd been anticipating. The interior was more like an interrogation room than a grandma's mobile home.

There was nothing and no one else inside.

"Thank you, Mr Chin," came a woman's voice.

She sounded young. And vicious. Her tone like someone who'd found half a caterpillar in her quarter pounder.

Jordi patted Aiden's shoulder just once then stepped off to the side and leaned against the trailer. "It's your rodeo now."

"And I guess I'm just another bull for them to ride." Aiden

sighed and stepped into the trailer with Jordi at his heels. The door closed behind him with a click of magnets activating.

"That's better," the woman said. Here in the sealed trailer, her voice was deeper, clearer, electric, and most definitely right out of the Valley. The dark glass on the walls flickered as she spoke. "Let's get those cuffs off."

A chime sounded at Aiden's wrists. The handcuffs clicked and fell to the floor with a clank. He'd thought they were standard cuffs, basic police gear. How did he miss that? His fingers felt numb, and his wrists immediately started to complain. He brought his hands around front and started to rub blood back into them, grimacing as pins and needles started in his fingertips.

"That's a neat trick." Aiden turned to the room. His dim reflections stared back at him from every wall.

"Please pick them up," the woman's voice said.

"You want me to pick up the cuffs you just took off me?" Aiden scratched his beard and stared at himself as he shook his head. "I'm not in the habit of taking orders."

"Mr Pearce, I'd very much like to get on with our conversation. It's something I've been looking forward to, so if you could please just pick up the cuffs."

After three uncomfortable seconds Aiden bent down and grabbed the cuffs. "You're not going to make me put them back on, are you?"

"I can be cruel, but I'm never banal," she said.

Aiden grunted. "All cruelty is banal in the end," he replied. He'd seen enough of it to know for sure.

"Place them on the table and sit in the chair."

"Who are you people?" Aiden asked. "What do you want?"

"We will get to that. Cuffs. Table. Now, Mr Pearce."

With a lazy toss, the cuffs flew from Aiden's hand and landed onto the tabletop. He dragged the chair out and sat. Jordi remained standing. Whoever had set this up thought to provide just the one seat. The metal chilled his skin through his clothes. They'd taken his coat and his hat before putting him in the car. January weather had a habit of cutting him right where it hurt, and getting older had not helped with that one bit. Some days he felt like a goddamned grandad.

The dark glass of the walls brightened, filled with millions of pixels, showing the illuminated image of a young, blonde woman in a navy blazer. Her blue eyes watched him like a raptor's.

"Happy New Year." She smiled and brought her steepled hands to her chin. "Aiden Pearce. This is… this is just the best day ever."

She couldn't have been older than thirty, just a little more than half his age. Thing was, she sounded genuinely happy.

"You're a couple of weeks late for New Year's. Are you a fan or a fed?" Aiden asked.

Her eyes got serious. She hummed, as if acknowledging the need to get back to business. "That's a good try, Mr Pearce. Give me choices to answer with, and I'll eventually reveal things. Right? But there's no need to pull mind tricks. For one, I won't fall for them, and for two, I'll tell you exactly who I am and what I want with you."

"So, you're a crazed fan." Except he knew he was wrong. There was a severe edge to her that spoke of training, of ambition and focus. And… was that panic at the edges of her eyes?

Jordi was quiet, further back, still by the door through which they'd come in. Why wasn't the dolt running his mouth like he normally did?

"My name is Sarah Leech, good to meet you. You have a choice to make, Mr Pearce."

"That's how life works," Aiden said, conscious of coming across like an annoying dad.

Leech hummed again. "Life. Yep. You could be spending the rest of yours in one of several different ways. Prison, for example."

"You're not feds," he said with conviction. The cold of the table was pleasant under his fingers, which were shot through with chronic pins and needles from the cuffs.

"No. I'm with the government." Her image repeated across the wall until there were three of her. They walked around the walls in different directions until they came back together in a single Leech standing there right in front of him.

Well, Aiden, he thought. How does it feel to have someone run your own game on you?

"Feds. Government. Isn't that the same thing?" he said, stalling.

If Leech's image was true to size, she stood at five foot four. Her fists were small, but the rough skin over her knuckles suggested she had experience using them with violent success. "If you're thinking of the FBI, they're part of the government. Just like the CIA, NSA, DHS, and all the other TLAs they love coming up with to describe themselves. Department this, department that. Me and the people I work with, we don't have an acronym. We're just with the government."

Aiden shrugged. "All the same to me. I should care because?"

"Boring you, am I?" Leech's image walked over the wall to

Aiden's right. She pointed toward a space directly in front of him. "Check this out."

The wall blinked to a live news broadcast.

A chyron title indicated the Black woman behind a news desk was named Jennifer Tills. A box beside her head showed Trevor Erins' black Papavero ripping through downtown Baltimore.

"After a dangerous high-speed chase late last night, authorities are reporting that Aiden Pearce, better known as Chicago's Vigilante, is dead today after police cornered the notorious hacker and domestic terrorist. More on this later…"

The screen returned to black glass.

"That's ready to air with the morning coffee." Leech sauntered over to appear in front of Aiden. "What's it like being dead, Aiden?"

He blinked at her digital eyes. "Same way it's felt the last two decades."

"This can be a fresh start for you. No more running and hiding. No more taking seedy contracts from Mr Chin."

Jordi kissed his teeth in outrage.

"That last one with Trevor Erins? I expected him to run. Still, I bet he doesn't get much of a sentence. Those corporate types never do." She paused, looked at her fingers.

"He's only delayed the inevitable," said Aiden. "The cartels will make sure he doesn't make it to his birthday. Being necklaced is not a good way to die." He'd seen people take twenty minutes to die from being set on fire with a gasoline filled rubber tire around their chest and arms. It was one of the worst ways to die he'd encountered and a specialty of the cartels.

Leech cleared her throat. "Don't you want a chance at a normal life?"

A normal life. Aiden had given up on that a long time ago. Even before Lena died. It was no offer he had any interest in. "I'm fifty-five," he said as if it answered everything.

"How about being able to keep all your freedoms and avoid a jail sentence? Retire in peace."

Bitch, he thought. He was getting older, but he wasn't fucking retiring any time soon.

"You just run the news, lady," Aiden said and nodded to the void behind Leech. "Everyone already thought I was dead, so your little piece won't make any kind of waves where it matters. You've got nothing to offer me. All I have to do is figure a way out of this current problem. Then, I'll be a ghost. You won't get a second chance at me."

Leech laughed and crossed her arms. "I won't need a second chance, Aiden. Everyone thinks you're dead now because that's what we've let them believe. We can come back tomorrow and say you're on the loose, and your face will be everywhere. Every lousy traffic cop in the country will be looking for you. The Fox is back on the hunt! Hide your loved ones! People believe what we want them to. More importantly, they'll do exactly what we need them to."

"We," Aiden repeated. "The government?"

"That's right," Leech said. "And your government has a special request for you, Mr Pearce. Perfect for you. If you believe in such things, you might even think it came along with you in mind. Cooperate and you get out of this intact."

"You think you have enough string to make me dance? You must not know me as well as you think."

"You're sitting here, aren't you?" Leech said blandly.

"So what then?" he growled.

"Everything that happened on the streets of Baltimore this evening was perfectly planned. It's amazing what you can do with mapping software and the starting framework of Baltimore's first ctOS network. Whatever control you think you have right now, Mr Pearce, I'm telling you, it doesn't exist. You're boxed in."

He wanted to object, but Leech was right. He was sitting in a trailer, having a video chat with a government agent while several armed people in SUVs waited outside. All Aiden had was Jordi, and that wasn't much. Even through his usual bullshit, the fixer had looked worried.

"Now, don't get me wrong," said Leech. "You pulled some awesome moves. Real Hollywood stunt level stuff. That thing with the crane?" She made a chef's kiss. "Beautiful. But ultimately you ended up exactly where I wanted you. I knew you couldn't resist the garage. I'd shut down everything else in the area, so what other choice did you have?"

There it was again. The illusion of choice.

Aiden stood and kicked the chair away. "What do you want?"

Leech's smile was broad and manic. It looked like it hurt. "Six days ago, a secret transport was hijacked. All assets on board were lost."

A video appeared on the wall to the left. From the point of view of the driver, it was a truck by the sound and look of the cab. It was heading down a curved single-track road at night. Ahead, a pickup truck and a van blocked the way.

"What the hell?" said the driver.

Another man to his right said, "Just slow it down, I'm calling for backup."

He didn't get the chance. Men and women leaped out of

the pickup and the van. They lined up on the road, shoulder to shoulder, and opened fire. Bullets crashed through the windshield. The noise was so loud it caused feedback on the recording.

The camera view grew hazy but kept recording. It was clear from the footage that both the driver and their passenger were dead. The truck door opened, and someone grabbed the driver's body and pulled him out.

"For America," a gruff, feminine voice said.

The speaker climbed up into the cab. They were wearing a hoodie. The bottom half of their face was covered in a mask, much like Aiden's, except this mask was vertically striped, red and white. They shuffled around for a minute and then leapt down and out of the cab. Noises came from the outside and, maybe, inside the truck as well, but no one else entered the field of view. Then someone shouted to bring in the big wheels. Aiden guessed they were busy unloading whatever the truck had been hauling.

Eventually, the screen went black. Leech's face returned on all the screens, and she turned to Aiden. "What do you know about human augmentation?"

"I suspect I'm about to learn a good deal about it," he said, not willing to admit he was curious. After all, no one would use that kind of firepower unless it was necessary. Unless it was worth it.

Leech's smile was icy. "The stolen assets were experimental technology for human improvement. Our experimental technology. It was on its way from a research facility to one of our medical centers. Maiden voyage. First time trying it out where our people could really see the benefits. We had soldiers, good people, who were depending on this tech."

"And what tech is that exactly?" Aiden asked. "Because I'd wager with this setup of yours it wasn't the kind of shit they fit people with after road traffic accidents. They had to have stolen more than pacemakers."

Leech smiled again. "The kind that makes people better."

"Prosthetic legs and arms?" he said. "'Cause I know a lot of people who would like some of those."

"Our people weren't just full amputees. Some were missing intestines, had collapsed lungs. They had no other option. Experimental treatment was the only way they might live anything resembling the lives they'd had before. We hoped they might even live better, to discover new ways of being human. We believe these men and women deserved to be upgraded. Each and every one of them earned it in service to their country." She took a breath. "The tech isn't simply parts – we're not talking individual prosthetics. We're talking about an adaptive mesh that integrates with whatever organ as if they were part of it."

"Software?"

"More that than hardware, yes. This is revolutionary Aiden."

For the first time, he thought he was seeing the real Leech – a woman passionate about a technology that would change people's lives. Everything else was an act put on just for him.

Leech continued, "We won't let something with such potential for good end up in the hands of whoever thinks they can take it from us."

Aiden's bullshit detector pinged in his mind. "It sounds like you found a way to get these people back into battle, instead."

Leech shook her head. "Who wouldn't want to continue serving their country? But you're thinking small. This technology is for the good of the whole country." She blinked a couple of times as if resetting. "Let's take a step back. We're a long way from a proper rollout. Years. Way before that, we have to make sure what we've got works. Make sure it doesn't malfunction or harm those it's designed to help."

"It's dangerous?" he asked, willing to believe this was exactly the kind of crap a corporation would pull on its patients for the sake of profit.

Leech shook her head. "No." She glanced away, as if checking the room before her eyes settled back on him. Aiden wondered who she'd been looking at. "Cards on the table–" she continued.

He interrupted her. "Why? You got me. I ain't going nowhere. Why not treat me like a mushroom?"

She stared at him nonplussed.

"Keep me in the dark and feed me shit," he clarified.

He was pleased to see a small smile flicker across her lips. "The big reason? Autonomy. These human augmentation pieces would have allowed us to test new routines to both allow it and see just how adaptive it was in the field. At the moment, this tech goes into people, and it has to be controlled remotely. Not by some jarhead in a booth, but by remote software access. It was designed so patients could use it with their tablets, smart homes, or" – she nodded to Aiden – "their phones and earpieces."

Images of metal arms and wires connecting to brain lobes flashed behind Leech. Pictures of scientific papers and patent applications together with graphs and even consent forms.

This was a project they'd been working on for years.

"We've branded it Wetware," Leech said. "Sure, it's on the nose, and yes, it can be used for military purposes. Every other sociopathic VP worth their share options asks that question.

However. Imagine people being able to jump higher, live longer in good health, without dementia or susceptibility to the diseases of aging."

Aiden felt a migraine creeping up from his shoulder blades. They'd become more aggressive over the years – his tolerance for stress was slowly ebbing, his body telling him the mileage was taking its toll. Aiden, being Aiden, hadn't changed his habits or his pastimes and so such headaches were pretty common these days.

"Uncle Sam lost a new toy to some candy-striper thugs and wants it fixed before word gets out. This sounds so far beneath me it should have a miner's lamp." Aiden snorted. "Why me?"

Leech spread her hands, as if she was laying it all out on that metal table for him like she'd wanted to. "You're the Fox, the Vigilante, the scourge of Chi-Town. I came up with that last one by the way, watch the news tomorrow."

"You can't just send in a kill team?" Aiden asked with a sigh. There was a shoe to drop, and he could see Leech building up to it.

"I prefer to work with a scalpel, not a shotgun. And let's just say you can get away with things we can't."

Aiden laughed and shook his head. "Like I said, you just don't want this getting out. Why else would you use all the cloak and dagger theatrics? The government isn't in the habit of hiring an old hacker like me – too much paperwork. You could have hired any three fixers for the price you've paid to find me." He thought of the helicopter crashing, of the cars overturning. Wasting people's lives surely meant it had to be more than a mundane fucking deniability clause. He was preparing to be disappointed.

"You're right. We don't want this getting out. It's not just that it would make us look incompetent. That it would appear we can't keep our own people under control. That ordinary citizens can steal from us. Nor the fact that if we don't get this back in time, it would slow or halt everything we've been working on. That we'd have to start from scratch, and it was tough enough to get the approval. But that's beyond the point, Mr Pearce."

"And what is the point?"

Leech blinked. "I hate the people who've done this. In general, we know what they stand for. If it was up to us, we'd have them killed and then their bodies paraded in front of every troll and wannabe Hawaiian shirt wearing libertarian prepper in the country to remind them that the government can, if it chooses, reach into your home and fuck you up."

"Someone's protecting them," said Aiden, putting it together. "You don't know who, but you don't have the know-how… no, you don't have the authorization, to find out."

She didn't respond. "You can either do this or get thrown away for the last time. You're a domestic terrorist. Focus on that word, Mr Pearce. Terrorist. Within it hides everything you need to know about the people we want you to find. Are you in or out?"

Aiden had taken on a lot of frustrating fixer jobs over the last few years, and when he wasn't fixing? Well, there was the running. Always the running. To a new city, a new climate, a new safe house. He liked to tell himself it was a choice, that he had the freedom to accept or deny a job, to punish or to forgive. He knew it was bullshit, but what other code could he live by? He'd made his bed as a young man and spent thirty years laying in it.

The United States government, this short woman in a suit, had him cornered. Thing was, he was also intrigued. But intrigue was no substitute for being in control.

"No," Aiden said. He tensed.

"If Aiden's out then our deal's off," said Jordi, stepping up level with Aiden.

For the first time Leech turned to the fixer, her face blank. "Jordi Chin. You think we brought you in and offered you a deal to help with Aiden because we give a shit? We've got more on you than you can imagine. The same fate awaits you if Aiden decides he wants to spend the rest of his life in solitary confinement somewhere in the Gulf of Mexico."

Jordi clapped his mouth shut.

"Now, Mr Chin, please, get out." The door opened, letting in a blast of cold air. Aiden ignored Jordi until he left.

"Don't fuck this up," he called back to Aiden as the door closed on him.

"Good," Leech said. The images behind her faded away. "We had an agent on the thieves' trail, but it went cold. I'm afraid he's probably ended up the same way. If you find him, his name is Miguel Henry."

An image of a Latino man appeared above Leech. He was buzz-cut and wearing a plain sweatshirt. It looked like an academy photo. As expected, there was nothing to signify which academy. A small file arrived in his VR. Leech had to have pushed it to his earpiece without letting him connect for himself.

"If he's still alive," Leech said, "get him out. But if he's already dead, focus on the Wetware and make his sacrifice mean something."

Aiden wanted to be sarcastic, to remind her he'd said no, but Leech wasn't someone who seemed to care about his attitude. Besides, Aiden figured, they both knew Henry was almost certainly dead.

"And the fucks who stole from you?" he asked, unwilling to say yes but knowing he had to find out more before he decided if he was going to risk saying a hard no.

Another file arrived in his personal space. He tried harder to follow it back this time but could find no obvious connection to the cloud.

Red and white stripes bled down from the top of the wall. It looked like the US flag missing its field of stars. Just the stripes.

"Did you notice the mask the attacker was wearing?" Leech asked.

Aiden nodded.

"We've found an uptick in this symbol on white supremacist websites recently. No name to go along with it. But the skinheads give them credit for several arsons and some gnarly hacks aimed at minority groups. You hear what happened to the NAACP site?"

"The burning cross?" Aiden asked. "These assholes did that?"

Leech nodded. "That's what we believe."

It had been all over the news almost a year before. Someone had hacked the NAACP's website, so that any visitor was inundated with the image of a burning cross and an audio roll of commands to burn Black churches, attack any non-white you encounter, and to remember to vote.

It was childish and racist as hell. Not even a hacker fresh out of high school would have wasted their time with small-fry stuff like that, even if they were fucking racists. But the hack hid its true purpose inside its ridiculousness. It hadn't been meant for the general public. The fear and disgust was a bonus, a neat distraction. The hack was a call to all those who had been waiting for the signal. The beginning of the race war they'd been having wet dreams about since the day segregation was ended, since the day a Black man entered the White House. In the weeks after the burning cross hack, countless hate crimes were reported all over the country. Churches burned, people lynched, hundreds died. And still, the group actually responsible remained silent, unknown, while all the usual suspects – the Freemen, the Aryans, the KKK – ran around doing whatever the fuck they liked while local police scrambled to tidy up after them, at best. Most telling of all was how no one had yet been convicted for any kind of involvement, not even a traffic infraction.

Images flashed across the screens of those who'd died in the resulting violence. There was no discrimination between the young and old, the strong and the weak. Aiden soaked it in. He knew he was being manipulated, that Leech was trying to get at his sense of justice. She needn't have bothered.

If she'd led with this I'd have been in, he thought tiredly.

Rumor said that DedSec were working to expose them, but nothing had come up.

Now Leech was saying it was Aiden's turn.

"I'll have full immunity?" Aiden asked. He felt like cracking his knuckles. He wanted to tell Leech she could have just called him, but then again, in some ways, being brought in like this was exactly as it should have been.

"You have the freedom to do whatever you need to do. Thing is, the police will still get violent if they catch you putting a bullet into one of these racists' heads. They aren't in on our agreement. No one outside my team is. We won't save you if you screw up. Act accordingly."

"I know how it works," he said politely. Did these people have a script they needed to follow? Was HR on the other line making sure they clearly informed the off the books contracted killer they were on their own?

A drawer slid out from one of the walls.

"Come get your things," Leech said. Her image held a hand toward the black drawer.

They had taken and destroyed his stuff. He'd seen them do it. What else did he have that could be returned?

Aiden stood, popped the ache out of his right shoulder, and walked over to the drawer. Inside were his hat, coat, mask, baton, phone, and 1911 pistol.

"Nice," he said. "Exact replicas?"

"You aren't the only one skilled at distraction. Before I ended up doing whatever you call this, I wanted to be an illusionist. Everything in that drawer is original." She sounded exceptionally pleased with herself, and he knew he should compliment her. Except he wasn't that kind of person.

"Wanted to make me feel small?"

"Nearly. Wanted you to feel powerless," said Leech. The humor in her face was gone. "Any weapons you need, Jordi can get for you."

"He's in on this then?" asked Aiden.

She shrugged. "That's between you and him. I can't think of anyone better to run support for you."

"He's good at a lot of things," Aiden said, "but working with me isn't one of them."

"Them's your choices, Aiden. Jordi has as much at stake as you do. You've needed him before and you need him now."

She was right, but Aiden wasn't about to let her know that.

"Where should I start?" Aiden asked. He slipped his phone into his pants and nudged his earbud further into place. The urge to hold his pistol came on strong. He was tired of being confined in this box with this digital fed.

"DC," Leech said. "As in the District of Columbia. Washington. Last we heard from Agent Henry he was at a bar on the east side, called Proud Patty's. I'd start there."

Aiden laughed under his breath and turned toward the door he'd come through, waiting for it to open.

"Something funny?" Leech asked.

"All of this is a bad joke," he said. "Only appropriate we start this off by walking into a shitty bar in a city of politicians."

Leech hummed her recognition. "Good luck, Mr Pearce. I'm afraid I won't be much help to you from here on, but your phone has my current details for when you complete the job."

Then she blinked out like an old TV.

The trailer door opened, and a wall of Maryland winter air wrapped around Aiden as he walked out. Save one, the black SUVs were gone. They were all alone.

Jordi lay on its hood with his hands cradling his head. He turned his head when Aiden came out. "Just how fucked are we?"

"All the way up to overturning democratically elected presidents," Aiden said as he walked around to the passenger side. "You drive. I need some sleep."

"Where to?" Jordi opened the door and climbed behind the wheel.

"Washington, DC. Some bar." Aiden sighed. "How much do you know, Jordi?"

"Know?" Jordi blinked as he put the SUV into reverse. "About what we're doing? All I know is we're headed to some bar in DC and only because you just told me. I also know if I don't help you and we don't succeed at whatever this is, we're fucked. Trust me when I say I have an out, but I'd like to avoid that if I can."

"What, a cyanide capsule?"

"Yeah, how'd you guess?" Jordi said.

Aiden shook his head. On top of everything, he had to fill Jordi in on this goose chase. "I'll tell you everything when we get there."

Jordi gave him a thumbs up and a stupidly broad grin. "Look on the bright side. We're finally getting to take that road trip we've always talked about."

Aiden leaned back in his seat and pulled the bill of his hat over his eyes. "Jordi, do us both a favor and try not to annoy me."

After a beat, where the only sound was tires crunching over the gravel road, Jordi said, "Would it help if I stop and get snacks?"

CHAPTER FOUR

The sun was up as they entered DC on Route 50 West. Aiden managed about an hour of broken sleep. Broken because Jordi wouldn't shut up. Aiden had tried tuning out the man's stream of consciousness – Jordi covered more topics than Aiden could track, from hacker kids in San Fran to how Leech dressed like a penguin – but it was useless. Aiden would sigh and pull his cap lower and grab another five minutes before the next topic shift woke him again.

Surrendering as the sunlight warmed the car, Aiden finally sat up in his seat and said, "Tell me everything you know about Leech."

"Hey, wakey, wakey, artichokey," Jordi said, looking off toward a Denny's as they passed. "Wait, is that how it goes?"

Aiden blinked tired eyes and let the silence stretch.

"Buddy," Jordi said, finally filling the quiet, "I can't help you learn more about Leech. I told you all on the ride to the trailer–"

"I know what you told me," Aiden said. "That doesn't make it true. We've both been doing this long enough to know you've got more. It's just us two here. You can talk."

Jordi made a popping sound with the side of his lips. "This

isn't like before, Aiden. This isn't some Southside gang or rogue Russians fucking about far away from home. I've seen enough spy movies to know it's not going to be just us two again for a long time. If ever."

"I already scanned the car for bugs," Aiden said. "It was the first thing I did. Spill it, Jordi. You were probably looking into Leech while I was in that trailer. Knowing you, you probably did it before you led them to me."

"It's an SUV," Jordi said.

"What?"

"You said you scanned the car for bugs. I wouldn't call this a car."

"Jordi. It's a vehicle on four wheels. Semantics."

"OK, fine. She's a Chi-Town girl, born and raised. Just like you, pal. When she was nine, a small tech magazine did a story on how she completely, and I mean down to the motherboard, took apart her dad's computer and rebuilt it in less than twelve hours. Eleven hours, twenty something minutes to be exact. Anyway…"

From Chicago. Tech wiz. Aiden absorbed it all like a sponge.

"…Stanford, top of her class. Twenty, maybe twenty-five. And aside from a few early social media pics with her elderly Schnauzer, that's it."

"What do you mean, that's it?"

"I mean for all my wonderfully wicked ways of getting the dirt on anybody and everybody crawling their way through this fucked up world, that's all I could get on Ms Sarah Leech."

Aiden groaned and rubbed at his eyes. "Which means it's all…"

"Bullshit," Jordi said in sync with Aiden. "Hey, jinx. You owe me a coke. Or a waffle. Nah, not quite. She really did Stanford. You can tell from the way she talks and the clothes she wears. You can take the ID out of the girl but not her alma mater."

"Latin now?" asked Aiden lazily.

"It's all I got. She ain't Sarah Leech any more than Sarah Leech attended Stanford, but she's trained, educated, and connected."

"That's enough for me," said Aiden.

"Right, you can track her down from there. Probably. But does it matter? Who she is now is not the girl who went to an Ivy League," replied Jordi, sounding relieved. "So, we good?"

Aiden laughed then, full and true. "Fucking hell," he managed as Jordi clicked his teeth. Whether it would be a bullet in the knee or leaving him strung up somewhere, Aiden hadn't decided yet quite what he owed Jordi for leading him to Leech like a lamb to the slaughter. Imagining the ruin he'd visit on the shitbag sitting next to him didn't satisfy, so for the time being he decided he wouldn't take the opportunity to pay back Jordi in full. Yet.

"We should probably find a better place to sleep than this SUV," Jordi said.

"Proud Patty's," Aiden said.

"Is that where you're buying my waffle?"

"It's a bar, dipshit. Leech said she had an agent go missing. Proud Patty's was his last known location."

Jordi huffed. "We aren't getting waffles, are we?"

"No, Dorothy, we aren't."

"And how do we know he didn't just stop there for a beer on his way to fight crime, cape fluttering as he waited for his drink?"

"I guess we don't," Aiden said, not caring. "We'll have to work it out once we case the joint. Spy style."

"Wow." Jordi whistled and shook his head. "I guess I shouldn't be surprised this is a government operation."

"Leech knows a lot more than she's given me. And that does sound like government."

"You think that's bad? You still know more than you're giving me," Jordi said. "I let you sleep, so now it's your turn to pay up. What's this job all about?"

Aiden watched Jordi focus on the road. He'd never been colorblind, and by Christ the last twenty years had been an education in just how divided his country was, but at that moment he wondered what it was like for Jordi. America, it seemed, was regressing more and more every day. "Some chickenshit white supremacists stole high-tech government toys and we're supposed to stop them." He checked himself. "Well, we're supposed to get them back."

Jordi was silent for a moment. "Well, you don't hear that every day."

"Come again?" asked Aiden.

"The government giving a crap about white people hating on the rest of us."

Aiden sniffed his agreement. There wasn't much he could say.

"What did the hog fuckers steal? Some laser weapons?" asked Jordi.

"It's not the Klan," Aiden said. "No one knows who they are or what they want. They hijacked a government truck carrying human augmentation tech. Leech calls it Wetware."

"Sounds like porn. Unoriginal, at that," said Jordi drily. "So, assuming it's not fake tits, is it like surgically implanted jet packs and stuff?"

"I don't think that's possible Jordi," snorted Aiden, and Jordi laughed. "Leech said it was medical. They were going to give vets new arms and legs. Maybe even replace their brains. Heal their organs. Hell if I know what Leech is really worried about or how any of it works without being able to connect to it. You gotta figure there's a military application for this stuff." The latter part was what really interested him, but it would have to wait until he had something concrete to examine. He tapped his phone in anticipation.

Jordi scrunched his eyebrows together. "They're weaponizing soldiers now? The weapons-grade shit they'll spew out should make you worry, even more so than whether you'll get back at the government for pulling you into this mess."

"You pulled me into this mess."

"I know what I'd do with that kind of tech," Jordi continued, ignoring Aiden. "So, I know what they'll do. Government or anyone else. What's the aim of any random guy who suddenly finds he can hurt people he thought were out of reach except in his basement fantasies? Look, Aiden, I'll give you a discount on the ammo needed to fuck their shit up. Not a big one, mind you. Business is still business. You think this bar is where – what the hell?" The SUV's tires screeched as they slammed to a stop at the corner.

The street sign said they were somewhere on North Capitol. Ahead of them, a battleship adorned in red, white, and blue sparkly tassels rolled down the street right across their path.

People danced on the sides of the ship, raising posters for a Senator Teddy Blake. It took Aiden a second look to pinpoint the pickup truck pulling the battle float. Behind it, a line of gaudy patriotic abominations followed slowly but surely, as a country song blared about America kicking ass.

They'd been cut off by a parade.

"It's seven-thirty on a January morning," Jordi said. "I wouldn't be out of bed if I didn't have to be, and I definitely wouldn't be dancing in a parade."

"A political parade," Aiden said. He flipped his phone over and did a quick search on Teddy Blake. As the parade rolled by, Aiden filled Jordi in on Senator Blake, reading aloud from the information scrolling in front of him.

Blake, forty-one, looked like a burger restaurant mascot: head too big for his shoulders, hair molded into plastic immovability. A walking Ken doll with blue eyes and properly tanned skin. He was clean and smiling, and the Right loved him like he'd been shat out of a Tea Party finishing school.

There was no shortage of footage of him speaking at rallies, and Aiden was impressed at just how charismatic the man was. He could hold an auditorium in the palm of his hand and have them spouting bullshit like it was God's own truth. Which meant he was as hated by the other side as he was loved by his own. He could see the way they fed on one another, each driving the other to new heights of emotion. Those that loved him were ravenous in his defense and promotion. Coming up through the ranks, he'd sponsored voter suppression bills, defended senators caught in questionable circumstances with minors, and worked tirelessly to ban critical race theory from public discourse. In fact, his policies would have been right on the nose a century before, but his push for robotic police drones, AI allocation of police resources, and draconian facial recognition technology in public spaces were entirely modern-day.

His supporters loved him for it. Blake said he loved God and America, that he was against their culture being diluted and against illegal immigration, which, when you listened for more than a moment, meant all immigration where people's skin was not Northern European in hue. He was clear he'd do whatever he could to protect them from the other guys and hosted more than one fundraiser at gun ranges where he got busy firing assault rifles at targets.

"God and America need protecting?" Jordi asked. "From other Americans?"

"The point is, these others, they're not Americans. Not really. People blindly follow the scent of the crap they like best," Aiden said. "Right or Left."

"Easy for you to say," said Jordi. "It's rare that people on the Left want to drag me behind a truck for ten miles just for having the wrong skin."

He has a point, thought Aiden.

"Look at these people," continued Jordi. "That guy in the star-spangled warpaint is flipping everyone off. And get a load of that woman riding a paper-mâché bald eagle. She keeps bucking like that, and it's not going to stay on top of that van for much longer. What's her shirt say? Oh. 'Love it or leave it.' Of course it does."

Aiden didn't respond. He'd never heard Jordi like this. Then again, they'd never talked about it before. Aiden hated racists as much as the next man except, it turned out, the next man was riding a papier-mâché bull in leather chaps and a Stetson while waving a confederate flag.

The cars and floats kept coming. The Blake supporters started honking their horns and screaming from every float: "Blake is great!"

"Oh, screw this." Jordi put the SUV in reverse, which alarmed the white coupe behind them. The driver lay on their horn and swerved to avoid Jordi.

Jordi spun around them and sped off in the opposite direction, ignoring the coupe driver's middle finger as he went.

"I guess I didn't make it clear," Aiden said. "We can still get arrested or shot if you pull any more of that IndyCar shit."

"We'll swap cars after we grab a room."

"I thought this was an SUV, not a car," Aiden said, with a tug of his hat.

"Ha ha, very funny," said Jordi, but he smiled. "You definitely need sleep. I'm thinking we check in somewhere discreet and cheap since Uncle Sam isn't footing the bill. I can make some calls. I think I might have some contacts around here if we need certain" – Jordi bobbed his head from side to side – "tools."

"The last time you made some calls I had to black out Wrigley Field."

"This isn't like that."

"No," Aiden said. "It's worse. Just let me run this."

"Look at reality," Jordi said. "Neither of us is running this. We're at the mercy of Old Glory."

"Well, the room is on me at least," Aiden said, putting his phone back into his coat pocket. "I just transferred two-fifty from the woman in the 'Love it or leave it' shirt."

"You know how to spoil a date," said Jordi, pulling into the motel.

The carpet and the beds had been cleaned with a cheap

detergent, and the room smelled like oranges and vanilla. It somehow did the trick, though, as they surveyed the room. For some reason, he thought about life after Chicago. It was a long time ago, but nevertheless, it remained the cloud under which he still lived. For a while, he'd had nightmares, but they were gone now, as if getting older had stripped their talons.

I'm not a backward-looking guy, he thought. He didn't think about those he'd left behind... not his sister, not his nephew, especially not anyone dead. Not really. A decade ago, he'd committed to never saying their names, never thinking of them after seeing a shrink talking about trauma on a late-night show while staking out some score in Phoenix. It had worked. Largely.

The future was his focus, although he was conscious of the horizon coming ever closer. At some point he'd run out of road, and recently he could feel it coming on like a distant shore whose sea he'd not be able to cross.

Even the present was a dangerous thing, a dog without a muzzle – as likely to bite him as give him love. So, he settled for getting through it until *tomorrow*. Always tomorrow, both a victory and an opportunity.

Instead of going to sleep, Jordi unrolled a mat of guns on the floor between their beds.

"Emergency supplies," he said proudly, and then continued more seriously, "They took them from me when they picked me up, and then gave 'em back when you were done talking to Leech. Go figure."

There was an SG-90, which Aiden regarded as an unreliable shotgun only good at close range, and an SVD sniper rifle, which Jordi tagged as his. There was also an M8-M revolver that Aiden slid into his coat as soon as he saw it. Not only was it the best weapon on the floor, it was the only one he could sneak into Proud Patty's without causing a scene despite the place advertising online that it was pro open carry.

The bar's profile also said they didn't really get rocking till around eight at night, so Aiden went to sleep, ignoring Jordi standing in a tank, boxers, and a pair of dark purple socks as he brushed off his suit and hung it up. He woke to the smell of ramen and found gyoza on the side table gently steaming. Jordi was an asshole, but he knew how to look after those around him.

Slowly slurping down the noodles, Aiden sat in the corner researching the red and white striped symbol. As always when working on the open internet, he set up a series of fake IPs and gave himself an onion-like online identity before he started. If people were watching for snoopers all they'd do is succeed in peeling back layer after layer of fake identities as Aiden worked in peace with no fear of being tracked or traced.

Leech had been right about there not being much to go on. It was a patriotic image after all, and an evangelical Christian one with the candy cane resemblance. Racists were good at hiding their hatred in plain sight, especially from those who couldn't decode their language – whether it was tiki torches or Hawaiian shirts, calling their enemies NPCs or all their talk about culture and socialism. Whoever was behind this particular set of symbols had hidden their affiliations well. Except it was only one short step to the same hateful websites and forums all these people congregated in.

A bad taste grew in Aiden's mouth as he read through the bigoted vitriol, like he'd drunk motor oil. Worse, it didn't take long for him to realize none of them knew a damn thing. They were nothing more than fan forums. The mob, following people they didn't understand but instinctively knew were their kind of people. Except they might not be. Aiden had come across more than one organization in his time that whipped up those willing to act on their behalf, while hiding behind symbols that could be read as innocently as they could be seen as dog whistles.

So much of it was rich people setting the poor against one another so they could get richer in peace.

The sites and forums offered no leads, not even hints to follow up. Each step of this was going to be done the hard way.

Still, Aiden liked that better than reading more from user *whytepryde2040* or *antiwoke18* and others like them. Just because he could, and couldn't think of people who deserved it more, he left behind a few viruses and set the sites to be shut down permanently over the next twenty-four hours. A second family of viruses would scan the storage of anyone logging in and send the contents to everyone on their address lists.

He dressed properly around eight. Jordi opened the window to their motel room and squinted up at the night sky. It was cold and clear. "So, how do you want to play this, Captain America?"

"Excuse me?" asked Aiden.

"He punched Nazis. It was literally his thing," said Jordi.

"You grab a new car," Aiden said, ignoring him. "Once we get to the bar, you hang back. We can't both be seen if things go sour. We'll stay in touch, and if there's trouble you know what to do."

"Sounds easy so far," said Jordi lightly.

"It always starts that way," Aiden said and wondered where the night was going to take him.

Jordi ditched the SUV and came back with a metallic blue 3.9T muscle car about forty minutes later.

"Sue me," he said when Aiden got into the passenger seat with a gruff look. "Why can't we do this with a little style?"

Aiden tagged the bar's address via his phone and let it connect to the car and provide them directions. They passed the Washington Monument on the way, standing tall and white, and finally arrived at Proud Patty's, sitting like a spiked, leather-wrapped pile of bricks.

Choppers and motorcycles were parked outside, but so were pickups and a rough looking utility van. Proud Patty's was a blue-collar compendium so rough Aiden could see the smell of old beer coming from the walls. There were stringy amber lights wrapped around every post, and music played from speakers fixed above the open front door where a big-bellied, bald man with a tremendous beard sat on a stool watching the traffic.

"Maybe you should leave your gun with me," Jordi said. "It looks more discreet than my options."

Aiden shifted the revolver to sit more snugly against the back of his belt. "Maybe you should've picked a less obvious car."

"Come on," Jordi said. "You have that stick thing."

"It's called a baton. And I'm keeping both, so save me an argument."

"Your funeral," Jordi said. "Don't you think I should at least come in with you?"

"I can handle it," Aiden said. "Besides, if this place turns out to be a lead, it's probably some kind of neo-Nazi bar, and I don't think they'd like you very much despite your addictive charm."

"Good point," Jordi said firmly. "I'll circle the block. But, uh, Aiden?"

"What?"

"If you're not out of there in an hour, I'm going to call all the DC gangs I can get ahold of, send them here, and watch the fireworks through my sniper scope from half a click away."

"That's funny," Aiden said, "I thought you'd burn it down."

"Fire before bedtime is my late-night cocoa, you know that," Jordi promised with a pat on Aiden's forearm. "This is more of a fast food fix."

Aiden left the car and dodged a taxicab as he crossed the street. He scanned the area with his phone, letting his profiler establish the electronic footprint for the bar. There was only one camera inside Proud Patty's, and it was in the back office. They hadn't bothered protecting themselves from incursions like his. Their ports were wide open. Linking to that single camera with his phone, he could see a safe, an ancient desktop, and stacks of paper set in metal trays. The office was otherwise empty. If there was a Patty, whoever they were, they weren't in.

Which made things harder. If Patty had been responsible, Aiden could have bypassed the bar and gone straight to the owner. Now, he was forced to mingle.

"You a member?" the bald man at the door asked as Aiden walked up.

"No." Aiden stared down at him. "Do I have to be a member to grab a beer?"

"Here you do." The bouncer, or whatever he was, reached behind him and grabbed a clipboard from the wall. A pen hung from it by a string and a piece of duct tape. He handed the clipboard to Aiden. "I'll need your ID."

"Don't have any on me," Aiden said with a shrug as if to say friends didn't ID friends.

The man looked up from the clipboard. His eyes looked like a doll's, disbelieving. "You don't have any identification?"

"I don't like the government knowing more about me than I know about them."

The doorman studied Aiden's face. "Couldn't agree more, bub. It's not like you're younger than twenty-one, anyway. All right, just print and sign your name and put an address."

Aiden wrote his name as one Jefferson Davis who lived at 1600 Pennsylvania Avenue.

The man at the door didn't look at the fake name and address before he tossed the clipboard back in its place.

Throwing up a thumb toward the inside he said, "Come on in. Behave yourself."

"Always," Aiden said, a little baffled as he entered the bar. No pat down? No metal detector? The guy hadn't even left his stool. Thank heaven for hole-in-the-wall bars and their retro vibe. Trying to bring back the good ol' days sure did leave them open to exposure.

An old jukebox was playing a Hank Williams song. With a swipe of his fingers through the air, Aiden changed the song to a Howling Wolf blues tune. If he was going to have to spend time among these bozos, he could at least enjoy a beer to some decent music. Around him people muttered about the shitty jukebox, but no one got up to change it back.

Aiden pulled his hat down and approached the bar. The room was an open sore of poor security, and within moments, Aiden's profiler had the IDs of just about everyone floating above their heads. He isolated the ones he thought might be top priority, shuffling some to the bottom of the list of candidates he should investigate.

The bartender was Brennan Crognale, forty-four. According to the IRS, he made thirty-five thousand a year, and had two credit cards maxed out. No record to speak of, no parking tickets, no medical insurance or dental, but a note floated across his vision about him needing root canal work. Poor fuck, thought Aiden, no wonder his cards were maxed out.

A loud couple in a booth by the back wall were Tom and Janice Rice. Their tabletop was cluttered with empty beer bottles. There was nothing he could find on them that connected them to a white supremacist group or anything to do with Wetware, so he took an empty seat at the bar.

"What can I do you for?" Brennan asked.

"Beer," Aiden said. "Domestic, not imported. Whatever your hand touches first." Best to lay the seeds of credibility from the start.

The drink appeared on the bartop with a napkin clinging to its side. A woman sat beside him, but before he could check her profile she reached over and touched the hand he'd used to grab the beer.

"Now that," she said, "is a pretty beard."

"I just let it grow one day." Aiden turned to her.

"Trying to look like a wolf?"

"Not really, but I'll take it," said Aiden.

She had green eyes and dishwater brown hair cut into a thick shag. She wore a worn tie-dye shirt under light blue denim overalls. She was at least twenty years younger than him.

Aiden knew he wasn't bad looking, but he'd also gotten older and wasn't under any illusions as to just how alluring he might be to a woman in her early thirties. Which was to say not at all.

"What's your name?" she asked, holding his gaze without hesitation.

"Jefferson," said Aiden, keeping his hand on his phone but out of sight in case he tipped her off. Paranoid people didn't need much to trigger them, and in this case, he literally was out to get them.

There were men sitting on her other side. "This here's Bill and Frank."

They raised their beers in greeting. Bill was the thinner one with a lazy eye, and Frank was built like a linebacker. They both wore thick tan work jackets.

"And I'm Gin," the woman said.

"Well," Aiden said. "You are what you drink." He turned back to the bar and briefly checked their IDs as the three of them chatted aimlessly amongst themselves. Both the men were felons but nothing that worried him: some battery, a smidge of fraud. For a place like this, it felt tame.

Gin was a nobody. No presence on police and federal databases. A clean DMV and no taxes paid in a long time. Her net worth appeared to be the clothes she was wearing. That piqued Aiden's interest. He needed to dig further.

"Funny enough," Gin said, "I hate gin with a passion. Bourbon for me every time, much more patriotic, you know?" She held out her hand to be shaken. "You're new here."

"Yeah. Just became a member," said Aiden with a knowing smirk.

"What made you pick Patty's?"

"I don't know," Aiden said. "Maybe I want to meet Patty."

Gin laughed. Frank and Bill grunted their amusement.

"You think someone named Patty owns this place?" Gin said. "You got it wrong, Jeff. It stands for Proud Patriots."

A patriotic bar that looked like a redneck dive. Yeah, Aiden thought. No wonder Agent Henry had wound up here.

"Why not call it that?" Aiden asked. "If you're so proud, why hide it?"

"I don't know," Gin said, as if thinking it over. "Doesn't sound much like a bar name, does it? So do you love your country, Jefferson?"

"This isn't my usual flirtatious bar conversation."

"Well, we've already established you're a newbie. Maybe this is flirtatious when you're at Patty's." She smiled.

"I'm guessing you're a regular," Aiden said.

Gin shrugged. "I'm here and there. Wherever the wind takes me. But yeah, I guess they know me pretty well."

Aiden nodded, while his eyes searched the rest of the room. "Anything important about this place I should know?"

Gin narrowed her eyes. "Not much to tell. I'm more curious about why a stranger would be asking questions about some shithole bar he'd just walked into." She yelled toward the bartender. "No offense, Brennan!"

Flirting didn't come easy to Aiden – it didn't feature in many of his jobs, and he hadn't had a partner in more years than he cared to count. Worse still was Gin, who was vacillating between saucy and paranoid. He couldn't come off as weak or uncertain or she'd eat him for breakfast. "Maybe I'm just trying to get to know you better."

Gin seemed to relax. Her smile turned less venomous. "Maybe you need to try harder."

Aiden nodded and excused himself, pretending he'd received an important text, tapping his temple to indicate he was distracted.

"I might stick around," Gin called after him.

Leaving his beer behind, Aiden moved toward the restrooms but stopped just short. He read the bubbles floating above Bill and Frank in more detail. They worked at the same factory for shitty wages. Frank had been medically discharged from the Marines but had never seen action. Bill was divorced and had an online handle of *alpha_pappa*. Apparently, he'd lost an eye in a bar fight, which was news to Aiden as the man clearly had two working eyes. Nothing fake about them.

Gin, or Ginny Whitmore, had more of a story once he unraveled whatever sheen had been keeping her as a nobody before. Out of the foster care system at eighteen, she'd made ends meet selling addictive painkillers, shopping neighbors to the IRS, and grifting abusive men. There was no indication she was involved with any paramilitary group, let alone this group that Leech was aiming him towards. Except. There in her profile, a vertical stripes pin on her photo. Easy to overlook, entirely innocent, unless you knew what it stood for. It was enough for Aiden to know he was in the right place.

When Aiden looked back at her, her eyes had that glassy look people had when they were using their earpieces to send messages.

Let's see what you're up to, Aiden thought, tapping on his phone to weasel into her life further.

The last message she'd sent was to an R Gatty and said, "You better wait for me tonight. I want to see if it works."

Aiden disconnected and backed further into the shadows to call Jordi. "I've got something. Be on alert."

"Oh? Got yourself a shot at getting laid?"

"No," said Aiden, grimacing at the thought. "Woman at the bar. Remember the red and white stripes I told you about? Her avatar has the same symbol."

"That's convenient," Jordi said. "But remember you're surrounded by people who worship the red, white, *and* blue."

"Maybe these people just worship the second one," Aiden said. "I gotta go."

Aiden cut the connection and strode back to the bar.

"Hey, handsome," Gin said. She flicked her hair back with the tips of her fingers.

Aiden's focus narrowed. If this place was going to offer any leads, it was Gin Whitmore. "What do you do for fun when you're not knocking 'em back here?"

"Skin cats and shoot cannons," Gin said, laughing. "Isn't that right, boys?"

Bill and Frank laughed but went right on drinking.

"I'm new in town," Aiden said, sliding back into his seat. "Just trying to find my kind of people, you know?"

Gin's mouth slackened. Her eyes grew bigger. "What kind of people are those?"

Aiden leaned closer to her. "I don't know. People like me. Like you. Proper culture, the right heritage."

"Is it just the outside of a person that counts, Jeff?"

"It's Jefferson," Aiden said. "And I'm not sure what you mean."

Gin cut her eyes to the side and began chewing on the end of a tiny red straw. "Someone told me how a person looks on the outside is a reflection of what they're like on the inside. Some folks are just clean and white. Inside and out."

Aiden saw his opening and took it. "My kind of people are red and white."

Gin pulled the straw from her mouth and looked to Frank and Bill. They were looking right back at her. The length of silence grew painful, until Gin spun her seat back toward Aiden, smiling. "Maybe we can help you with that."

"You can?"

"Sure. How far are you willing to go?"

This was moving a lot faster than he'd expected. "My view? There are plenty of states that don't belong in the Union. The stars on the flag show just how far we've fallen. Better off without them. Should just be the stripes if you ask me."

Gin nodded and smiled. "Couldn't agree more, handsome. One question though, you know, before we go too far."

"Sure thing," said Aiden.

"Who was that you were talking to just now?"

Aiden's stomach went icy. "Friend who lives in the city. Arranging dinner."

"That was important enough to blow me off?"

He smiled. "Rest of the evening's all yours."

"Ain't how it works, Jefferson." Gin's tone went cold. "You don't come in here and ask questions like these and then take calls. If you're not a fed, then I'm Bill's bastard love child. I'm not stupid. You all seem to think we don't have eyes and ears, that we just float through life without observing anything."

Gin brought her right leg up and kicked Aiden in the chest. He flew from his stool, knocked into the empty one next to him, and skidded across the floor until he was at the front door.

His chest felt caved in. He sat up wheezing and rubbing at the spot, trying to focus. How was such a kick so powerful?

Gin pointed to Aiden. "Tear that son of a bitch apart, Stripes!"

The bar's inhabitants moved in as Gin, Frank, and Bill shoved past them and ran for the back.

Someone from behind grabbed Aiden under the arms, dragged him to his feet, and shoved him forward. Aiden drew his baton as he flew forward and used the momentum to stab at a man coming right at him. His baton connected right in the man's solar plexus and sent him crashing to the floor, eyes wide with surprise.

Aiden spun on his feet as the rest of them charged, trying not to overbalance.

A bearded man in a biker vest swung a broken bottle at Aiden's head. He ducked and it crashed against the incoming doorman's neck, gashing him open and sending him reeling away. Aiden shoved the end of his baton into the unbalanced biker's gut and sent him sprawling as well.

Two of the mob grabbed Aiden's arms and held him in place long enough for a snarling woman who'd been sitting in the booth with her partner to clock him across the chin with her ringed fist.

Aiden's vision snapped white. Blindly, he kicked out in the direction he thought the woman was standing and connected with her ribs. As the pair holding him pulled him back, he butted his head against the guy to his right and got his hand on that side free.

He snatched his revolver from his belt and pointed it at the man holding his left arm.

"Whoa!" The man threw his hands up and moved off. "Easy, buddy. No need for that."

The crowd backed away as Aiden turned in a circle, gun steady. He watched their angry, scared eyes looking down the revolver's sight.

"Damn it, Carl!" Brennan shouted, eyes on Aiden's gun. "You've got one job."

Carl was groaning from where he'd fallen to the glass-covered floor. Blood was slowly pooling around him.

Revolver steady, Aiden pointed his baton at the ones blocking the back door. "Out of my way."

They didn't move.

"Bub, you ain't getting out of here," Brennan said, raising a baseball bat from under the counter.

Slowly, Aiden lowered his baton and took a moment to think things through. Fighting was rarely the only option. Besides, he was outnumbered, his head hurt like he'd been punched repeatedly, and the fight had escalated beyond hands and feet. If they continued, people were going to die.

Time for a left turn, he thought.

Still logged into their network, he shut off the lights. Using the sudden darkness as cover, Aiden rushed forward through the confusion with his baton swinging, hitting anything in his way. People shouted in pain, bodies tumbled back from him, and then he was past them, using his VR to find the door.

Finding the back door, Aiden stumbled outside, where Jordi was waiting in their new ride.

"Where have you been?" Jordi said. "Three just took off down 23rd. Come on!"

Aiden ran, slid over the hood, and was in his seat by the time Jordi punched it forward.

"Your lip is bleeding," Jordi said, his foot on the accelerator. He jerked the wheel to the left then pulled a handkerchief from his suit pocket, holding it out for Aiden with a nod.

Aiden held the cloth to his suddenly stinging mouth, his chest still complaining about that single kick from Gin. "Didn't think any of them got me."

"From what I saw through the windows," Jordi said, "it looked like a geriatric battle royal."

"You saw what was happening and you didn't come help?"

Because of course Jordi hadn't.

"Whoa, there, cowpoke. You told me to stay in the car." Jordi pointed. "Look! There they are. Look at that cute little pink Wildebeest they're driving. How much you wanna bet they take it off road?"

The boxy pink car was veering all over, swerving between slower, more sedate traffic before sliding over the central line onto the wrong side of the road.

"Aiden," Jordi said, hands tight around the wheel.

"What?" Aiden wanted to close his eyes until it was over. He scrambled for his phone, even as his body throbbed in pain.

"I'd buckle up."

His chest still hurt like hell from Gin's first kick, but he clicked in by the time Jordi crossed the median.

Whoever was driving was headed for a large, white truck coming the other way. The truck driver laid on the horn and flashed their high beams, but the Wildebeest didn't change course.

"She's fucking crazy," Jordi said, but he was following right in line. "I love it."

"Get back in the right lane," Aiden said, his backside tense enough to crack walnuts.

"You want to catch them or not?"

All Aiden could do was brace his hands against the door and the dash as Jordi swerved around car after car. Gin's Wildebeest looked like it would crash head on with the moving truck, and while that would solve one problem, it would create a hundred more. Chief among those problems was that Aiden and Jordi were about to be a part of that crash.

The Wildebeest cut to the right at the last second, narrowly finding an empty hole and speeding up the on ramp to 395.

Jordi pulled out of the truck's path, but there was a golden sedan in their way. The driver's wild eyes stared at Aiden as they slammed into his side, sending the sedan through orange cones and down an embankment off the road.

"There," Jordi said. "That's better."

Aiden got an alert that a dispatch had just gone out for their location – a high-speed chase causing trouble and collisions.

"Jordi," Aiden said.

"I got it too," said Jordi.

"We have to get off the freeway," he said.

Jordi sighed, as if his fun had been cut short. He rolled the window down and said, "Say no more."

He pulled a small submachine gun from under his seat and held it out the window.

"Jordi!" Aiden, panicked, reached over to grab the steering wheel, but Jordi still had an iron grip on it with his other hand.

The fixer let the bullets fly. He might have been driving like a fool in love with death, but Jordi's shot pattern stayed tight on Gin's Wildebeest, smashing up its rear windshield and filling the fender full of holes.

"Damn it," Jordi said. "I'm trying to get the tires. You want them alive, right?"

"That would be optimal," said Aiden, as drily as he could manage.

If he and Jordi didn't disappear down a back alley in the next five minutes, it wouldn't matter what condition Gin and her cronies were in. The cops were on their way regardless of the outcome.

"That big guy is crawling out of the window," Jordi said.

Frank pulled himself halfway out. He had a pistol in his hand, the barrel waving in the air. Balancing his phone in one hand while steadying the steering wheel in his other, Aiden brought up the car's electronics systems and sent a shutdown order – except it was rejected by a security system it shouldn't have had.

"What the…" Aiden muttered. "I can't hack into her car's electronics."

"Do something, Aiden!" Jordi yelled back.

Gin swerved to avoid an oncoming car. Frank buckled, dropping his arm as he shot, popping a bullet into the 3.4T's hood.

"Fucker's got no respect," said Jordi.

"Keep it steady. You know, if you can." Abandoning his attempt to hack Gin's car, Aiden lowered his window, unbuckled his seatbelt, and leaned out, resting his elbow on the sideview mirror. Jordi took over steering. Aiden grabbed the revolver from the dash and found Frank, who was struggling to steady himself, in his sights.

Aiden squeezed two shots from the revolver. They punched through Frank's chest, where expanding red circles appeared on the front of his work shirt. The big man fell from the Wildebeest and landed right in Jordi's path.

Aiden slid back into his seat as two big bumps racked the bottom of the muscle car, knocking his head on the window frame as he came back inside the car. His headache was back.

"Fuck," Jordi said, with a glance in the rearview. "That kinda makes me feel bad for him."

"Don't be. If he wasn't dead from the gunshots or the fall, you made sure of it," said Aiden, and Jordi laughed.

Aiden heard a helicopter in the distance. He was sure he could hear sirens somewhere out there, getting closer. The ctOS network told him they had three cars en route, ETA less than three minutes.

Gin took the next exit off 395 and began to drive more erratically, cutting over a sidewalk, through a gaggle of tourists taking pictures of the lit-up Capitol Building from a distance.

"Get me closer," said Aiden. "If we can't nab her for information, I can get it from her network connection before she disappears."

"How close do we need to be?"

"Closer than this." His earpiece was picking her up, but her ID kept flickering as the profiler struggled to maintain a lock. "And quickly, I can't run two sets of hacks at once."

"Two?" asked Jordi.

"I can get us away from the police or I can get her info. Not both at once. You choose."

Pedestrian screams blocked out any hint of inbound police, but he knew time was almost up. Their car bounced as if it was falling apart, making his teeth shake. Jordi swore as he followed Gin up a wide shallow stairway and back onto an actual road. "Where the hell is she taking us?"

She led them to a large roundabout. A sign said it was Dupont Circle. Aiden readied his hack and his revolver, but he'd have to use one or the other when Gin eventually pulled out of the roundabout.

But she didn't. She continued going round and round. Cars split from her path and they either took the first exit or crashed into nearby bushes.

Jordi held the wheel to the left as they remained in the curve. Round and round they followed the pink Wildebeest. Soon, Gin and Bill were staring at them from the other side of the circle where Aiden couldn't tell who was chasing who anymore.

Gin pulled out a pistol. It was bigger than the one Frank had been holding, nearly the length of her forearm and finished in the same color as her eyes.

"She's going to shoot!" Jordi yelled.

But while Jordi had been driving, Aiden had been riding the city's ctOS.

Gin was staring out of her window, gun leveled right at them. She didn't see the three blocker poles spring up in the middle of the roundabout. The pink Wildebeest slammed into the barrier like a soda can against a brick wall. Gin and Bill flew through the windshield and flopped across the sidewalk like rag dolls in the hands of an angry toddler.

Jordi slammed the car to a stop just behind the crumpled 4x4. He wagged a finger at the carnage. "And that, children, is why we wear seatbelts."

Aiden got out, shakier than he'd expected, gun held out in front.

"Hey," Jordi called. "Where are you going? Didn't you say the cops were coming?"

As Aiden hurried over to the bodies, he checked on their pursuit. Selecting a point as far away as he could scroll with his thumb on his phone's screen, right over by the Smithsonian, he sent a dispatch out requesting urgent support. He didn't wait for the sirens to grow distant, just trusted it would work.

"I bought us some time," Aiden, said without looking over at Jordi.

Bill was dead. At least, if he wasn't he was going to regret it in the morning. The right side of his face had smeared blood across the sidewalk and his body was bent all wrong and open to the elements like he was in a horror movie.

Gin lay unmoving five feet away, flat on her front. He couldn't see her face, but he figured that was a good thing.

Her clothes had been ripped up from landing on the asphalt, and through the rags covering her legs Aiden saw a gleam of shining steel.

"What the hell?" he murmured to himself.

Her earpiece was still in place. Aiden bent over and grabbed it, wondering why people always had to do things the hard way.

A burst of gunfire came from behind. Aiden turned around, gun raised. Bill staggered up to a stand, back from the dead, his face in bloody ruins and what remained of his left eye glaring. Then, with a blast and a wet thump, he fell to the ground to reveal Jordi behind him holding his SMG. Jordi walked over to Bill, putting another burst into the man's head.

"He was dead," said Aiden. "I was sure of it."

"You should be thanking me then," said Jordi. "Not like you to miss something like that."

"He was fucking dead," said Aiden, angry and confused. Bill's head had been caved in like a melon.

"Well then, he just got up all Lazarus-like right behind you."

"How was he not dead?" Aiden said, as much to himself as to Jordi.

"Maybe you can ask her?" Jordi ran past Aiden and began firing.

Against all the odds, a blood-soaked Gin scrambled upright and limped toward the Benedict Bank on the other side of the street, holding one arm to her side.

"Stop!" Aiden shouted. Gin looked over her shoulder and then up at the building. With a grimace, she jumped into the air and latched onto the front of the bank like it was a climbing frame not a sheer wall. Her metal foot dug into the brick up to the toe.

She groaned in obvious pain but kept climbing.

Jordi started shooting, leaving a trail of holes as he tried to correct his aim. Gin jumped again, barely making it onto the roof and disappearing out of sight.

"We have to get out of here," Aiden said, staring after her. No amount of distraction would keep the cops away forever.

Jordi was out of breath. He stomped toward Aiden, pointing his empty machine gun at the bank's roof. "Are you kidding me? She just climbed that building like a grasshopper. A grasshopper with a metal leg. You did see it, right?"

"Yeah, I saw it," Aiden said. More importantly, she'd been as good as dead a moment before. The bank's alarms were going off, and he marked multiple video cameras inside and out. "Get the car. I'll sort the feds."

Jordi looked at the man on the ground, then at the crushed Wildebeest against the blocker poles. "I don't have time to clean this up, Aiden."

"No," Aiden said. "You don't."

CHAPTER FIVE

Jordi was adamant. "I'd rather not get caught by the cops no matter how nice the car."

They abandoned their newly acquired car at Dupont Circle after searching for and then picking up a very specific telecoms van Jordi was after.

While Jordi was looking for his van, Aiden got busy scraping Gin's earpiece for whatever info he could get. When the radio traffic suggested they were free to travel unmolested, they drove until Aiden insisted they stop at a small diner out of the way down by Rock Creek Park. When Jordi asked why, Aiden didn't care to answer, instead promising him waffles.

Now, Jordi sat on the other side of the diner's booth, staring at the waffle Aiden had bought him. The butter had melted, and the maple syrup had soaked right in. He'd taken one sip of his coffee before letting it cool untouched to room temperature.

Opposite, Aiden had Gin's earpiece laid out on the table. It was encrypted to the moon and back, and its messages had been remotely deleted, as well as any call records. Aiden could dig them out by penetrating the service provider, but that would take time.

Their waitress passed by, ignoring them and Jordi's untouched coffee for a third time. Jordi put his elbows on the table.

"So, we're going to talk about it?"

"You can talk all you want, Jordi. I'm trying to find these candy stripers."

"First," Jordi said. "That's a horrible name. We'll work on that. Second…" He lowered his voice to a whisper. "We just saw a dead woman scale a two-story building faster than an Olympic speed climber, after she'd been thrown through a windshield. That is not medical prosthetics, and if it is, sign me up because I deserve it."

"I saw," said Aiden, still focused on the task at hand. Why was it so hard to tune Jordi out?

"Is that what they stole? Robot legs?" Jordi stabbed his waffle. "You know what they could do with tech like that, right? Fuck me, you know what I could do with it?"

"Sell it," said Aiden.

"Well, yes. But I'd have my own all geared up to make life easy, which means deadly for others and extra safe and cozy for me. What else do they have, Aiden? What exactly are we facing?"

"Leech didn't give me a grocery list, but it encompasses something that could kick a grown man across the bar without breaking a sweat." Aiden looked up and rubbed at his beard as he thought about what they'd seen. Jordi wasn't wrong. Leech had, perhaps as expected, undersold the value of what had been stolen. Adaptive tech. He'd assumed she had meant it integrated with people's bodies without the normal risk of rejection or could be melded into multiple uses. What they'd seen was something of a different order. It seemed to him there were two parts – the replacement limbs and organs, and then the technology controlling them. He guessed the control tech was where the real value was. Without it, everything else was just lumps of dumb metal.

There was no doubt in his mind that Gin was fitted with one of the items Leech was so eager to get back. Leech's finding him and forcing him to help her made more sense now – multiple deaths and crashed helicopters weren't something you accepted for run of the mill fake arms and legs.

However, legs that had you leaping over buildings in a single bound? That was worth his time.

The trash file in Gin's cloud shifted codes every sixty seconds. He'd scraped it as soon as he'd fished it from her, but he wasn't going to get anything else. Fortunately, there was enough there to get them one more step along in this strange investigation. All he had to do was wait.

"We won't know what exactly it was they stole until we retrieve it, and we can't do that until we find them. And if we don't hurry, and if you don't let me work, they'll have moved on. This isn't a marathon Jordi, it's a hundred meter dash, so shut the hell up and let me work."

Jordi threw up his hands. "Hey, don't let me slow you down. I'll be here thinking of, you know, *consequences*. And guns. And everything else we need to take these fuckers on. You think EMPs will work better to stop that tech in its tracks?"

Aiden gave him a look. Jordi turned away, muttering loud enough to be irritating, something about how EMPs were the kind of thing that worked in movies.

Aiden didn't have the luxury of considering consequences.

They would arrive whether he thought about them or not. That's the kind of hell life is, he thought. Of more concern was figuring out where Gin would be heading, and who she might have been able to bankroll an operation with – someone with the know-how to attach cutting-edge medical tech and make it work.

And he didn't have a clue. The list was either far too long to be useful or no one except Leech could do it. Either answer was unsatisfactory.

"And to think" – Jordi leaned back in his seat, linking his fingers behind his head, speaking his thoughts aloud – "I'm considered a criminal for providing a recognized community service. The government, on the other hand, fucks up and lets the Klan get ahold of some super soldier shit and they're the victims."

"They certainly came crawling," said Aiden, without looking up.

Jordi snapped his fingers as a thought struck him. "Hey, no wonder she was able to kick you across the bar like that. I'm surprised she didn't break your ribs."

Aiden wasn't sure she hadn't. His chest glowed with low-level pain, and he was trying not to breathe too deeply because when he did, it felt like someone was squeezing him tight.

"I'll add some painkillers to the order," said Jordi, watching his face.

"Got them," Aiden said triumphantly. "At the bar, I found out Gin messaged somebody named R. Gatty. She wanted to 'be there' to see if something worked. And wouldn't you know it if I didn't trace the call." Aiden grinned and sent a message.

"Gotta be more super soldier gizmos," said Jordi, waving a fork at Aiden. He'd finally started on his waffle in earnest.

"Maybe a pizza oven for all I know. But it's looking like Gin's earpiece is a bust. She only used it to contact Gatty, and no one else."

"Gatty. What kind of name is that? Think it's her boss?"

"Nope. From her message I think she's in charge of Gatty, not the other way around. They're careful, Jordi. All I got is fragments before the wipe, but they used their phones to set up meets, different places, different times. Not a lot to pick over." He hummed, musing on the pile of data he'd managed to extract. "Except for this, there's mentions about some guy named Abraham. Nothing much, just too often to be coincidence."

"Abraham?" Jordi asked. "Shit, now they're religious, too?"

"While they love talking about Christian purity, no, not that Abraham. And not President Lincoln either, before you try."

"There's also F. Murray Abraham."

"Whoever it is, I bet he's their linchpin. But that's a guess 'cause whoever they are, they're good. No addresses, no personal details, and no other names. These are their own devices, and you still couldn't doxx them from scraping them."

"The robot lady was our only lead. We let her get away." Jordi shook his head. "Remind me to double tap anyone we kill from now on." He mimed shooting with maple syrup coated finger guns.

"We're not killing anyone if we can help it," Aiden said. "And she wasn't our only lead."

Jordi put his fork down. "Did… did Aiden Pearce just say we're not killing anyone? Tell me now how our robot overlords replaced you and where I can find the real Aiden."

At Aiden's bland look, Jordi said, "It's either that or getting old has softened you up. I thought we're all supposed to get more right-wing as we get older."

"Dying's easy, Jordi. Salting the land, destroying a legacy, those things take time and effort."

Jordi whistled his approval.

We're not going to have the time on this one, thought Aiden suddenly.

He raised the orange juice he'd ordered and glanced at the door. The straw still had paper on its end. "Maybe you can work on getting us better equipment."

Jordi swept a hand at the mostly empty diner. "You can say guns, Aiden. This is America. Hell, you can ask me to get you a bomb and nobody in here would bat an eye."

The waitress, who'd been heading toward them to offer a refill now that Jordi was actually eating, spun on her heels and went back into the kitchen.

"Get us guns, Jordi. Actual guns," said Aiden, eyebrows raised. "I sent Gatty a message."

A smirk came to Jordi's lips. "We gonna go see him?"

"Absolutely." Aiden nodded toward the diner's entrance, which opened as they spoke. "That should be him walking in now, thinking he's coming to see Gin."

Gatty didn't look like anybody they'd seen at Proud Patty's. He was clean cut, dressed in a dark fleece jacket, light brown hair recently cut and groomed like a man ready to read the news on TV.

Aiden dragged the man's info down from his profiler.

Richard Gatty, of 1209 Massachusetts Avenue, Apartment 5. He worked as a scrub tech at DC General Hospital, making a decent living and, according to online records, spent an enormous amount of time playing video games online. At least until seven months ago.

Gatty looked around the diner, searching for Gin. Aiden lowered his head, removed the paper from his straw, and sipped his orange juice. The diner had a camera pointed at the door, and Aiden shared its feed with Jordi.

"That guy?" Jordi whispered. "He looks like a youth pastor."

"He's in medicine."

"That's even worse. I wouldn't want people like him operating on me. Some racist with a scalpel? That'll give you nightmares." Jordi made a show of shivering.

"Unless she has deep wells of talent and resolve she keeps well hidden, Gin didn't attach that metal leg herself."

"Jesus," Jordi said. "And I thought accessing healthcare was bad. So what do we do with the boy scout?"

Aiden routed a message through Gin's earpiece. "Gin's just told him she changed her mind and to meet back at home. Got spooked. Ruckus at Proud Patty's. Simple."

"Home?" Jordi said. "Didn't you pick up his address already? Why do we have to follow him?"

"Because 'home' is what they call their base of operations, I think. He'll know what it means."

Gatty's expression was all scowl. He cursed at the waitress when she asked if he wanted a table and turned to leave. Viewing him through the camera, Aiden noticed a gun holstered inside his jacket.

A moment later the welcome bell rang as Gatty rushed outside toward his pickup.

"I think you ruined his day," Jordi said.

"It's about to get a lot worse," said Aiden. "Give me the keys. I'm driving."

They followed Richard Gatty, who drove his truck like he was someone's cautious grandmother.

"In case I didn't get a chance to tell you this already," said Aiden to Jordi, who was wearing the ctOS-branded hard hat he'd found on the dash, pushed back so it looked like it might fall off if he needed to slam on the brakes. "As a pursuit vehicle this sucks."

Aiden hoped it didn't come to an actual chase because they'd be left behind like a lame dog watching a hare leave it in the dust. The point of the van was the stash of usable equipment and parts in the back, all neatly numbered, packed and stored by whoever ran the truck day to day. At first, he'd been irritated at Jordi for taking so long to choose their next vehicle but having seen the stash in the back, he understood completely why Jordi had been so picky.

There were boxes of wires, generic circuit boards, and even a drawer of cheap processors. He'd found five remote control cars, six tablets, and, for some reason, a bag of fireworks with a receipt inside dated from the previous July. There was more, but Aiden hadn't had time to rummage around and do inventory.

Plus, who'd suspect a ctOS maintenance guy of being up to no good?

He laughed. People like him, maybe, people who knew just how intrusive the network was, how much it offered up to anyone willing to take a moment and search.

"It's comfortable," Jordi said. "And sure, I know most people are basically going to screen us out as invisible, but you're not wrong. It's not very stylish and definitely not capable of anything but steering like a two-ton turd, but that's kind of the point."

"You got your chance with the last car," Aiden pointed out.

"And that worked out great," said Jordi. "Oh, hey, look." He gestured out the window. "See that wall? You know what's on the other side of it?"

"Humpty Dumpty?" Aiden said.

"Have some respect. It's Arlington Cemetery, Tomb of the Unknown Soldier. That's the grave where there's always an Army guard on duty to watch over it. They do it at night, in the snow, the rain."

"Unknown is just another word for forgotten," Aiden said bitterly, eyes on the wall imagining the other side. "I can see why there'd be someone on the watch."

"We ain't quite the same kind of unknowns," Jordi said.

"I wouldn't need a guard."

Jordi sighed and Aiden knew he'd pissed him off.

He kept the van back from Gatty's red pickup. Aiden was linked to the man's personal ID, so if they lost sight of him, it wouldn't take long to catch up.

Gatty led them off Highway 50 and into a town called West Falls Church. It was a cookie cutter suburb with gas stations, grocery stores, and power lines as far as Aiden could see. There wasn't much to say about it until Jordi saw their destination.

"Sleepy Hollow Road?" Jordi said with a huff of resignation. "Is this the place where the headless horseman comes to decapitate you?"

"No," Aiden said. "That's in New York. Tarrytown. I don't know where the hell we are."

The road wound on through dense woodland. Gatty's lights blared red as he came to a stop outside an old gate with a large sign in front of it proclaiming, "First United." There had, once, been other words but they'd been scrubbed off. On the other side, a dirt road led deeper into the woods.

Gatty got out of his pickup and approached the gate. He stood before a panel built into the side and gave them wary glances when they approached in the van as the gate opened.

"Ask him for directions," Aiden said, lowering Jordi's window as they slowed to a stop just past Gatty.

Jordi didn't miss a beat. He leaned his hand out in greeting before adjusting his hard hat. "Hi there, young man. I was wondering if you could tell me if we're going the right way to the local burger joint."

Gatty looked disgusted. "Get out of here. Leave me alone."

"Well," said Jordi, "that's not very neighborly. I just moved in down the street. Me and my family. Navigation isn't working for me. I just need you to point me in the right direction."

Gatty smiled and raised a middle finger. "Here's some direction for you."

"Let me kill him," Jordi whispered, turning back to Aiden. "World's average IQ will go up."

But Aiden was already out of the van and walking around the back. Getting close enough to jump him, Aiden said, "Behind you, asshole."

Gatty turned and took Aiden's baton across the face. When Gatty hit the ground, Aiden dug through his coat. He took the gun, a simple P-9mm, and found a mask tucked in his inside pocket. It was striped, red and white. Aiden ripped Gatty's phone from his hand and stomped it to pieces.

At the sound of whining metal, Aiden looked up and saw the gate closing.

"Shit." Leaving Gatty on the ground, he raced for the closing gate and, sucking in his gut as he slid sideways through it, made it to the other side as it clinked closed.

His hat had gotten knocked askew, but he was otherwise fine.

"What did you do that for?" Jordi climbed out of the van and walked over to Gatty's unconscious form. Jordi's SMG hovered over the man's face as he kicked him in the ribs. Gatty let out a burst of air but didn't move.

"The gate was closing, and we didn't have time to get in the van and drive through. Take him with you and see what he knows," said Aiden.

Jordi kept his gun over the man's face. "Why don't I tie him up and we can both see what's at the end of that road?"

Aiden tried to tap into the keypad, but there was no way he'd be able to unlock it. "I can't open the gate from here," he said. "No network connection, all hardwired. I have to find the main server."

"Fine," said Jordi unhappily. "I'll just get our guy in the back of the van and find a way to hop over. Give me a moment while I get the rifle."

Aiden looked at the fence with his VR. "That's not going to work either."

"Why not?"

"C'mon man, you could do this yourself. The whole run of it is electrified."

"Bullshit," said Jordi, but he didn't move. "It touched your hat, and nothing happened."

"It engaged when the gate closed."

Jordi laughed. "You can't Lone Ranger this, Aiden. Help me find a way over."

Aiden sighed and pointed to the top of the gate. "Test it out if you think I'm lying."

Jordi glared at the gate, then shook his head. "So what then? I'm just the backup driver?"

"Listen," Aiden said, "I can slip in and out of whatever's up there. No guns. Promise. If I see the stolen goods, I'll contact Leech. Then we can both ride off into the sunset and let the government handle the rest. You can do the most good by asking Gatty what he knows. He knows what I'm going to find, get him to spill it so I don't walk headfirst into the barrel of a shotgun."

"Whatever you say. You want me to toss over anything from the van?"

Aiden patted his coat pocket and the gear lodged there. "Already grabbed what I needed."

Jordi grunted as he lifted Gatty over his shoulder. "How will I know you aren't dead?"

"I'll call you." Aiden heard the van door open as he turned and headed into the trees.

CHAPTER SIX

There was a second gate.

This one came with the added protection of barbed wire. It was the only way through a high mesh wall that surrounded a clearing in the trees with a church at the center. Built from wood and bleached gray from age, the gate's fabric had been fortified with boards and sheets of corrugated iron. Aiden thought it looked like a patchwork quilt, if one sewed with steel and hate. The clearing around the church was occupied by multiple vehicles between which wandered guards sporting assault rifles and blue jeans. Aiden picked up a server somewhere near the church, underground if the magnetic fields displayed on his AR were anything to go by.

Basement, he thought, as he watched from behind a fallen log. Just my luck.

He pinpointed cameras placed around the church, but everything was hardwired, which meant he had to get to the server if he wanted to access them. He wasn't sure if these people were brilliant or just old fashioned.

The gate itself didn't appear electrified like the first one, but the wall was high, and if he tried to climb it the noise would bring people pretty quickly. He waited to hear from Jordi, wondering if Gatty had woken and Jordi had gotten any layout information from him.

But, when it became clear the patrols were both slender and infrequent, he decided he could make a start and use whatever Jordi sent over to fill in the gaps. Whenever that would be.

Time couldn't be wasted.

Tim Yarlsley was on guard duty ten miles from the main road, passing the time peeking through the back window of a Brubeck Polar and checking out the upholstery. A fine SUV, in Tim's opinion. They'd gotten it from one of the test goonies downstairs, and it should have been his. He'd waited his turn, worked his time, done as he was told by a string of dipshit bosses. That's what he'd been told to expect if he was to succeed.

Except, when it came to it, life hadn't turned out that way. Everything he learned in school was horseshit. It was Abraham who'd shown him that democracy didn't mean anything if you didn't participate with voice and sword.

So, Tim had staked his claim. The community would be voting on the ownership of the Polar that night, and everybody had put in for their chance to win it. Bad odds, but he'd been asking people to vote for him. Against the rules, sure, but he'd learned you needed to take before it could be taken from you.

He looked at the wheel arches, the placement of the headlights and sighed. Driving it would rock.

His mask fogged the window as he imagined pulling up to his house, climbing out of his new acquisition as people stared, pretending he didn't see them gawking. They'd probably wonder how he afforded it and would take back all that crap whispered about him being white trash. He was just about to wipe away another puff of condensation when the clamor of a muffled male voice set against some awful urban background music caught his attention. He rushed over, rifle up like he'd trained, but there was no one around. He couldn't believe anyone among the community would listen to such degenerate nonsense.

Where was everybody else? Had the livestream started already? Someone was pulling his leg. Or was it a test? He looked around in case Abraham was there judging him.

Whatever was making the noise remained out of sight. Then he heard the whine of small tires as an RC car rolled backward from the gate. The music was coming from its open windows. How was a toy doing that? Probably some ridiculous Bluetooth nonsense. Like children needed to listen to music like that while playing.

"What the hell?" Tim said. He raised his walkie to his lips. He had to tell Abraham.

The cough and purr of a second engine came from behind him. Tim spun and raised his rifle as the back of his prized Brubeck Polar SUV rolled toward him at increasing speed. Still trying to figure out what was happening, Tim realized he was in trouble far too late. The SUV rolled right over him without slowing before running into the gate like it was made of grass. The Brubeck crushed the RC car under its tires like it was a soda can, killing the noise squawking from the car's stereo.

Aiden rolled out of his spot behind the tree as he tapped his phone and put the Brubeck in park. The gate had crumpled in a groan of bending steel loud enough to attract anyone awake. More guards would be coming. He climbed over the demolished gate and kept low to the ground as he ran for the back of the church.

Jordi called. "I was going to ask if you were still breathing, but it sounds like you're fine."

"I'm busy," Aiden said. "What have you found out?"

"Yeah, so am I. I kind of had to kill that guy."

Fucking hell, Jordi, thought Aiden. "Gatty? How difficult is it to keep someone alive after you've got them tied up?"

"Yeah, right, that was his name. Wasn't my fault. He woke up and came at me. Almost made me crash the van. Anyway, I'll have to take care of this. Shout if you need me."

"Damn it, Jordi, now I have to do this the hard way." Aiden hung up before Jordi could answer.

Gatty hadn't just been a way to find the red-and-whites and learn about why they called this place home. He was a way to learn about the church and its layout in detail. Plus, he was a fallback in case the compound proved a bust. Something concrete to hand to Leech. Now, Jordi had mucked it up.

No pressure then.

Tracking around the edge of the church, Aiden came across an angled cellar door. Thankful he wouldn't have to sneak through the building to get to the cellar and the server housed there, he knelt to open it up.

There were shouts in the distance from the direction of the wrecked gate. He didn't have long before the distraction he'd served up would end and they'd start a proper search of the site.

The plan was to get inside and out again before that happened.

While the church looked like it had been built in the 1950s, the door to the basement was recently installed and sealed with a digital lock. Pretty standard, even for condemned buildings, but this one was strange. It looked like they weren't trying to keep people from getting in as much as they were trying to keep what was inside from getting out.

As much a prison as a lair, he thought, suspecting something grim waited for him below.

Either way the lock was a pain in the ass. Aiden tracked its connections and saw it was connected to an alarm, had a trip switch in case of tampering, and would call for help if an unauthorized entry was detected. He needed to manage each of these and do so at the same time, so they all went offline together before one failsafe had a chance to rat him out.

All while the compound searched for him.

"Check around back," someone shouted.

Come on, Aiden thought, trying to line up each of the different hacks he needed to deploy and synchronize them to attack at the same moment.

He nearly had it. Just a few more seconds and he could duck inside. Footsteps came from the side of the church. They were walking, not running, but he couldn't tell how many there were and couldn't use the cameras to find out.

Letting the work on the lock continue without his oversight, Aiden got ready to fight. He'd have liked to attack them with the baton, keep it quiet, but if there was more than one, he couldn't risk getting distracted trying to subdue them. It was going to be a gunfest whether he liked it or not.

Finally, the lock unlatched. No alarms went off, with no call for help. Aiden pulled at the cellar door and fell into the basement. He caught the falling hatch just in time to lower and close it quietly before he heard voices above him.

He hung by the door, breathing hard and hoping no one had seen him enter. His profiler software latched neatly onto all four of the people searching for him and fed him their conversation.

"This is some bullshit," one said. "No one else is here. I'll tell you what happened. I bet Tim was being a dumbass and slobbering over the Polar and got himself crushed by it. Twenty dollars. As if anyone was going to vote for him. Now we gotta tell Abraham and fix the goddamned gate."

"Don't use the Lord's name in vain," another said.

"I'm not. God did damn that gate. Look what Tim did to it. What did he think he was doing?"

"It looks bad on all of us but you're right, it's Tim who's damned."

"This ain't the time to be joking. Y'all can bother Abraham during his livestream if you want, but I sure as hell ain't."

"I… well… we can't just leave Tim like that. We have to move the Polar."

"Abraham's the one with the keys!"

"Tim managed to move it," said the first voice doubtfully. "Besides, you sure Tim's dead?"

"I don't know, Francis. A whole ton of American metal and rubber ran over him and smeared him across a steel gate. What do you think?"

"Did you check his pulse?

"I didn't get his pulse because I couldn't reach under the tires."

"If he's alive Abraham will want to talk to him," said the first voice, sounding the calmest of them all.

"Fine. We can go try to pull him out, but I am not telling Abraham anything until he's done inside. I'm not getting it in the neck because Tim acted like a bag of dicks. Agreed?"

"Yeah, yeah. Come on."

Aiden smirked as the voices retreated, and ensured his profiler logged the data on the men for him to recover later. He turned to focus on what was in the basement. The air was rancid and sweet like rotting flesh. An unwise gulp of it made his stomach churn, and he resisted the urge to wipe at his watering eyes. Pulling up his mask he breathed through his mouth, but the smell only receded a touch. It was going to stick in his clothes like used gum.

Feeling his way forward, Aiden kept his hand on the wall as a guide. The only things he could see were two tiny dots of red light somewhere ahead. Sometimes they'd disappear as he moved, but then they'd appear again, closer. He couldn't tell if the basement was an open space or a winding maze of walls, and he decided not to find out until he could see.

The VR provided by his phone and earpiece didn't help – he had no map of the room that it could overlay. The smell of death grew as he moved toward where his phone was telling him the server was located. He stepped into something slick on the floor and flung his hands out to make sure he didn't fall.

This must be where they dump their garbage, he thought, wrinkling his nose under his mask. It certainly smelled like someone had left last week's chicken out to decompose.

Moving on, he found the ctOS box. It hummed in his earpiece, and his hand went to it like it was a long-lost pet. It wasn't Wi-Fi enabled. Another smart decision by the people who'd installed it, but he forced it into open mode using a short-range radio frequency ID protocol all these boxes had but which were rarely activated. The factory login was "Admin" and "Password." He shook his head. Most people never changed them because all they really needed was to plug them in and forget about them. Maybe these people were more old fashioned than he'd perceived.

"Come on," he whispered, and then grinned when the system opened for him.

From there, it didn't take him long to navigate his way through. Whoever put the church together had assumed that by being offline they'd not need to install network protections, so once he was connected, the entire system folded open before him like an all-you-can-eat buffet.

The server was busy – something elsewhere on site was using a mad amount of bandwidth.

What do we have here? he thought and remembered what the men before had said about a livestream.

The livestream was being broadcast across multiple channels. He followed the initial upload and saw how they routed it through proxies and VPNs to ensure it couldn't be traced back to the church, and then funneled it across multiple social media and video hosting sites including those publicly committed to banning this kind of thing. Two million viewers and growing. That was a lot for a group that had taken great lengths to ensure anonymity.

Let's give it a watch, thought Aiden, as he plugged into the feed.

"Hail to the Chief" played as the camera zoomed in on the silhouettes of a group of people standing in the shadows at the back of a church's stage. It sure fit with the shape of the building above him.

As the presidential song came to a close, lights brightened to reveal a large group of people wearing red and white vertically striped masks, bandanas, and caps. Many of them wore sunglasses to cover their eyes, reflecting the glimmer back at the camera. It looked like a gang photo op or terrorist stream. Most of them held big rifles against their hips, or stood there with crossed arms, chins jutting. To one side, a big man in a tan baseball cap held up his shiny metal arm, repeatedly opening and closing his fist.

A tall older man with long gray hair falling to his shoulders walked out and stood in front of the others. He wore black slacks, and a white shirt with red suspenders. No tie. His beard was covered by a longer striped mask.

Aiden's ear pinged with new signals, but none of them made any sense. The crew inside were putting out some kind of disruption to keep their feed anonymous. Aiden's profiler couldn't identify any of the people he saw on the pulpit. His analysis slid off them like they were shadows. For the first time he wondered just how good they were and whether he and Jordi had been unwise to barrel in without doing more background work first.

Not that we were given any choice by Leech, he thought darkly.

They weren't racists of the Christian variety, he thought. There was no cross or dying Jesus hung up behind them. Instead, nothing but a United States flag hung vertically with the stars burned off. The flag looked thick, military grade, like one picked up at the garden store to resist winter storms and hurricane season.

The older man at the front spread his arms as if to welcome the viewers into their midst. The group behind him grunted, "Haroo!" and stomped their right feet against the church floor in unison.

"Do you hear that?" the man asked, with eyes clear, jaw firm, and arms still raised. He clapped his hands together and brought them to his chest as if in prayer. "Things are out of control in our glorious country. We are no longer united. I don't remember a time we ever truly were. Do you?" The people behind him haroo'd their agreement.

"Our founding fathers would be outraged at how far we've fallen. We have let this nation slip into the hands of the greedy, the sycophantic, the unclean. It's on you and me. We've let this happen on our watch. Our forefathers would be speechless if they saw how their glorious plan has been desecrated. How dare we stand by and do nothing."

The camera zoomed in on the speaker.

The words were like acid in Aiden's veins.

"You may be sitting there wondering who we are. We do not keep our identities hidden because we are cowards. No. We stand behind these stripes because rich liberals, traitors, Jews, and their vassal races deny us the right to speak the truth. Every day of our lives we have had to give up who we are or face persecution and violence for saying the things no one wants to admit are true. I say this to you: you wear a mask every day. Look in a mirror and see how they've made you hide who you are.

"We are the Brotherhood of Stripes. We hold the original plan of this country in our hearts. From Franklin to Jefferson, all those who came before knew what we know to be self-evident.

This country was meant for us, for our culture and our traditions, and using our property as we see fit. We are here to inform you that the backsliding stops with us. It stops now. We are willing to suffer the lashes, to earn our red stripes against white skin in the fight to come. There will be no stars of miscegenation to water us down. No blue sky of cultural genocide. Our problem is here, right where we are, and we are going to fix it.

"I say to you: this country will become great again. My flesh and blood came over on the *Mayflower*. They helped fight to create these beautiful states, driving out those who knew not what they had, who did not deserve it. Our kin shaped this country without guidance from those too weak to hold their own, to stop their own people from giving them to us. We made our own rules, rules which the rest of the world only dream of using as their own.

"The men and women you see before you will no longer sit back and watch our legacy be trampled on by the inferior: nonwhites, Jews, homosexuals, men-haters, ladyboys, and politicians who continue to take our money to uphold a demonic agenda. Their conspiracy is uncovered and will be destroyed in fire and blood. God will bless us as we become His purifying fire."

Jesus, Aiden thought, feeling sick to his stomach. Jordi had been right when he'd predicted these people were nuts.

Smart and nuts was never a good combination in Aiden's experience.

The man pointed at the camera now. "Unlike them, with their back biting and infighting, we are willing to bleed for this country, united and with one voice. The America we knew is dead, the America we dreamed of nothing more than ruins. It is up to us to forge a new beginning. With that comes an end, and here before you are its harbingers. Witness the future as it was destined to be since the time of our forefathers."

The man with the metal arm moved forward, metallic palm up. A short woman wearing a black bandana brought out a cardboard box and waited in front of the speaker. He opened the box and removed a human skull.

"What the hell?" Aiden whispered.

The skull was placed in the metal hand. It sat there for a few seconds as everyone in the room went quiet. The man with the metal arm looked down and stared at the hunk of bone in his hand. With a quick squeeze, he crushed the skull into a million pieces.

"And that's just one—" The speaker was interrupted by the sound of a heavy door swinging open and crashing against a wall.

"Abraham? Where is he?"

"What are you doing?" the older speaker said, eyes darting left but his face resolute as if the interruption had to be temporary. "Get out of here. Not now."

If Aiden had been watching in the comfort of his own home, he would have laughed at such ineptitude. The person who had interrupted the live feed stepped forward, the camera catching the shoulders. He recognized Gin's back on the screen, blocking out the pulpit. "You can't keep me waiting like this. I've got important shit to tell you about—"

The feed went dead.

CHAPTER SEVEN

Shit, thought Aiden. Time to go.

The Brotherhood of Stripes. He'd have to call Leech, let her know he had a lead on a name, but that couldn't happen until he got out of there. With the feed going out to two million viewers, she most likely would have seen it already, and his claim of intel might be seen as a ploy to escape. After all, the job was still only half done and the easy half at that.

Where was the Wetware? It might be at the church, but the chump upstairs with a metal arm suggested the Stripes had access to high-grade medical facilities, which sure as shit weren't in the rickety wooden building overhead. Even so, he needed to be damn sure the Wetware wasn't sequestered here.

It also means they've had this stuff for a while, Aiden thought, suddenly pinpointing a huge gap in Leech's story. No way had the Stripes been performing major operations in the last few days on people like Gin, especially if they recently got the tech.

The designers of this compound might have kept everything

off grid, but they'd then created an entire network linked to the server, connecting everything from water to lights to the air conditioning. Even the fridge upstairs in the kitchen was connected. Aiden brought up the lights in the basement, eyes blinking as he tried to adjust to the sudden illumination, determined to search the area for anything suspicious.

The server room was tiny with a single door in, surrounded by slatted wooden walls through which he could see other rooms beyond. Turning around, he finally saw the source of the stench and nearly gasped in horror.

Bodies had been piled in a corner. The corpses were in different states of decay, some bloated blue, others missing various limbs, their clothes stained the brown and black of old blood. Mostly they were in a state of undress. On the verge of vomiting, Aiden locked onto his breathing and counted his breaths in and out until his mind buried his revulsion.

The Stripes had murdered these people and left them here. But why? Over the initial shock, he looked harder. The man lying at the top of the pile looked untouched except for a device wrapped around his throat. A red indicator light blinked in the device's center. Aiden stepped closer and away from the server. He recognized the man. Miguel Henry, the agent Leech had lost contact with.

His profiler dinged. Henry's details floated above his head. The first detail glared at him in bright red – terminal throat cancer. No wonder he'd been willing to take such risks in infiltrating a white supremacist group. He hadn't cared about the consequences. There was no suggestion Henry had been voluntarily fitted with whatever was around his throat before he'd started the job.

What are you? thought Aiden, getting close enough to bend over and inspect the device.

A bubble of air and bloody pus grew on the man's lips, and Aiden gasped as he realized Agent Henry might still be alive.

Heart in his throat, fingers trembling, Aiden reached down and took the man's pulse. It was there. Faint, intermittent. Was he mistaken? He shook the agent as gently as possible.

"Henry," he hissed. "Agent Henry."

Henry didn't respond, his body cold and floppy.

"Fuck," Aiden cursed and looked around, trying to figure out what to do. He had to get Miguel out of there. He leaned down to take Miguel's pulse again when the agent gasped, taking several gulps of air, and blinked at Aiden.

"St… st…" His Adam's apple bobbed as he tried to speak.

"It's OK," Aiden said. "You're in shock. Stay still. I won't harm you." He knelt and pulled the mask from his face. "Sarah Leech sent me. Can you walk?"

"Str… str…" Miguel tried to sit up. He seemed to still be in his Proud Patty's attire of flannel and jeans, but without shoes. The man had been deeper into it than Aiden and Jordi, and probably more careful, and yet he'd still ended up here.

"What is that around your neck?" Aiden asked, offering his hand and strength to the man.

"Str… str… stripes."

The device made a whirring noise. The red light blinked faster. Miguel slapped both hands against the device, trying to remove it.

"Just stay still," Aiden said, "I'll get it off."

There was no way he could pry it off by hand. Miguel jerked violently. Aiden's earpiece rang a warning that the device was emitting a signal, just like the interference the Stripes used during the stream earlier.

Miguel Henry was heaving, crying out as he tried to take desperate gasps, his eyes on Aiden. Aiden scrambled with the device, seeing it squeezing tight around Henry's neck, reducing his pleas to whimpers.

"Hold on, hold on." Aiden moved quickly, fingers shaking, pulling up his phone to see if he could terminate the signal. Even if he couldn't manhandle the device from Miguel, he could do what he did best. The device around Miguel's throat wasn't controlled by the server – if it was remote controlled, the source could be literally anywhere in a hundred miles.

Miguel was turning blue.

Aiden was almost there. He just had to plug in a few–

The device clamped shut with the sound of snapping twigs, and Miguel flopped back to the floor.

"Miguel?" Aiden said.

The hack he had in play fell away. The device shut down, the signal evaporating like it had never been there.

Standing over the dead government agent, Aiden saw that the thing around Miguel's neck had closed tight as a vise, crushing his airway before clicking open like a pair of handcuffs.

Aiden clenched his fists. He felt desperate for something to hit.

He swallowed his rage. Saved it. Another entry into the ledger for these fucks. They'd be paid back, that he swore to himself.

"I'm sorry," he said, looking down at Miguel and feeling utterly useless.

He finished his profile of Miguel. It felt wrong, but it was his only remaining option, and he knew that the agent would want him to obtain any evidence he could and use it against the bastards who'd killed him. In death, Miguel might still offer guidance, on Leech as well as the Stripes. As the program ran, Aiden checked the basement, making sure they weren't about to be disturbed, churning over the events.

The agent had said the group's name. That's what triggered the device. Maybe it had been keeping him alive before then, but the Stripes didn't want him talking. Bit fucking elaborate, thought Aiden. Why bother when a bullet would have worked?

For an undercover government agent, Miguel seemed profoundly normal according to the profiler. Married without kids, he lived in Mechanicsville, Maryland. Banal apart from his stage four lung cancer diagnosis just over three months ago.

That's a disease you don't walk away from, thought Aiden. It seemed the device helped deliver medication to the agent, such as low doses of his treatment throughout the day. The technology seemed advanced, but nowhere near the Wetware Leech was after. While the device could help him breathe in the event the cancer overwhelmed him, it seemed to have been manipulated enough to become a threat. Someone had the ability to reprogram it. But who? And why would such a thing be done?

The time to think it through further was up. Gin was talking to the perceived leader of the Stripes, most likely about her interaction with Aiden. It was time he got out of there as fast as possible.

As he snuck toward the cellar doors, he checked the security cameras the server gave him access to. He wanted a sense of the compound – to get out, but also for when he and Jordi came back with big, messy guns.

The security feed caught his attention. Now that the livestream had ended, it showed the hall, and in the main part of the church, Abraham and Gin were arguing.

"I told you to stay away," Abraham shouted. "You could have led them right here."

"I didn't join this cause to sit in a house all damn day," Gin said. "There's no way anyone knows where we are. Even anyone watching wouldn't lift a finger against you."

"You lost your piece, Gin."

"I was always careful," she replied, ignoring the comment. "I never said shit about anything."

The other Stripes watched nervously. Aiden wondered how important Gin was and where she ranked in the hierarchy of this fucked-up group. She didn't seem to care about Abraham's message but clearly bought into their goals at some level.

"Careful is you staying where I told you to stay." Abraham ripped away his striped mask.

His face looked younger than his gray hair and beard. The tension lines at his eyes were permanent fixtures. A man used to fighting, thought Aiden, memorizing his features.

"I gave those pricks the slip, Duncan." Gin slapped the side of her metal leg, now covered in a pair of khakis. "The way we intended." She looked around at the other Stripes. "Have you seen Gatty? He hasn't been answering my calls."

Abraham rubbed his face with both hands. "Saints alive. This is what I'm talking about. Who gives a shit about Gatty? It's not him we care about – you do understand that? I don't care how tight you are with him, he's a means to an end. If this kind of shit keeps happening, the influence he brings to the cause isn't going to help us." He turned to the others. "Everyone. Pack it all up. We have to go."

Aiden bit his lip, worrying at his beard. The "him" Abraham referred to didn't seem to link with Gatty. From his research, Gatty didn't have much influence, despite his appearance.

"Now, I said." Abraham's voice boomed without yelling when the Stripes didn't move fast enough for his liking. "Everything in the truck. This house of righteousness has been compromised. Someone needs to go downstairs and burn the remains. You know where the fuel is?"

The Stripes scattered, grabbing everything in the room. The first thing to go was the desecrated US flag. They didn't bother with properly folding it. One of the Stripes handed Abraham a radio. He'd be alerting the guards, no doubt.

"Damn it," Aiden whispered. They were coming, and time was of the essence. Still, he couldn't leave yet. Not without ensuring the Wetware wasn't stashed somewhere, even though he doubted it.

Aiden scrolled through the other cameras. It wouldn't matter if he called Leech and told her about the Stripes. They'd be gone by the time anyone showed. He put tags on their earpieces and phones, concentrating on Abraham first. They'd stopped emitting their interference, and he wondered if they'd been doing it simply to cover their tracks during the broadcast.

Either way, if he could get out without alerting them, then it would be easy to follow on at a distance. Especially if Jordi hadn't done anything stupid in the meantime.

And if he could get out without being noticed.

Someone was relaying the fate of the guard near the wrecked gate to Abraham. The leader looked exasperated and shouted commands for the other Stripes to check out the accident. Four of them ran from the church.

Aiden grimaced, knowing he would have to take a few of them out, and yet not feeling sorry in the slightest. *Almost like you planned for it to turn out this way*, he chided himself.

Watching the compound via the camera feeds, he saw the Stripes start up an SUV and reverse it to the church where they began emptying the building. Footsteps sounded from the stairs at the other end of the basement.

They're coming to burn the bodies, he thought.

"Hello?"

Fear gripped Aiden, and he swung around with his pistol. He couldn't see who'd called out. The tone of the voice – desperate and weak – was far from threatening.

Was some poor bastard down here all alone?

The footsteps sounded louder in the distance.

"Who's there?" the voice cried out again. "Let me go. Please, I just want to go home. I helped you like you asked." Whoever it was broke down in tears.

Aiden gritted his teeth and stepped into the next passage, following the voice with his gun ahead of him.

A young Black man was huddled inside a chain link dog kennel. He had his face buried against his thighs, arms wrapped around his shins. Something was wrong with his right arm. He was breathing shallow and fast. Soft whimpers emerged from his mouth, and he couldn't look up to see Aiden.

"Hey," Aiden said quietly.

The young man looked up, and Aiden bent down into a crouch. The man's eyes were watery, but there was defiance in his face. Yet, when he saw Aiden, his teeth separated, and his jaw went soft, the fight draining from his expression. "You're not one of them. Are you?" He touched his own chin. "Wrong mask."

"No," Aiden said. "I'm not."

The cage was secured by a heavy-duty padlock looped through the door latch. Mechanical. There were four empty kennels stacked side by side next to the first.

Not everything can be hacked, he could hear Jordi say.

"Don't worry. I'm going to get you out. How did you end up in there?" Aiden asked. He yanked on the lock to no effect.

"Fuckers took me off the street. I don't even know how long I've been down here. They've been doing stuff to me. Making me do stuff. Please get me out of here." The young man wore a light purple dress shirt whose sleeves had been ripped off and smeared with muck.

"Working on it," said Aiden, conscious of the growing clamor from the other end of the basement. "Keep your voice down, kid. We have company."

"I don't care. Just get me out."

A Stripe whistled nearby.

"We gotta hurry," the young man urged, standing. "You have any shotgun shells on you?"

"Fresh out of those," Aiden said, wondering what difference that would have made. "This is what we're going to do. I'm going to shoot the lock."

"But they'll hear…"

"No, they won't. Just step back. I'm going to kill the power and shoot at the same time. They'll think a transformer blew."

"How are you going to do that?"

Aiden pointed the pistol at the padlock. It was too dim to see clearly despite the illumination. With his other hand, he waved through the commands to bring up the church's power grid on his phone.

"Scotty Shotty," called a voice behind them. "It's your lucky day!" Whoever was speaking dragged out the name like a schoolyard taunt. "I have good news and bad news. Good news is, you're finally going to get your wish. We don't need any more medicine from you, so I'm going to let you out of that cage."

Scotty pressed himself against the cage. He reached out and grabbed Aiden by the front of his coat. Aiden looked down at Scotty's right arm. Black metal squares had been embedded into his forearm, top and bottom. Dry blood and raw tissue met the edge of the metal.

Scotty's lip trembled when he said, "He's going to kill me."

"Not today. Drop to the floor, OK?"

"Hey!"

Aiden kept his body still as he turned his head. A blond man hoisting a 12-gauge stood behind him. His eyes popped with a mix of fear and determination and fixed on Aiden's open hand.

"Stay completely still," the Stripe commanded, shotgun moving to nestle against Aiden's shoulder. He called out, "Carl! I got somebody."

Back to Aiden, he said, "I said, stay still."

"Sure thing," Aiden said and closed his fist as his phone executed its directive.

The lights went out as Aiden fired at the lock and dropped to the ground. Hot shot blasted through the air above him as the Stripe tried to take him out. Rising into a squat, Aiden fired three times. The Stripe cried out and collapsed to the floor.

The door to Scotty's cage swung open. "Shit. Did you get him? Sir?"

"Don't call me that," Aiden said. "I'm Aiden. Come on." He wasn't sure if Scotty would be able to run. After all the death in this room, he figured the young man would be hurt or starved. "Put your hand against the wall and feel your way along."

"Yeah, yeah," Scotty said, sounding achy and ecstatic all in one. Aiden found his way into the hall down which the Stripe had approached him. Behind him, he heard Scotty stumble over the body.

Aiden held on until Scotty's hand found his back and shoulder. They stumbled through the dark as sounds from above told them both the Stripes were trying to abandon the church as fast as possible. The young man was in better condition than Aiden had anticipated – the Stripes had kept him confined, tortured even, but they hadn't done him any great damage, and Scotty was walking almost normally.

"Thank you, man," Scotty whispered. "You saved my life. But now I've got a shotgun, them motherfuckers are gonna pay."

"If you want to thank me," Aiden said, "stay alive and get out of here. And toss that shotgun once you get through the trees. You don't want anyone seeing you with it on the street."

Aiden felt embarrassed at telling Scotty what the man clearly already knew much better than him. He wondered if Scotty had picked up the Stripe's gun.

"Ain't no one going to see a thing," said Scotty.

They reached the short passage leading to the cellar exit only to find the doors wide open. A man the same size and rough dimensions as a mountain stood there shirtless, flexing arms that were attached to a metal chest plate. Where the metal met flesh, dark veins webbed throughout the skin.

Aiden raised and fired his gun, but the bullet ricocheted off the man's chest. The Stripe reached down and slapped the gun from Aiden's hand, forcing Aiden to stumble back and into Scotty. Tapping his earpiece, he used his network access to scan for entry to the man's Wetware. There was no other explanation for it – Leech's tech had to be integrated into the Stripes' bodies. How else would Gin and the others have such advanced technology on them?

With his other arm, the Stripe grabbed at Aiden, catching his wrists. The robotic fingers clamped down hard and lifted Aiden up into the air. He shoved Scotty away as Scotty leveled his arms, hands folded in a strange gesture Aiden didn't understand. But Aiden didn't have the time to think about it – the man pulled him close, and Aiden got a breath full of cigarette ash in his face.

"You're fucked, little man," said the Stripe.

"Let him go, Carl, you prick!" Scotty cried, rifling through his pants pocket before diving for cover when Carl tried to push him further into the basement. Carl stepped out of the cellar.

Aiden concentrated on hacking the Stripe. As he tackled the entry protocols, the same strange code designation appeared as he'd seen before on Henry, emitted by the Wetware. Ready for it this time, with a breath of thanks to whoever might be listening, Aiden peeled open the Wetware's code like a banana and went to work.

"Come see what I found," shouted Carl over his shoulder at people Aiden couldn't see. "Rats."

Aiden hit the motor controls on the Stripe's limbs with a jumble of meaningless code. His hands twisted although they didn't open up and release Aiden.

"Cut out that shit, asshole," Carl growled.

Somehow, the jumble Aiden had hoped to create was being undone by an onboard defense system. Aiden yelled as those hands crushed his wrists and he had a vision of his bones breaking under the pressure.

Desperate to get away, he kicked Carl in the chest, which did nothing more than jerk his wrists painfully. Aiden tracked back the hack, unwilling to risk his own bones to experimentation.

The grinding of Carl's hands stopped. Carl held Aiden locked in a torture grip, laughing at him through his mask.

A click came from Carl's back. His shoulders shifted, and his arms widened like a human can opener. He pushed Aiden's arms away from the torso, bending them until Aiden's chest was unprotected.

Scotty ran out from where he'd taken cover, arms still raised in that weird stance. "Let him go, asshole," he shouted at Carl.

"You got nothing," Carl said simply.

"Is that so?" Scotty showed Carl a shotgun cartridge.

Carl stepped back, putting Aiden between them. With one arm still raised, Aiden watched as a patch of skin rolled back to reveal a black square in Scotty's forearm. The square popped out and Scotty loaded the slug.

"Last chance," he said, but Carl made no move to release Aiden, swinging him around and using him as cover.

From where Scotty's hand was supposed to be, a light blasted out, dazzling Aiden. Blood, bone, and brain suddenly splattered across Aiden's face, and then he was falling to the floor as Carl's body tumbled lifeless the other way.

On his ass, Aiden's ears rang, and in shock he rubbed his sore wrists, making sure they hadn't been broken. Scotty ejected the used slug from the middle of his forearm and extended the same hand to Aiden.

Aiden stared at it then, uncomprehending, before taking the offered hand. "Did you just … ?"

"This is what they did to me," Scotty said, covering the squares in his arm. "I ain't the first either. They cut every one of us. Didn't work for everyone. I saw some of 'em die on the table, and others passed after they brought them back down to the cellar." He looked at his arms. "I got lucky. Didn't get sick, didn't get taken away to wherever people went after things went wrong."

Aiden focused on keeping his breathing calm. No goddamned military application, eh, Leech? he thought. And now, such tech was in the hands of white supremacists. No wonder she'd been shitting her pants enough to bring him in with the offer of a pardon.

But at least he had located the Wetware. And Scotty was the key in making sure Leech could authorize whoever she needed to take this place down once and for all.

"I'll make sure they pay for it," Aiden said fiercely. "All of them." He grabbed his own gun back from where it had fallen on the floor. "First, you've got to get out of here."

"What about you?" Scotty asked. The man's eyes were wide, his pupils small. He was ready to rumble. "I'm going to take down as many of those fuckers as I can."

"I'll be fine. I've got more to do here, but you're important. Do you understand that? I need to see if I can find more evidence of this, but believe me, I was sent here to locate that tech." He pointed at Scotty's arms. "And others need to understand what's been done to you and others."

"I can stay," Scotty said. Revenge burned in his eyes, and Aiden felt a strange pain lance his heart. He knew what it meant when such a flame was lit.

"You're important, Scotty," said Aiden. "You want to help burn these fuckers alive, then I need you in one piece."

"OK," Scotty nodded. "If that's a promise, then I'm in."

"I'm at the Lazy Inn in DC. Room 103. Got it? Don't go to the hospital and don't go to the police. Don't make any calls, don't message anyone until I've had a chance to clean you up, right?"

Loud voices came from inside the church. "I heard a shot!"

"I don't give a damn," another Stripe said. "Somebody get to the fuse box. Burn the basement."

Scotty wouldn't get another opportunity to run.

"Go," Aiden said. "Head for the gate and get in that SUV. They won't see you until you're driving away. If it's too overrun, head for the first gate and look for a ctOS van. My... friend is there."

"I don't want to sound ungrateful," Scotty said, "but what about when they do see me? They've got other people on their side who have worse than my arm."

"You leave that to me." He slapped Scotty's back as they both fully cleared the cellar. "Go!"

Scotty took off, visibly in pain from his imprisonment but still able to move with determination and speed. Within moments he was lost to sight.

Footsteps came from the church door. Aiden crouched and moved around the corner. Cars sped through the compound, their lights flashing across the building as they turned and drove down the road and out the gate's front. Aiden slipped closer to the front. A glance through the window seemed to indicate the Stripes had fully left the building, leaving him alone to scope out who might still be alive or what Wetware was left. The smell of smoke filled the air, and he could see flames licking the inside of the church near the back. Behind him, more gray smoke pressed against the cellar door, straining to get out.

A tall man emerged from the front of the church, hands on hips. Aiden snarled silently and stood, ready to take out the leader of the Stripes. But before he could, he needed answers.

Abraham turned, and when he saw Aiden's gun raised, he took a step forward, pressed his forehead against the barrel, and smiled.

"Hi there, son. My name is Duncan Abraham."

Before Aiden could speak, a blur came shooting past Abraham, a fist landing on Aiden's shoulder, and as he stepped backwards, a boot swung up and into his face. Aiden tumbled backwards, landing hard on his back as the air left his lungs in a whoosh.

Gin Whitmore stood over him. The church had fully caught fire now and outlined her in a halo of flame. She ripped his mask away and nodded. "You've got a bad habit of walking into places you don't belong, handsome."

Abraham joined her and stared down at Aiden. "Well, now. Can it be? This day just keeps getting more and more interesting." He squatted and spoke low enough that Aiden felt the message was only for him. "The Lord, he sure does work in the most mysterious of ways."

CHAPTER EIGHT

Zip ties cut into his wrists. Aiden was tired of this shit.

Here you are again, speeding along to parts unknown with people you'd rather be shooting, he thought. The Stripes had faced him backward in the truck so he couldn't see anything of where they were headed.

Aiden sat on the floor while Gin stood in the corner trying to get into Aiden's earpiece and phone, which they'd pried away the moment they had him secured. Abraham held onto a handle in the ceiling, leering over Aiden, watching him as if he were a prize catch. He snapped his fingers toward Gin. "Are you getting anything?"

Gin continued tapping away at Aiden's tech but shook her head. "He's got it locked down pretty good. Right now, I'm having to clear out a fake spam attack that keeps popping up to distract me."

"Gotta love the classics," Abraham said. "Hackers are a sentimental sort, aren't they, Aiden?"

"You're a hacker and a racist cult leader," Aiden said slowly, as if listing titles.

"Me?" Abraham said. "No. But we have a few of them in our ranks. Our white hats." His laugh sounded like a rusty door hinge. "We have a few of everybody to tell the truth. People you wouldn't suspect of being kin, people the media would tell you were upstanding citizens, educated, family people. People who get called progressive, liberal but have been forced to wear those costumes to keep employed, to avoid persecution. High places, Aiden."

"Spare me," Aiden snarled.

"Thing is, we're not racist. We're the minority now. We're the ones who are oppressed. We're fighting for the truth. We're fighting for what's ours and those like us who are systematically seeing everything we built dismantled and taken away. White genocide, White decline because we were magnanimous and granted freedoms to those who hadn't earned them and ignored the corrupting influence they brought with them, their greed and their desire. We only see what's really there. We want to live, to prosper. We're proud of who we are and won't step back in the face of those who demand we become something else."

Aiden knew it didn't matter what anyone else said, Abraham lived in a world in which anything that disagreed with him, that challenged his assumptions, was automatically filed as suspect. Abraham knew in his bones he was right, and no one and nothing could come close to challenging that.

"Then how about I call you what you are – traitor?" Aiden asked.

Abraham clenched his jaw. That one hit deep. "I'm anything but."

"Yeah? You like to quote Jefferson. What do you make of 'all men are created equal?'"

A smirk came to Abraham's lips. "The Declaration! Do you think he was talking about anyone other than white men?"

"I resent that," Gin said.

Abraham flapped a dismissive hand at her. "Unlike many, you've earned your equality, my dear. Many times over."

Aiden rolled his eyes, refusing to speak with them, and instead tried to make sense of the sounds of the road. It felt like a highway, but that didn't make things clearer on where they were going.

"Shit," Gin said angrily, and she struck Aiden's phone against the side of the cab.

"The only thing you're going to get out of it is a headache," Aiden said.

"Keep at it," Abraham told Gin. "We've got time."

He turned back to Aiden. "I have to say I'm surprised to see you, the actual Vigilante, bastard of Chicago, enemy of the state in the flesh. We were already planning to burn our camp back there, but you coming along certainly provided us, what shall I call it? Motivation, impetus. The way Gin made it sound, I thought you were some fed hot on our trail."

"He's not?" Gin asked, peering at Aiden.

"No, no," Abraham said lightly. "Not this one. Gin, say hello to Aiden Pearce, the Vigilante. The Fox. Which do you prefer?"

"Never heard of him," said Gin, like he was a disease she was pleased to have never caught.

"You have to forgive her," Abraham said. "She's young and careless and doesn't pay attention to the happenings of the world. How can she when the mainstream media is full of lies? But I do, Aiden. In fact, I'd go so far as to say you inspired me. That mask of yours, the mission to fight the corrupt powers that be. By God, this is serendipitous."

"Then why don't you tell me what you're planning on doing with me?" Aiden said.

Abraham waved a finger. "Is this how you think it works? You just ask and I'll answer? You should be glad Gin didn't kick your head in. A head for a head, right? I'm sure Carl would agree."

"Life isn't fair," Aiden said flatly.

"You got that right," Abraham said, as if Aiden hadn't presided over Carl's decapitation. "You have to fight to make it fair."

"Is that what you think you're doing? Fighting? I saw your circle jerk livestream. You're nothing but a bunch of hog-fucker hillbillies who got lucky knocking off a government truck."

Abraham was full of bullshit. Gin's legs, Carl's chest and arms, and even Scotty's shotgun hands testified to that, but Aiden was determined to get some answers even if he ended up getting beaten en route.

"Oh…" Abraham reached out to touch Aiden's face. He tried to turn away, but Abraham grabbed him by the cheeks and forced him to look into his eyes. "Did you think that livestream was an accurate representation of all we are? A bunch of backwoods bigots? We're soldiers, Aiden. Disciplined and ruthless in the pursuit of our goal. Your childish antics won't stop us. We are legion."

"You do know you're referencing a demon in that story, right?" asked Aiden.

Abraham laughed and looked over at Gin. "Do you care?"

She shook her head.

Abraham stood. "All men are not created equal. And when the dust settles, we'll bestow our technology on those we deem worthy. And someone like you could serve us well."

Aiden stared at Abraham.

"No?" Abraham asked. "I've seen footage of your time in Chicago. You would have done anything to accomplish your goals, regardless of who got in your way. If I'm a villain, then what are you? Fortunately for us both there are no heroes and villains in this world. There are only those who hold onto their beliefs and the purity that brings."

"Tell that to the bodies below the church," said Aiden, but speaking to Abraham felt dirty, as if giving the man any kind of response only fed the monster.

Abraham tutted. "We avoided using people to experiment upon, Aiden. We're not monsters. No human being was harmed by what we did."

"You killed a government agent. They'll be coming for you."

"And here you are," Abraham said. "Are you happy? You've had me say more to you on this trip than I've said to anyone in weeks. It's fun talking to you because nothing I say matters. Either you side with me, and we move on, or you don't and then no one will ever know this conversation took place."

Gin gave him a big dose of side-eye, but Aiden knew she'd been brainwashed with the same rhetoric. Despite Abraham's proclamations that she'd earned her place, Aiden knew it was precarious at best.

"This planet placed us in easy categories for our own good. It went wrong when we convinced ourselves everyone was equal. We ignored nature's warning about mixing, about breaking the codes she'd given us. I know you get it."

"Because I'm white?" asked Aiden.

"Of course," said Abraham. "You know how white women cross the road when they see a Black man on his own coming toward them? That right there's hope for us. We're so much closer to a great awakening than people are prepared to believe."

"Just going the wrong way," piped up Gin from the other side.

"Exactly!" said Abraham. "We've lost so much progress in the last fifty years. You think it's any coincidence that corruption is endemic now?" He raised his eyebrows as if it was so obvious even a child would agree. "You can fit right in, Aiden. They say all saints have a past and all sinners a future. You're on the wrong side right now, but you could be on the side of the angels if you wanted."

"If you think I'm going to join your cause…" Aiden said, but then shut up because there it was again, feeling sullied by even speaking.

Abraham frowned. "It's always disappointing when someone doesn't get it. I wonder if I've not explained myself clearly. Are people like you so damaged, so corrupted already there's no way back? I don't know, Aiden. I wish I did, because then maybe more people could be shown the truth." He pulled out a knife from his belt – a hunting blade with a handle carved to look like a bald eagle. "If you're not going to even pretend to understand, then I have no need for you."

Gin, who'd been focused on Aiden's phone, spoke with excitement. "I got something."

"What is it?" Abraham asked, the knife still in his hands.

She frowned. "He just got a message. It says, 'Get down and hold on.'"

Aiden threw himself to the floor.

Something heavy slammed into the back of the truck. Abraham stumbled, nearly falling. His knife skittered into a corner as he slammed into Gin. Aiden rolled to his side and pushed toward the knife, using his boots to shuffle across the floor. The truck was pulling wild maneuvers, weaving left and right. The knife slid away just as his fingertips reached it.

Someone up front fired a heavy caliber rifle.

"Sonovabitch!" shouted Gin as she struggled to find her feet.

Bullet holes ripped through the back of the truck. The rifle went silent.

"Don't stop," shouted Abraham at the driver as he tried to climb out from under Gin.

Aiden wriggled after the sliding knife, but it slid around with each swerve. Then, when a small oblong bounced past, he thought, screw the gun. Aiden popped up to his knees and dove for the plastic, landing well enough to cradle it and grab his phone.

A huge bang crashed through the vehicle. The back doors blew off in a ring of flame and smoke. Aiden fell sideways and bounced deeper into the truck, but he could see Jordi at the wheel of the Brubeck Polar from the compound and Scotty crawling out the passenger window, right arm flailing to line up with the truck.

Aiden shoved the earpiece into his ear with just enough time to hear Jordi scream, "Jump now before your rescue falls out the goddamned window!"

Every inch of Aiden's body ached. He coughed against the smoke blowing in from the back of the truck. His hands were still zip tied. His knees didn't want to cooperate, but he stumbled into a standing position and faced Jordi's SUV as the bumper closed the distance.

Something behind him clicked – the distinct sound of a

revolver hammer being drawn back. Gin lay there, holding the M4-M with both hands. "I got you now."

Aiden knew he was done for, but the truck veered left and threw both of them to the side. Gin squeezed the trigger, the shot slicing deafeningly past his ear.

From the SUV's passenger window, Scotty leaned out and pointed his arm toward the truck.

"Ah, shit," Aiden said. As Scotty leveled his arm Aiden jumped onto the Polar's hood.

Scotty's arm blasted a gout of flame. Inside the truck, Gin threw herself to the floor, but Aiden couldn't see if she'd been hit. Aiden scrambled to hold onto the slick paint with his tied hands, and saw Jordi give him a wink through the windshield.

Scotty let out a cry of frustration as his arm jerked like a stuttering robot toy. "It's moving by itself!" Scotty's shotgun arm pointed at Aiden then away then back again, as all the while Scotty tried to pull himself back inside the car.

Aiden pressed his face to the hood, arms ahead of him straining to stay on the car. He wouldn't be able to dodge if Scotty fired his way. Not with Jordi driving so fast.

"What's the matter, Scotty? Arms playing up again?" Gin called from inside the van. She held onto a handle as she aimed the revolver. "Never figured out how to shoot, did you?"

The Polar's tires screeched as Jordi hit the brakes. Aiden felt his body start to slide off the hood and, with gritted teeth, hoped he wouldn't end up rolling along the road at seventy miles per hour.

Another shot sounded from the Stripes' vehicle, but Gin's aim was off, and the bullet punctured the hood next to Aiden's head.

Jordi backed up the van and then pulled off the highway down an exit ramp as Aiden watched the Stripes' caravan of vehicles speed farther away. Gin and Abraham stood in the open maw of the truck staring down at him as they shrank from view.

As the convoy disappeared out of sight, Jordi gently brought the Polar to a halt. With a groan, Aiden rolled off the side of the hood and onto the dirt where, shoulder sockets and forearms in roaring pain, he lay without moving.

"Aren't you glad I keep an eye on you?" Jordi shoved Aiden with his foot. Aiden rolled over to let the fixer snip the zip-tie handcuffs with a small pair of pliers.

"How'd you blow those doors off?" Aiden asked.

"Oh," Jordi said, "I put a little C4 in some sticky putty and threw it on the van."

"Jesus," said Aiden, thinking how easily Jordi could have blown him up instead. "You did know I was inside, right?"

Jordi shrugged. "Hey, it worked, didn't it?"

Standing, Aiden stared at the highway, no longer able to see the Stripes' vehicles. Turning back, he pointed at Scotty. "You were supposed to meet me at the motel."

"Hey, eyes over here," said Jordi. "If I hadn't run into him on his way from that church, you'd be toast. And we got to upgrade vehicles. You know, since you were so worried about not being able to participate in a car chase." He smiled broadly and then fiddled with his shirt collar. "He's got a gun in his arm, Aiden. Remember when I said what I'd do with Wetware if I had it?" He rubbed his hands together in a way that clearly said, *money*.

"Believe me," said Aiden, "I'm fully aware. There are a lot of them, Jordi. More than a single truckload, and they've been working on this for a while. It isn't some accidental hijack – they knew what they were doing. They call themselves the Brotherhood of Stripes, and they've got a plan."

Scotty walked around to join them, cradling his right arm. "I'm sorry I almost shot you. We never could get it to work properly."

"What do you mean, 'we'?" asked Aiden, fixing the young man with a penetrating stare.

Shaking his head at Aiden, Jordi put a hand around Scotty's shoulders and walked him toward the Polar's back door. "I bet those clowns said a lot of things, Scotty. Maybe you can help. Tell us everything you heard. Sing like that bird out of the Loony Toons show. Don't listen to grumpy old Aiden. He may be my friend, but he needs a nap after today."

Aiden sighed. He knew that would come to bite him in the ass at some point, and he looked off into the distance while rubbing his numb hands. Why hadn't the Stripes stopped when Jordi pulled off the highway and killed them? While it wouldn't have been easy to deal with Jordi, Scotty posed no threat while his arm was malfunctioning. He wondered why the Wetware had misfired. He didn't think Abraham or Gin had the ability to manipulate the tech while in the back of the truck. Aiden's frown deepened.

The Stripes needed to get where they were going, he thought. He'd counted three trucks and half a dozen cars in their convoy. They'd been loose lipped enough to tell him they were burning the church anyway, so they had another base of operations, and it was clear Abraham was reporting to someone else. Someone with great influence, thought Aiden, with a sense of foreboding.

We've got to find out what they're doing, he thought, and then we've got to stop them. Their livestream, their public coming out – they were planning something extreme. Whatever Abraham wanted with him didn't come before whatever it was they were going to do next. Maybe Abraham wanted Aiden to help tweak the tech. Make sure it didn't act out, like he'd seen Scotty's do.

And then there was Leech, withholding vital information and deliberately sending him in half prepared. Had she expected him to die as well? What kind of game was she playing?

It was clear he needed to talk with the woman. He hoped she'd give him an excuse to shoot first.

CHAPTER NINE

The Old Mammot Grill, founded in 1673, was the rumored oldest saloon in DC, even though most boasted that the Old Ebbitt Grill, founded in 1856, claimed that particular fame. The Mammot was the go-to spot for DC's elite and the kind of tourists who had more money than sense. It was a place whose booths were backed with red velvet and mirrors glossed with white lead lattice work. The army of hooded lamps and dark ambience gave it the feel of Victorian London, if Victorian London could serve up a cheeseburger at forty dollars a pop.

Stuffed antelope heads hung above the bar where mirrors lined the back, and illumination underneath the bottles of top shelf booze shone a tainted golden glow onto the ceiling.

Tonight, the place was closed. Nearly the entire staff had been given the night off. Just a bartender, a waiter, and the sous chef had been told to stay.

Sarah Leech sat at the bar, running a finger around the rim of a whiskey glass when Aiden entered. She had a guard detail of two men, standing at either side of the polished mahogany counter.

"Another round?" he asked her. Both guards moved to intercept him, but he waited calmly as she commanded them to step back. He was impressed. She turned to him. "You look like shit," she said.

"You're shorter in person," Aiden replied.

"You haven't aged as well as expected."

"Age gives no shits about who you are when it arrives. Plus, after what you've put me through trying to find this Wetware, I feel like I've aged an extra ten years since we last spoke."

She smiled then. "Must be my observation skills. By the way, good job on finding me, but this is my night off. It isn't easy to have the place to myself, too many damn politicians trying to stab each other in the back in the private rooms of every restaurant I actually like. So, what can the United States do for you on this, my one night of peaceful contemplation in three weeks?"

"Stop jerking me around," said Aiden. "It makes doing my job unacceptably difficult. I know you left clues for me to track you down and meet you here. I expected it after the livestream."

"Where's Mr Chin?" Leech looked around the saloon as if expecting to see him pop up from behind a banquette.

"He's keeping busy, and you have other problems," Aiden said.

"The livestream's a problem for us all," said Leech.

"Who are the Brotherhood of Stripes?" he asked, knowing his initial assumption was right. She would have seen the livestream as soon as it launched.

She screwed her mouth up. "You'd think knowing their name would help us find them, but it's only made things worse. You were listening when I said this needed to be dealt with, right?"

He stared at her and put his elbow on the bar. "It was never my job to keep this under wraps. You told me to find the Wetware and then we'd be square."

"Well, then," Leech said as she raised a hand toward the back of the bar. "Do you have the truck with all my Wetware out back with a gaggle of racists tied up in a bow for me? Or are you playing bartender and wasting my time?"

"You've mistaken me for someone who gives a shit what you think," he said. "You didn't tell me everything and hey, that's your call, but when it can get me killed? That is not OK, and it won't get your job done."

"I told you about the deal from the beginning," Leech said. "You're on your own. We've all got someone curb-stomping us when no one else is looking, so consider yourself lucky. I even had to talk with that wet blanket of a vice president and explain how the livestream reached that many viewers. You made me look bad."

"I'm sorry your life is so difficult," said Aiden, although he wanted to ask if Leech meant the actual vice president of the actual country. "In the meantime, you put me in harm's way without telling me what was going down. That stops."

Leech finished her drink and set the glass down softly. She sighed. "Tell me what happened."

"I found your missing agent," Aiden said.

"And?"

"Put it together. I'll wait."

Leech looked down to her empty glass and tapped the side with a finger. "Damn. Give me the location, and I'll send in a team to collect his body. Maybe we can find something there that'll help us find the Stripes."

Aiden stepped behind the bar and reached for the whisky bottle. He refilled her glass.

"It wasn't just him, Leech. They had a pile of bodies, and they burned them all. They torched the whole place." He gave her the location and waited while she checked it out via her own feed.

"A church?" she asked.

"You saw the livestream," Aiden said. "They're experimenting on people, trying to figure out how to work the Wetware. It's some bad shit. They aren't looking to help others. They're looking to make soldiers. From what I learned, they simply picked up randoms off the street. None of them white, all of them cut open, jammed with tech and discarded when they were finished with them."

"Jesus Christ."

He was gratified to see her genuinely horrified. He placed the bottle of whiskey next to her glass.

"I saw a lot more. These people have weaponized your Wetware, and they're planning something big. Unless the Wetware was always meant to be weaponized in the first place."

Leech rolled her eyes. "Go to the movies if you want that story."

He tried to access the network and found it beyond reach. "I've got two names," he said, raising his eyebrows at her.

"Oh," Leech said, smirking. "Sorry about that. Can't have you freewheeling through my network. Give me a moment, and I'll give you an appropriate amount of access."

Aiden waited and pulled his phone out, scanning until he saw what must have been Leech pop up.

"You should be able to do whatever you wanted to do now.

Assuming it wasn't to come for my network connection," she said.

Aiden slid a screenshot over to her. "Duncan Abraham is their leader." He sent a second picture, showing Gin and her metallic leg. "Gin Whitmore, who seems to have reasons for being aligned with the Stripes, but she's taking orders from someone else. Your influence peddler, I suspect."

"It's impressive, isn't it?" she said softly. She gazed at Gin's leg and the footage of her climbing the building after the car accident.

"Sure going to make hunting down a cabal of mass murdering racists easier, that's for sure, so thanks for that," he said.

"I've never heard of either of them," Leech said, ignoring him. "If I hear anything I'll let you know. The leader, Abraham, sounded like an old-fashioned tent revival preacher."

"He's anything but. He's smart, charming, ruthless, and with a complete grasp of what the offended and insecure want to hear. Last I saw of them, they were heading this way."

"You think they're in DC?"

For the first time the mask slipped enough that Aiden saw the worry in her eyes, a stark contrast to the manic woman he'd met in the trailer what felt like months ago. The two probably fed each other – worry transforming to desperation to protect her reputation and that of her country.

"I don't know," Aiden said. "If they are trying to overthrow the government, I guess they'll start at the strip clubs down from Congress."

"You're not funny."

"I'm hilarious," Aiden said. "What they have planned isn't as simple as race war. There're dozens of other groups itching for something like that. They're trying for something else, Leech." He referred to the images of Gin. "You said this was civilian tech with a medical purpose. That it was supposed to help people. You didn't mention weapons-grade legs or bulletproof chests and shotguns for hands. You want this done right? Then you tell me everything."

"I haven't been forthcoming," said Leech and gave him a wry look before filling up her own glass. "A baseball bat has several uses. You don't blame the sports store if it's used to smash someone's head in."

Aiden thought about it. "You've simply ensured heads need to be smashed."

"The beauty of Wetware…" Leech took a breath before starting again, "… is that it can be implemented in several ways. The tech isn't just the metal or the wires. The big part of it is the adaptive control and integration program – an AI system that learns and syncs perfectly with the biorhythms of its host, which can be overlaid on any connected prosthetic."

"Sounds parasitic."

"Symbiotic is a better term," said Leech quickly.

So you've had to defend this before, Aiden thought.

"Why can't I hack it?" he asked. "When I tried, their pieces emitted some kind of nonsense signal, made it impossible to get a handle on."

"It's doing its job," Leech said. She couldn't help smiling. "What kind of prosthetic would anyone want if, while they're shopping for milk, someone could take control of them? If, in this world of fixers and hackers, your augmented lungs could be seized for the fun of it, or taken over by another country and used against you? Not many think of that… they're just grateful for the tech that can save their life. But I'm sure you've figured it out beyond the basic person's intellect – the protection is designed to stop serious hackers along with drive-bys... for the most part."

Aiden huffed at just how infuriatingly reasonable she sounded and leaned over the counter. The guards at each side took a cautionary step closer. "How am I supposed to stop them if I can't stop them from being half-cyborg?"

"Not my problem," Leech said. "What is my problem is that they have my tech and that they are using it in such a... disastrous way. We've taken steps to ensure they won't get any more, but right now? I want what they do have back. Your focus is on finding and retrieving the Wetware, Aiden. Not who wears it or utilizes it. For all our tech, Aiden, they remain human. Flawed, maddeningly individual and predominantly flesh and bone. You're good at exploiting and overcoming humans to get down to the bottom line." Leech flashed that wide smile, the one that left a chill running down his spine. "So do what you do best and stop them."

Aiden backed away from the bar, her barbs sliding over him without landing. "And when I find the Stripes again?"

"When you find them again, stop them. Get me my tech back, and try to keep at least some of what you're doing out of the news channels, yes?"

"That's your job," Aiden said, remembering the bogus news she'd already orchestrated against him. "You don't mind me taking them out? Does the government approve of this?"

She stared at him. "I am the government, Aiden." She waved her glass, dismissing him, then poured another drink and looked away as if he wasn't there.

Aiden walked out from behind the bar, not sure what to think. But just before he left, Leech's voice floated towards him.

"Were there any survivors at the church?" she called.

Aiden stopped but didn't turn. "No," he said.

CHAPTER TEN

"She likes you," Jordi said when Aiden got back to the hotel.

"I knew I shouldn't have let you dial into the feed," Aiden said.

"How else would we begin to unravel the mysteries of love?" Jordi said and shot Aiden a feral smile. "Although, when the conversation cut off midway, I wasn't sure if that was deliberate or something on her end."

"She wants the tech back, Jordi. The Wetware that the Stripes were sporting."

"I won't mind a bit of butchery in this case." Jordi shrugged.

"You know a guy?"

"I know a gal. Runs a cleanup crew who can make sure we get what Leech wants and tidies up after themselves. Sunlight Cleaning. You know, after the film. Wait. Sunbeam Cleaning? Whatever. They clean. That's the point."

"We just gotta find them and create a mess then," said Aiden with a sigh. He sat on a chair in the corner of the room. His entire body pleaded for more rest, for time to recover.

"Where's Scotty?" he asked, noticing the young man had

gone. Jordi handed him some industrial strength painkillers, which he washed down with tap water. His eyelids were heavy like lead pillows.

"Taking a walk," said Jordi in a light voice. "Couldn't sleep. He kept waking up screaming. I sent him out for my sake as much as his. Boy's got issues, and no shrink's ready for a client with shotguns for arms."

Aiden wanted to care that Jordi had let Scotty go wandering by himself but couldn't even raise his head. As his eyes closed, he thought about how, twenty years ago, he could power through the night on barely any food or sleep.

"I think you did the right thing," Jordi said oddly. "About keeping Scotty from Leech."

Aiden meant to pop an eye open at that, but sleep overwhelmed him, and he drifted off.

The smell of coffee woke him up.

"You're not any more beautiful," said Jordi, putting a Styrofoam cup next to him. Aiden sat up in the chair he'd fallen asleep in and felt a painful tweak in his lower back.

Scotty stood behind Jordi, a full head taller, and peered at Aiden.

At least he's not dead, thought Aiden blearily. "Think there's food that comes with this gut rot?" he asked, taking a sip of coffee and grimacing.

"Only one way to find out," Jordi said and motioned Aiden to his feet.

They checked out and drove a couple of blocks to a diner. Scotty seemed nervous when they sat down on the bench, keeping his arms crossed and close to his chest. They ordered, and when the waitress came back with fluffy pancakes stacked three deep, each as big as his plate, Aiden's stomach growled.

Aiden stared at them with abiding love before pouring maple syrup all over until they turned from a light brown to a dark sodden earthy color.

"You are disgusting," said Jordi who'd watched him drown his breakfast with a horrified expression. "Waffles are far superior to pancakes. These are just flour circles. There's no joy in them." He sighed and leaned back.

Aiden knew a diatribe on the merits of breakfast selections was imminent. He wasn't sure he could put up with another rambling conversation. The drive to DC still haunted him. "It's food, Jordi. I've been busy and my body needs refueling. That's all."

"Right," said Jordi, dragging the word out, digging into his sausage and mushroom omelet. "You just don't want to be proven wrong."

Scotty listened intently while picking at a pile of eggs, bacon, and grits. "We gonna talk about them?" he asked quietly.

"Sure," said Jordi brightly. "What you got?"

Scotty laid down his cutlery and cracked his knuckles. The expression on the young man's face was so earnest, Aiden found himself leaning in. He recalled that fire he'd seen in Scotty, that burning for revenge.

"They didn't grab me at random, you know?" Scotty started. "They took me with a crowd of people all in one night. I volunteer at a rehab facility a couple times a month. We were coming out of a meeting when I was shoved into the back of a van. Scariest shit I've ever lived through. And then, I ended up there, in that church, surrounded by people from all walks of life. You'd think they'd target the homeless or drug addicts. Nope. I met doctors, cops, lawyers, teachers. I thought they'd made some big mistake, except everyone was missing something, you know, from accidents or birthing defects or genetic diseases. Men, women, anyone."

"How'd you figure that out?" asked Aiden, feeling like he was missing something.

"I'm a medic," said Scotty, and for a moment, his whole body seemed to beam with pride in the statement. But then, that glow diluted. "It's why they kept me alive when all the others were killed."

"They made you work for them?" asked Aiden.

Scotty nodded. "Things went off pretty quick after that but before they separated us out." He took a deep breath and recounted a tale of torture, pain, and cruelty.

"And you helped," said Aiden, as plainly as he could.

"I didn't want to," said Scotty hotly. "I never wanted to do something like that."

"I'm not judging you, kid. You'd be dead if you hadn't. And we would have been none the wiser to stop it."

Scotty hung his head. "I ended up managing the anesthesia. It isn't my specialty, you know?"

Aiden could see it was costing him to talk, but they needed the information, so he stayed quiet. The kid was strong, and Aiden felt in awe of him. If it were Aiden, he'd probably already be on a rampage.

"Then they tied us down and left us on the table, let us lie there when we woke up groggy with the drugs." Scotty shuddered.

"What about people like Gin?" asked Aiden.

"Didn't see no sign of her, or any of the other white folk except those who came down to feed me once I was finished with helping them. They kept masks on." He looked apologetic.

"You didn't operate on her?" asked Aiden.

Scotty shook his head. "No, but there were a lot of them. The surgeon was some white fella with a West Coast accent. He made me stand back like I'd give him cooties. The one with the metal chest, Carl, would come down and crow 'bout how his augmentation was the reason we were being put through all of this. Like, he was making some profound point out of our suffering." Scotty shook his head. "Dickwad. Glad he's dead."

Jordi laughed and snorted into his coffee.

Scotty ignored Jordi and looked right at Aiden. "I know I said it before, but thanks, man. Without you, I'd be barbeque right now. Carl had been telling me all week about how they were going to torch me alive when they were done. I just never knew when."

"Did you learn anything else?" Aiden asked. "Anything you can remember?"

"I don't know," said Jordi drily. "Sounds to me like they could be anyone. Well, anyone white."

"They've definitely got people in government," chimed in Scotty, face deadly serious. "To the Stripes, it's not just about being super-soldiers. It's like those that deserve the augmentations adhere to the correct standards of living. No one should suffer if they have the belief to make the country stronger, better, and the augmentation is supposed to reflect that. But, of course, there must be sacrifices made first, to ensure that that ideology can actually work," Scotty finished, his last words a mixture of sarcasm and deep bitterness.

Aiden took a sip of water and rubbed his face, trying to digest what Scotty was telling him. If the Stripes knew what they were doing, and Abraham's organizational skills suggested they did, then they'd be structured as semi-autonomous cells whose members knew no one beyond their handler. Each handler would be part of a smaller cell all designed to protect themselves from giving the farm away if caught but also to protect the leadership from spies and informants.

Catching anyone but a handler or someone belonging to the upper leaders would yield them nothing and certainly wouldn't lead to Leech getting her tech back. Abraham might not even be the most important person in their network, he thought, filing it away for later examination.

He had no issues taking down Gin or their goons, but just how many of them had this tech? Was he going to be asking Jordi's cleanup crew to be dismembering a dozen or a hundred bodies? And how were they able to integrate it so quickly, especially if the tech was stolen a week prior? He glanced at Scotty's arms. Were those part of Leech's Wetware, or possibly mimics created by this surgeon Scotty had mentioned, in preparation for the real Wetware?

"How many did you operate on?" he asked Scotty.

"Nineteen," said Scotty immediately. "Every operation was different, but they were all people like me." He stared at Aiden then and his message was clear.

"Fuck," said Jordi.

Scotty took a deep breath. "Just to be made clear, I don't want to go to the cops," he said with such conviction that Aiden felt something tug at his heartstrings. "Those bastards were going to burn me alive. There ain't no forgiveness for that, no matter what my mama sings in church."

Jordi lifted his empty glass. "Amen."

Scotty fixed Aiden with a straight stare. "I want to find them and make them pay."

"Sirs, your check's arrived," said Jordi mockingly. "The price is death."

"I get that you've been hired by the government. And I appreciate you letting me listen to what that Leech lady said. But I will not be sidelined or told to go home and deal with my trauma." Scotty shook his head. "I'm going to find the Stripes with or without you. I'm going to make them regret everything they've done."

The ache in Aiden's heartstrings became a piercing pain. For a moment, he saw his nephew, Jackson, in Scotty and wondered with sharp clarity what he would have done had these Stripes taken his last remaining link to family. "You've no idea what you're getting into," said Aiden hoarsely. "I know you want to help, but–"

"Fuck you, man," said Scotty, hands flat on the table. "I'm thankful you hauled my ass out of there, but I don't know what I'm getting into? You think I don't know what these cocksuckers want?"

"I didn't mean that," said Aiden. "They're going to get what they deserve but you're not that kind of man. I am."

"I don't know what kind of man you are, Aiden," Scotty said. "But I know who I am and something like this will not – cannot – be left alone. I refuse to let that happen. You ever been pulled over just for driving your car in the wrong neighborhood? You ever had a woman call the police on you for smiling as you passed each other in a park? You ever been put in detention for fighting back when five white boys attacked you?"

Aiden shook his head, desperate to speak, to try to make one of those wrongs right, when Jordi jumped in.

"I can play this one. Hey, Aiden, you ever been called Yellow Peril? You ever been asked to order at the restaurant because you must know the food? You ever been asked if you're good at karate or told that Japanese people and Chinese people all look the same? You ever been asked if Vietnam is in Africa or if you know someone's niece who's visiting Tokyo on their year out? You ever been asked where you learned to speak English or where you're from, you know, originally?"

"This one time I was asked to take my hat off inside a church," Aiden replied.

Scotty laughed in a short gruff burst. For a moment, it seemed his anger had been quenched, but Aiden knew his need for revenge would resurface.

"By the way," said Jordi, poking Aiden in the shoulder. "I'm much better at ordering food than you."

"I get it," said Aiden softly, knowing his earlier response wasn't meant to compare what both Jordi and Scotty had been through. He looked at Scotty again, seeing the same flame that had driven Aiden in Chicago so long ago. It was a flame that had burned bright ever since, and one that had left him alone without family or friends, chasing one gig after another, staying hidden all the time.

"Good," said Scotty.

"But it's the worst idea," Aiden finished. "You better be sure,

Scotty, because once you do this there's no coming back. You dig two graves when you go looking for revenge."

Scotty's eyes wavered.

"You've never killed anyone before Carl, I bet."

"What's your problem, Aiden?" interrupted Jordi. "Kid wants to help, where's the issue? Not like you haven't killed before. Not like I'm a saint."

"You say I only killed one person but you're wrong," Scotty said. "Everything that happened to those people in that basement was partly because of me. I'm not going to let anyone else die because of what I did."

Aiden sighed. Would it matter if he insisted that the actions of the Stripes weren't his fault? Scotty wasn't Jackson. He was a young man removed from a successful career and thrust into a nightmare. He was a resource and an ally. Aiden needed to stop getting tied up in worrying about whether the kid was going to come out of this fine.

Fuck, he's got shotgun arms, thought Aiden. Shotgun arms that he sometimes couldn't control, sure, but they were still shotgun arms.

"Let me be clear: you killed Carl in self-defense, and I'm pretty fucking glad you did, but from here on out, you're choosing to kill others. It's different." Aiden took another drink of water.

"No polite company for you, my son," said Jordi with a grimace. "We don't do dinner parties, and mothers don't want us at the school gates. You already got the sleeping badly part covered. Good news? You'll sleep fine after a while. Bad news? You'll sleep fine after a while."

"Not a problem," said Scotty. "As long as the Stripes are dead."

You haven't got a clue, thought Aiden.

"Anger makes a lot of things seem fine in the moment," said Aiden. "I'm older than you. You could be my kid. I've seen a whole lot of shit and trust me… when we go this way, we cut ourselves off from others."

Jordi eyed him. Memories washed up again for Aiden. Again, he wondered about his nephew, about what remained of his family.

Not now, Aiden, he thought, closing the door on those images and with it, a certain surprising sense of comfort at being around Scotty.

"You think I don't know that?" asked Scotty.

Aiden didn't want to dissuade him. Not really. They were going after murderous bigots, and the young man across the table had every right to take them down. No one would stop him if the situation was reversed. But it seemed important that Scotty understand everything.

"My life's been a bag of dicks, Scotty. I've been hiding, running, and fighting for nearly all of it. Here I am, fifty-five, and I'm still up to the same old bullshit. You want revenge? Good. I'll show you. But there's no way back from this."

"Would you do it differently?" Scotty demanded. "Now you know, looking back?"

Aiden didn't hesitate. "No."

The memories surged, but he pushed them back where they belonged – far from him.

"So, you know how I feel then," said Scotty.

"Revenge it is," said Aiden.

CHAPTER ELEVEN

After that, Aiden asked Scotty every question he could, looking for identities, reasonings, locations, anything that would give him a trail to search for. Scotty recounted everything until he became frustrated and exhausted.

"The only thing I can remember came out of this clerk from Santa Rosa County," Scotty said, accepting a coffee refill. "Bug, he wanted to be called. Was his first big trip out of state and he was happy to talk, even to me. He mentioned this place…" Scotty rubbed his forehead, trying to remember. "The Washingtonian, he called it."

"It's a start," Jordi said, but Aiden was already searching the place.

"Probably some underground club, or a hideout the Stripes go to," he muttered, already knowing he would have to come up with an infiltration plan to crack some heads when his search brought up an upscale restaurant close to the Capitol.

Stunned, he flicked the place's details over to the other two, and they sat in silence, reading up. The Washingtonian, a steak house, frequented by political aides and tourists, a favorite of those living their sunset years in the District of Columbia.

"You sure this is the place?" Aiden asked Scotty after reading a handful of reviews, which praised it for the service and ambience.

"Sure am," said Scotty.

"Maybe we're looking in the wrong place," mused Aiden and he began to search outside DC for a lead. A Pentecostal church or maybe a veteran's club, perhaps.

"Nah," said Scotty. "Bug said he'd come to Washington to take in the sights. That this was where he'd meant to come all along. Maybe they want to hit it? Make a scene? Hurt some people?"

"Dumb move," said Jordi dismissively. "Who's going to care about a joint like this getting blasted? Sure, it'd make the news, but only alongside whatever school shooting happened that day."

"You'd be better off suggesting a sex ring was run out of there or something," said Aiden. "You'd take it down online with a few photos splashed across a dozen of the right forums, not by landing an armed mob on the doorstep. The Stripes are smarter than just blowing up a place for show."

"I'm telling you it's the place," insisted Scotty, growing heated.

Aiden sucked his teeth. "Look, I want to believe you but it's a nowhere place. People go there for dinner and pay too much just to be near the Capitol." He blew out a breath between barely parted lips. "You could see them using it as a staging post. If you squint."

"What else have you got?" asked Scotty.

"Nothing," said Aiden, sitting back. With time, he knew they would track down the Stripes, eventually. But, given how hot

Abraham had been to get to DC, Aiden knew they didn't have the luxury of time.

He looked at Scotty. "Fine. A wisp of a lead is better than none. We go see."

"I'm gonna have to pass on another meal," said Jordi, patting at his belly. "I'm not eating again until dinner."

"I'm going alone," said Aiden.

"I'm coming too," insisted Scotty.

"No," replied Aiden and stood. "You're a young Black man with unpredictable arms. We don't understand who might be able to use your augmentations against you. We don't know if there's a time limit, or anything that could hurt you or others. Plus, you're known to them. How do you think this plays out? We go there, this Bug or the surgeon spots you, and then what?"

"They've seen your face just as much as mine," said Scotty.

"Gin and Abraham, yeah. The others? Not so much," said Aiden. "I can get in there without being noticed. Let me do this and come back. Then we go in with guns."

"If it's not just a restaurant, that is," Jordi chimed in.

"If it's just a restaurant, then we try something else," said Aiden. "We'll be back to where we started."

The drive took twenty minutes. The day was icy and the sky a metallic blue. The Washingtonian was tucked in at the bottom of a swanky hotel, although Aiden, walking around the block a couple of times, saw it had a separate entrance.

The hotel was called the Founding, which Aiden infiltrated first, passing through revolving doors loosely manned by two young men in sharp uniforms of cream and brown with peaked hats and brocade on their shoulders. In his dirty clothes and baseball cap, Aiden felt like he stood out, but they paid him no attention as he went past.

As he'd suspected, the hotel had an entrance to the Washingtonian inside through a couple of wood and glass doors at one end of the lobby. The doors opened onto an unattended concierge's desk from which the rest of the restaurant was roped off with a moveable stand for a private event.

Aiden found a spot and took in the view. He pulled up the menu on his phone, seeing that it was aimed at people with money looking for solid American fare… if done well enough to justify eighty-dollar price points and descriptions half in French.

He scanned the hotel's booking system and found the list of those attending. They were united in hailing from the Midwest and South, with a vast majority over forty. Over two hundred guests were present, but from the check-in software, Aiden was able to compare it to an invite list about twenty percent longer.

Which meant there were plenty of identities for him to rifle through in order to select one he could use for himself.

Aiden settled on a veteran called Alex "Sascha" Makarov. Forty-seven, three tours in Iraq and Afghanistan. Discharged with honors after driving over an IED. Made a full recovery but had problems running and sleeping. Like countless others.

The restaurant's first room curved away out of sight, heading out toward the front of the building. From there came the sounds of celebration. A hubbub of noise. Aiden slipped into the restaurant and made his way toward it. He tried to make himself more presentable – undoing his jacket, removing his cap, and running his hands through his unwashed hair. He felt grimy and wished he'd taken time to become more presentable.

Easy jazz played in the background, the tinkle of a piano playing ragtime at half the normal tempo.

Gun kept well out of sight, Aiden repeated Sascha's name to himself and turned the corner. He stumbled into a densely packed room full of people drinking champagne and beer, eating canapes, and dipping into a huge buffet that ran the length of one wall and reminded him of the better ones in Vegas.

There were a couple hundred people in attendance. Above them and on every table, hanging from every wall, were banners in bright red and white.

Aiden was unable to see what they were in aid of, but there wasn't a hint of racist nonsense anywhere. A waiter handed him a bottled beer, with a soft sad look, and Aiden held the chilled drink out in front of him, crossing through the crowd with a dozen or so *excuse me*s as he went. He wondered if his appearance fit the bill for a struggling veteran, which led to no one wondering about how he looked.

He soon noticed one of the guests, an older woman with gray hair, had a prosthetic arm. Pausing, he saw the two people she spoke to also had prosthetics.

Were they all like this? What was going on here?

He made it to the buffet table, ready to sequester himself in the shadows and start profiling when he bumped into another guest, this one dressed similar to him.

"So sorry," the guest said, before holding his hand out for a shake. Aiden took the offered hand without a thought. "Looks like you've served. Fallen on bad times?"

"You could say that," Aiden said, not sure how to navigate the conversation.

"What did you have?" the man asked in sympathy. He had thinning blond hair and dull gray eyes.

"A brain," Aiden replied before thinking it through.

The man nodded as if it were completely normal. "Lungs for me. Like something out of the movies. I'll never stop thanking the senator for his support." Scars reached up past the man's collar, just short of wobbly jowls.

"How long ago did you get yours?" asked Aiden. Leech's shipment had been stolen only a week before. There was no way these people had all received transplants from that same shipment.

"About six weeks," said the man. "Mikey. Mikey Hay, by the way."

"Sascha," replied Aiden. "About the same for me."

Mikey looked grateful. "We're so damned lucky. The first lot had some glitches, but they took them back to the drawing board, and me? I'm breathing like a teenage quarterback." He took a huge lungful to demonstrate, his shirt straining at the buttons, and breathed out with a loud "ah."

"I figure I'm smarter than I was," said Aiden, unable to resist jerking him around.

"Where are you from?"

"Chicago," said Aiden. The Windy City was his home even if he'd not been there in two decades.

"Tough gig," said Mikey, whistling. "Too many liberals up there for us to do much good. I'm from Florida. People like us know the score down there."

"How'd you end up here?" asked Aiden.

"Lung cancer. Senator Blake's aide found me and asked if I wanted to be part of a program." Mikey shook his head. "I wasn't sure, you know? I'm suspicious of vaccines and chemtrails and big pharma so was ready to turn him down, but then Senator Blake came to see me himself. Can you believe that? He talked about how America needed people like me to stand up and be counted."

"Were there any tests?" asked Aiden.

"Lots," confirmed Mikey. "Medical, as well as making sure I wouldn't waste this gift. You know how it is. I'm sure you had a tough time of it."

"What do you mean?"

Mikey smiled, genuine and happy. "I don't mean to be offensive. Lots of Americans would take this opportunity as if it was their right. Like they deserve the technology that will save their lives without being grateful for it."

"We're not like them," said Aiden encouragingly.

"Hell no. I know what America is and why we're important, why the whole world looks up to us." He chinked his beer bottle against Aiden's. "Here's to us, to Senator Blake and to America."

"To true patriots," replied Aiden, feeling sick. He and Mikey had very different ideas of what the word patriot meant, but despite Mikey's beliefs, Aiden didn't get the sense that he was associated with the Stripes. Looking around, he knew that if he profiled all of the people attending this event, he'd see a smattering of backgrounds and views, all pulled together with this technology gifted by Senator Blake in exchange for honest fundraising support.

"I'm encouraged every day, Sascha. That newsletter of his is so damned heroic. To think there are tens of thousands of us in line for this tech." Mikey shook his head in disbelief. Aiden had a hard time not joining him.

Before he could ask more questions a voice to Aiden's left said, "Ah, I'm so glad you could make it."

A large, manicured hand rested on Aiden's shoulder. A thrill of fear ran through Aiden as he turned to see the senator. "I honestly didn't know if you'd come," Senator Blake said cheerfully.

"Wouldn't miss it for the world," said Mikey. "I heard that there was an authorized neurological assistance ability now. Amazing, senator. Simply amazing."

"Thank you," Blake said with an award-winning smile, and nodded at Mikey, then steered Aiden away from the other man and across the room toward the entrance.

The crowd thinned as they neared the doors.

"Alex, although my friends call me Sascha." Aiden held out his hand.

"Nice to meet you again, Alex. Although, the last time we met you had less hair."

Which wasn't how Aiden remembered Alex's ID image. Was he being tested?

Blake didn't wait for an answer. "Don't panic, I'm not going to have you thrown out, but you'll not find anything here to report on. Go back to whichever paper sent you and tell them exactly what you saw: a room full of happy constituents whose lives have been made better through access to medical care their insurance companies denied them. It's your job to report the facts, after all."

"Sure," said Aiden. "They must love you here." Aiden was more than happy to roll with Blake's assumption that he was from some paper trying to dig up dirt.

"It's amazing what looking after people can do. I doubt they love me, but they're certainly grateful, and that will do. I have a constituency to serve, after all. If they're not happy then I'm doing it wrong. The man whose shoes you're pretending to wear? He's got new knees because of me. Didn't cost him anything either."

"And I suppose it doesn't hurt if they donate to your campaign or support you during the election. It used to be they elected people to do what was right, not popular," said Aiden.

Blake laughed softly, and Aiden stiffened at the sound, resisting the sudden urge to punch the man in the face.

"What is popular is right. *Panem et circenses,*" said Blake.

Portraits of Blake twice the size of the real thing flanked the entrance. They were set just to one side of the doors and looked at the room as much as they greeted people entering the restaurant.

"You don't believe then," said Aiden.

"Oh, I believe with all my heart. America the great, Sascha."

Aiden's mind whirred with possibilities. Leech had been clear someone was protecting the Stripes, but Blake? Seemed like a long shot. A senator wouldn't have access to the briefings needed to run the hijack job on Leech's assets. And it seemed like a lot of these augmentations weren't weaponized – they seemed to be part of an initiative to help those that would likely die without it. How were the two connected? Were they even connected? Maybe Scotty's Bug had hoped to be part of the initiative and gotten sucked into the wrong place with the wrong people.

"How'd you get these people the tech?" Aiden asked. "Seems cutting edge. Expensive. Far outside the fundraising capabilities and allowances for a senator's campaign."

Blake smiled and put a hand into the small of Aiden's back as if he needed guiding across a busy street. "I'm a senator, Aiden. I have friends, connections, and above all I have constituents I want to make happy. Americans. Patriots. People who are proud of their heritage and their culture. If I do nothing else, I want to unite us under one banner. I could go on, but I'm not on a podium and you don't need me grandstanding." He smiled and gestured behind him. "You can see for yourself."

And Aiden could. A room full of people drinking sparkling wine and beer, smiling and laughing. If he didn't know the darkness lurking underneath, he might be dazzled by the possibilities. He might even believe that Blake was a good man.

Blake waved at a guest walking with crutches. "But you don't need what I'm offering. I don't think you're the kind of constituent I'd like to spend too much time with."

In other words, we're done, thought Aiden. He couldn't have agreed more. He didn't have concrete evidence that Abraham was involved with the senator, but it seemed there was more to Leech's Wetware than he knew... and that the appearance of both types of augmentation might be linked. Maybe Abraham looked after the nastier side of the operation while Blake was the power, but Aiden knew if they were working together that taking just one of them out wouldn't work – it would have to be both of them.

"I'd wish you luck, but it's not going to help," said Aiden.

If Blake heard the threat in his voice, he ignored it. "Luck is for those who aren't prepared. I do have one question though. If you're willing."

"Shoot," said Aiden.

"Are you proud to be American?"

"Some days more than others," said Aiden, and he pushed out through the restaurant's doors without looking back.

CHAPTER TWELVE

"So, what was it?" Jordi asked. "A den full of tattooed bastards or a muumuu-filled all-you-can-eat buffet?"

Aiden's jaw was clenched so tight he couldn't give an answer, but Jordi apparently didn't need one. He had more answers than ever before. It was time Leech explained some of them. When they returned to the motel, Aiden opened up his network and began scouring for the same links that had led him to Leech at the restaurant. There they were – still active and waiting. A way to communicate with her if he was smart enough to figure it out and follow the breadcrumbs she'd left.

He called with video feed off. He didn't want her to see Scotty, but he wanted to ensure Scotty and Jordi were present for the conversation. Scotty sat on the bed, and Jordi lounged in a chair in the corner of the room while Aiden paced, unable to calm himself enough to sit down.

The connection clicked, becoming live, and Aiden rushed to fill the space. "You lied to me. Again."

"What was it this time?" Leech's tired voice cut across his.

"How long have they been stealing the Wetware?" he demanded.

Silence. "Three months. This was the third shipment. Once is careless and embarrassing. Two is a problem but we thought we had it under control and had found the leak."

"How much stuff have they taken, Leech?" Aiden asked. He said her name like it was contagious. "How many people could they have augmented with your tech?"

"Should I care?" she asked, her voice turning cold.

"You lied to me and withheld vital information. Now, you need to tell me the truth because I counted upwards of two hundred people, Leech. Some of them aren't even associated with the Stripes, I bet. Many of them will die if you take their prosthetics from them. They're nothing more than harmless fools, or people desperate to live, believing in some kind of miracle. They don't deserve to die for being easily deceived."

"I'm not taking the tech back. You are. Don't talk to me like I'm some fixer you've fallen out with, Mr Pearce. In this, you work for me, but in the same way someone whose life is in danger holds onto the edge of the cliff. Let go of me and watch how you fall."

"What do you suggest? Ask them nicely?" he hissed at her.

"The goal's clear. Work it out. You're famous for improvising, Vigilante. Do so."

"Innocent people are going to die," he said, although he had no intention of killing anyone if he could help it. "People whose lungs or hearts have been augmented won't survive without your tech."

"What is it that's so hard to understand? We want our tech back."

Why was she veering down such a hardcore path? Did he need to give her an out and allow her to save face?

"You don't get it," he said. "This isn't a slaughterhouse you're setting up. None of us want that. Not you. Not me. You want me to bring these people in? OK, let's talk logistics. You want me to scramble them so the tech is dead inside their bodies? Fine, maybe we can talk. But you cannot be serious about killing unwitting civilians. If you're seriously talking about crossing the line, maybe you can explain how a senator has access to what I can only assume is your stolen tech."

He flung her the location of the fundraiser for Teddy Blake.

Leech didn't respond. For a moment, he thought she'd hung up despite the line being still open, until he heard a heavy sigh.

"Start with the Stripes first. You seem to stomach killing them," she said, her tone flat, almost defeated. "The others I'll leave to you. Do what you feel is right. Just make sure it stays quiet, Mr Pearce. And don't send me anything else. You are on your own, understand?"

Aiden grimaced. He'd deliberately broken protocol by sharing the info with her, had put her at risk if things went sideways because there was now a hint of a paper trail in Leech's direction. Leech represented a part of the government, the very piping of the country. She'd scrub herself clean the moment they broke communication, leaving nothing for anyone to trace.

There was no walking away. He could either work toward his pardon, or let Leech set the whole world after him.

"Find a way, Mr Pearce. The Wetware is already being used in ways it was never meant to be, and if it becomes associated with the Stripes, there will be no polishing the tarnish off it. It won't be able to make the real difference we'd planned for it. Fix it." She hung up.

Aiden closed the connection and saw that any link to Leech

had been wiped. He turned to see Jordi and Scotty.

Jordi sat back as if slapped. "Whoa, dude. She reached up your ass and ripped your heart in two or what?"

"She doesn't give a shit about the people," Scotty snarled and smashed his hand against the dressing table. "Fuck her, man. Fuck her."

"She's got a point," said Aiden and held his hands up when Scotty shot him a murderous look. "You're a big name government research and development department. Your stuff is weapons grade, and you've spent who knows how many billions developing it. It'll see your troops fighting alongside drone strikes, running, jumping, and surviving injuries that would knock out regular Joes. It can bring back soldiers to fight another day. It can reinvigorate faith in the military and government. Suddenly, all that work has gone missing and to the worst kind of people. You want anyone to know that stuff was on the streets? You want anyone to know it even exists?" Aiden closed his eyes and took a breath before continuing.

"As long as it remains inside old Betty, keeping her eighty year-old heart beating, she's a risk to everything you're doing. I can hear the Senate Appropriations Committee wheezing with joy at the investigation that would follow. What has Betty done to deserve the tech? Shouldn't it go to someone who can serve a purpose – say, the Purple Heart hero who fought on the front lines who has heart disease?

"Would the Senate look at the deaths of a few hundred people spread across the country who had their prosthetics harvested after their deaths? No evidence of cutting-edge tech, and no evidence of government black ops, means no interest from anyone who matters."

Scotty shook his head, disgust written on his face.

"Well, that's fucking grim," said Jordi.

Aiden nodded. Across from him, Scotty fiddled with his implants, grinding his jaw back and forth. Aiden didn't blame him. He itched to put a bullet in Leech and call someone to come clean up her mess.

Except that someone was him.

How the fuck did I end up here? he thought.

"I'm not killing those people," said Aiden with finality. "The Stripes? Not a problem. But people whose only crime is to accept the gift of a lifetime?" He put his hands together. "The question becomes, how can we regress the tech so it's not useful anymore?"

"Man's got an idea," said Jordi, looking at Aiden.

"Maybe. Let me work through it." Aiden paced, letting the thought wiggle in his brain. It all came down to degradation. Getting older. Bodies failing with use. Diseases. Sickness. And how to eke that much more life out of one's existence.

"The jewels Leech wants are the components that drive the prostheses, not the prostheses themselves. These drivers are software, which means they can be hacked. It also means they're using a common operating system and are susceptible to viruses. I don't have to remove each piece. We can just make the Wetware fail. Their owners can have them removed, Leech can organize her own collection operation, or disposal crew. Or, if they're stagnant, then she doesn't have to worry about any further complications in their use."

"People with new hearts and lungs are still gonna die, Aiden," said Jordi.

"Those people with systemically important gear? Their stuff

will keep working. Or we can make it glitch an appropriate amount. We can easily set something to seek and destroy only the prosthetics we're interested in." He looked at Scotty's arms, his mind fixed on them like an arrow, remembering how his arms had misfired when the Stripes had captured Aiden.

"How's Leech gonna take that?" asked Jordi.

"Do we care? She'll get back every piece of dangerous tech. We'll be free of her and live up to our promise. It just won't be via a bloodbath. Sure, she'll be letting a few dozen people live their lives in peace as the price. I think she understood that, at the end."

Jordi shrugged as if it didn't matter. "Long as I get my leash taken off, I'm fine with it, bro."

"I lose these then," said Scotty, holding up his arms, and it was a strange mixture of hope and regret.

"You'll be surprised how often revenge doesn't actually involve a shotgun to the face," Aiden said.

"How are you going to control the Wetware?" asked Jordi, cutting back in. "You said when you tried to hack them before they had self-defense mechanisms that kept you out."

"That's what I need Scotty's arms for."

Aiden didn't like it, having to use Scotty for experimentation for his own devices, but he also didn't know any other way of getting to the prosthetics without everyone dying. He hated being out of options.

"I'm OK with that," said Scotty. "So long as we get the Stripes, shotgun hands or not, I'm good."

Something clicked inside Aiden. He sat down on the edge of his bed, opposite Scotty.

"No," he said. "We should rethink this. Capture a Stripe and do this on them."

Jordi's eyebrows raised. "You finally grown a conscience? Fifty-five years late but better than never, I guess. Scotty here's a resource first, best use him as such."

"Fuck off, Jordi. I'm not doing this to you, Scotty."

"What other options do we have?" asked Scotty.

"You'll as likely end up a cabbage as you will a hero," Jordi said, crossing his legs.

"They're my arms. I'll do with them what I want."

"What if it leaves you crippled?" said Aiden, frowning. "I plan on developing a virus to turn every one of those prosthetics into a brick. It could affect your whole hand in ways I'd never be able to anticipate."

"You saved my life," said Scotty firmly. "I'm going to do this, and if you refuse then we're fucked. We have to stop the Stripes no matter what. Sure, we could kidnap one, but that might put our lives in danger. It's smarter for us to develop a virus now, and then release it on the Stripes as soon as we can."

Aiden took his hat off and ran his hands through his hair. He understood Scotty's argument. The young man was their best option. But he felt that ache in his heart again. Scotty might be a resource, and Aiden could respect his decision. But he could also give him time to consider his options.

"Right," said Aiden, making his decision. "This is what we're going to do. Jordi, I'll write you a list of what I need, but a powerful cyberdeck is the starting point. I want food, drink, and electronics components. Lots of components. While you're at it, a couple of cases of my favorite firearms."

"Oh sure, and what are you going to do while I'm hunting and gathering for you, huh?"

"I'm going to see what Senator Blake is up to. Time we pulled back the carpet there and see what's hiding underneath. And see if there really is a concrete connection between him and the Stripes."

CHAPTER THIRTEEN

It felt like second nature for Aiden to co-opt the rented sedan of a corporate power couple attending a conference for his use that evening. He'd return it when he was finished without anyone being the wiser – or the large-scale hotel seeing that their records weren't exactly correct.

Emerging from the underground parking lot, Aiden turned the car south, crossed K Street and passed Franklin Park, driving a few blocks down until he hit New York Ave. Meanwhile, he parked and began tracking sightings of celebrities and persons of interest – with Senator Blake's rising stardom, it took about ten minutes comparing news briefs and social media before he tracked down the senator's location.

Most of the photos and comments from users were focused on the meet at the Washingtonian, but soon the senator was seen entering a restaurant called Hamilton's House, two blocks east of his office, and a swanky establishment at that. Aiden smiled and thanked social media user @hoppin. in.DC for taking a picture of her photo-bombing the senator. Unfortunately, he didn't think he'd be able to get into the restaurant without dropping a few hundred dollars on a suit and tie.

Aiden inched the car along until it was on the far side of the same block as the restaurant and accessed the restaurant's booking system. From there, he discovered discreet surveillance of the public eating space, which ended abruptly up against the member's area. He confirmed no sign of Blake in the main room.

If he couldn't eavesdrop on Blake via the restaurant, he'd need to take a more direct approach. Blake's phone was encrypted, but it automatically signed into the restaurant's network, which was significantly vulnerable. From there, Aiden piggybacked into Blake's surface layer of activity that included his phone calls and his voicemail whose password was, surprise, surprise, the one put there by the manufacturer.

Aiden downloaded Blake's messages, then turned on his microphone and recording system, listening in on the ongoing conversation.

A waiter greeted Blake by name, and they exchanged pleasantries. Then Blake was standing, greeting someone. Whoever it was broadcasted static on a range of frequencies, and Aiden had to fight to strengthen his connection or risk losing it from the interference. Someone clearly valued their privacy, but such caution only enticed him more. It didn't seem to be broadcasting across the restaurant's network, and so he recorded a sample and gave it to a learning algorithm he'd installed in his profiler for exactly this purpose. The algorithm quickly revealed the interference was modulated to obscure the speaker and countered the sound of their voice like a pair of noise canceling headphones.

Impressed, Aiden ran a piece of software to decode the static and nearly swallowed his tongue when Leech's voice came through the filter.

Had Leech decided to take the investigation into her own hands and set up a meeting with Senator Blake? Aiden had given her a sizable bone to chew on when he revealed Blake's intentions from the private event. His fingers drummed on the wheel.

The conversation was mundane – Blake had bought a place in Montana that was entirely off grid and sustainable. He was proud of his five hundred acres, fresh water well, solar panels, and ground source heat pumps. He had a tech billionaire as a neighbor, and they went hunting together.

By contrast, Leech withstood such banal talk, which surprised him more. The woman he'd come to know would have balked at such trivialities. Leech declined dessert, but Blake, as if reading from the politician's playbook, ordered homemade apple pie. Aiden wanted to stick his finger down his throat at their performances.

"How long?" asked Leech, and Aiden sat up, noting the question signaled a change in their conversation. "How long has your initiative gone on for? I knew you were popular, senator, but I didn't realize you'd been playing the role of a god."

"I can only apologize," Blake said. "I'm not sure I understand the question."

"Don't pull that non-sequitur shit with me," Leech hissed. "We had a leak, but I never thought it would be you or your people. One of our own, sworn into office. You've taken highly classified tech meant for certain citizens and doled it out as a way to win votes."

"I'm saving lives, Ms Leech. I am not really given to waiting, because like all good men I have plans, and those plans will not be delayed. If I was a god, it would be a red-blooded American one, standing up for my people."

"You're saving lives of the people who will give you money or uphold whatever values you believe in," Leech snarled. "Meanwhile, you've destroyed the integrity of a project that has taken years of time and development, tons of taxpayer money..."

"And given it back to the citizens." Blake coughed politely. "Isn't that the point? If it was somehow leaked that you were responsible for hoarding technology that would change the world, while I have given it to those in need immediately and without question, I think I'd still be voted into office, Ms Leech."

"I want the Wetware back," Leech said. "The project has intentions. You don't have the authority of handing it out to whoever you want because you think the public will approve..."

"I am in the privileged position of being given miles of rope with which to hang myself," said Blake. "To paraphrase a president, I could do very bad things in broad daylight, and my constituents would not blink. Let me worry about who is noticing me and who is not. In the meantime, I'll investigate this so-called leak you've brought to my attention and ensure it is fixed. Your future shipments will continue unharmed. I'm sure this whole misunderstanding can be handled quietly now that we both know there will no longer be any further bumps in the road." Blake paused. "Can you do that, Leech? Can you see a smooth fresh road in front of you? Perhaps there's even a way we can do further business together after this. I'll help you, of course, since you've so kindly helped me, even if you didn't fully agree to it."

Aiden could hear Leech's teeth grind together. "Only if I get the Wetware back. All of it."

"And leave hundreds of Americans to suffer?" Blake tsked. "Not the kind of openhearted kindness I'd expect from a government employee."

"I don't care who has the tech, but I know where it belongs."

"Then expect that to be written on your grave," Blake said. "The tech belongs to us, whether we are stars… or stripes."

Aiden shivered at the man's cool tone, happy to threaten a senior member of a secret government agency as if she was some schoolgirl. Aiden fully expected Leech to come back with her own threat but she said nothing.

Just what depth of shit has she waded into? he wondered, even as he wanted to set the world on fire. Leech didn't care who was hurt in the process, only that she got her Wetware back. If she knew about Scotty, she'd scoop him up and bag him, checking off one mark as a recovered asset. Both he and Leech might be on the same side, but she was ruthless, down to her core.

Leech's problem now was that Blake held all the cards, had all the leverage. Blake had taken the Wetware from her, leaving a trail of dead bodies in his wake, all with the easy, moral explanation that would still leave him shining in the light and Leech taking the fall.

The sound of movement came through the static, and Aiden wondered if Leech or Blake had gotten up and left.

In the beginning, Leech had had no choice but to find someone like Aiden to clean up her mess. If he died in the line of fire, no one would give a shit and no one would trace it back to her. If he succeeded? Blake would be dead, the tech returned, and Leech entirely safe.

His phone pinged.

"Jordi, now is not the time," he began but a voice cut him off.

"How dare you?" Leech's words were sharp as a blade. "Do not listen in on my conversations ever again."

"How'd you know?" he asked, not bothering to deny it.

"You didn't hide your presence on Blake's phone," she replied. "I'm not an idiot, Mr Pearce, but let's make one thing clear. I don't care what you think you heard. The goal is to take the Stripes out and return the Wetware to its rightful owner – the United States government. I don't care who it was used by previously. Do what you do best and don't make me decide you need dealing with as well."

"Honestly, I'm surprised you didn't take him up on his offer in full," Aiden said casually. "You could have been selling restricted technology for your own profit off the books to him. Sounds like you might still if he gets you out of this mess."

"I'm not a fucking traitor," Leech growled. "Why do you think I've given you such freedom to mete out violence in the first place?"

It was as close as he was going to get to an apology. He believed her. She was ruthless and trying to unwind the shitshow set in motion, but she didn't seem like a traitor. Now however, Aiden had others to protect – people who Leech would kill given the chance.

"First thing to do is get Abraham," Aiden said. "I get it. Then, we cut Blake's knees out from under him."

Before Leech could respond, Aiden cut the connection.

Luckily, he'd tagged Blake and waited for the senator's next move. The senator was a fool if he didn't think at least half a dozen agencies were tracking his movements and his unencrypted communications. He probably expected it as part of the price he paid for having power. Aiden hoped his following the senator wouldn't be noticed.

Teddy Blake had been so smooth when they'd met – he'd easily adapted to handling Aiden when he thought he was an invading journalist. Perhaps Blake knew who Aiden was all along and wondered if Abraham had told Blake to watch out for the Fox to infiltrate their den.

Maybe he should go to the press and expose both Leech and Blake. Yet, Aiden couldn't see how publishing the truth about Blake would do him any harm at all. Those who voted for him would double down, and those on the other side would only screech about their suspicions being proven true while doing nothing definitive to tackle the threat. Like Blake had pointed out – down to brass tacks, the senator had saved lives with the tech. That would hit the public harder than any other message.

No. Aiden wasn't going to expose him. He was going to shoot him dead.

Aiden's phone pinged, indicating that Blake's cell phone GPS had him being driven toward Springfield.

Aiden slung the sedan into action, dropping onto 395 and catching up until he could see the taillights of a typical black SUV. Passing Springfield, they continued onto I-95.

Where were they headed? Aiden wondered. If the Stripes had a base of operations out here it would make striking at them that much easier – with fewer civilians in the way – and that much more likely any police response would be delayed or perhaps not arrive at all, especially if it was a private compound.

They came off the interstate at Newington and headed west. Aiden noticed an unusual number of bikes on the road. Blake's car caught up to a handful even as others approached them from behind. He let the sedan drop back, not wanting to get caught up in a biker gang's desire to ride together. It was then he spotted they were holding stationary around the senator's ride like an escort.

A couple of them slowed down, dropping back until they were level with Aiden's sedan. One rider on the passenger side wore the Stripes' bandana across his face.

Shit, Aiden thought. They weren't like an escort, they were an escort.

Just play it cool, he told himself, willing his heart to slow down and his hands to stop sweating on the steering wheel. They have no reason to suspect you're here for him.

Aiden had prepared for dealing with a couple of bodyguards to take out the senator, with plans to wipe whatever security systems they hid behind. Right then he could see a dozen bikers, five ahead, one on either side and one behind Blake's SUV with the last two still lingering on either side of the sedan. Not exactly the security he was expecting.

Aiden reached slowly for his pistol, leaving the other hand on the wheel. The bikers were sitting steady, eyes ahead but not budging from either side of the car.

Then the cohort ahead accelerated, the bikers speeding up to match the senator's SUV as it pulled away.

Aiden cursed and put his foot to the floor, swerving left as he did so, right into one of his own pair of bikers. The car crunched. The bike's front wheel gave way, and the biker disappeared in a cloud of wreckage.

The other biker wasted no time in pulling a shotgun and firing on the sedan.

Aiden flinched down in his seat and accelerated. Ahead of them the SUV made some distance – a bigger engine, a newer model, and just all around better than the car he'd taken for his own. Bullets pinged against his door. The rear window shattered. The steering wheel pulled to the right – the car must have snagged something on the bike he'd driven off the road.

"Fuck," he said. There was no way he'd be eliminating Blake tonight.

Another shotgun blast made Aiden slam on the brakes, and the biker shot past, their eyes meeting for a moment as they swapped places. Aiden flipped him off then swung in behind the bike and accelerated. The biker, looking over his shoulder and trying to level the shotgun in Aiden's direction, pulled ahead.

The front bumper tapped the rear of the bike, which wobbled then swerved ahead of him. Aiden was about to ride over the biker when a spray of automatic fire raked down the driver's side of the car.

Two more bikes headed back in his direction, lights on full beam, blinding him and forcing Aiden to swerve out onto the other side of the road. The bikes shot past, pulling tight circles to come back in his direction.

Aiden wasn't having any of it. He swung the sedan into a braking turn, bringing the car around to find the bikes were just starting their own run back toward him. The three of them accelerated, the two bikes falling in alongside one another, lights on high.

Aiden returned the favor so that all they'd be able to see was the dazzling white of his high beams as he barreled towards them.

He had no intention of hitting them both. He'd been in enough collisions to know that even if he managed to wipe them both out, the car would be totaled as well – the bikes weighed upwards of five hundred pounds each.

Winding down the window and keeping one hand on the wheel, he leaned out, aimed as close as he could to the spot directly in front of his car, and opened fire.

The first three shots went into the dazzle and were lost. The fourth made the bike on the right slide off the road ahead of him. The engine roar was deafening. Another biker aimed for him, and Aiden threw himself back behind the wheel as the air right next to him was cut through with roaring bike and biker.

Holding tight, Aiden cut around the other biker and was back into darkness with the bastard behind him, the red light the only sign he was there.

The guttural fury of a two-cylinder piston engine opened up in his blind spot. The third biker, the one he'd nudged, was back there, having waited for him to pass before pulling out and giving chase.

If he'd been in DC, he'd have been safe enough to maneuver the city blocks and escape. But here, there was nothing but a long stretch of interstate without help. No one was coming to save him, and the bikes they drove had barely a hackable silicon chip between them.

The shotgun blasted again. The back of the car jumped then sank down as the rear tire gave way. Aiden smashed his head against the roof of the car, only just holding onto the wheel, then he was freewheeling, out of control across both lanes, praying no one was coming the other way.

With no choice but to slow down, Aiden struggled back into the right lane, and felt the rear wheel's rim grinding on the road. He tried his best to keep driving in a straight line. "This isn't how I expected the night to go," he growled to no one.

Another blast and the rear driver's side window blew in.

Aiden blindly fired behind him until his pistol was empty. There were two beams in his rearview – no chance of getting away from them. If he stalled, they'd shoot him. The senator was long gone. He had one choice left.

On either side, intermittent trees and a pitch of unlit fields surrounded him. He drove off the road and straight into the field, keeping the wheel steady as much as he could. The bikes wouldn't do well off-road. The car squealed as the ruined rear wheel slid from pavement to dirt to grass. The car jolted and from under the hood came a loud bang as the engine gave out.

The car rolled to a stop halfway up a row of foliage – grass and fields and greenery.

Aiden was thrown against the steering wheel, his ribs smashed hard, and his hands pushed into the dash. He'd bitten his tongue. His head ached.

Vision spinning, Aiden tried for the door, arms numb, and then he fell out the side of the car, grasping for his empty pistol. He had more rounds but couldn't immediately say where they were. In his pocket? The glove compartment? He could remember putting them in the car, but the images of where he'd last seen them swam across one another and refused to settle down.

The roar of motorcycles filled the background, rumbling in

idle. A long corridor of smashed vegetation trailed back from the rear of the car. He watched as the bikers stopped at the edge of the field and turned their headlights off before dismounting.

The bikers were coming for him on foot. They were armed with shotguns and semi-automatic weapons. Probably jacked up on Leech's tech, too. All he had was an empty handgun.

Still, look on the bright side, he thought wryly. He had an advantage – they didn't know if he was alive or dead, whether he was armed or not. They didn't even know if he was trapped in the car.

If they were smart, they'd take their time. Approach quietly and finish him off right there. Aiden only had a few moments to find cover and hide. Moving away from the wreckage, he hunkered down close enough to see the car's outline in the darkness, but with enough space between it and any curious bikers. His phone was clutched in his hand, and he tried to find a connection, but there was nothing he could find. He couldn't even profile these bastards.

Soon, he heard the crunching of heavy boots on foliage. They weren't even trying to be stealthy. Instead, they stomped in the ruin the car had left behind.

Aiden thanked his lucky stars and waited for them to pass before he tried jumping them.

A large shape passed a few feet from him. Aiden held his breath, thinking of one time when he'd been laid out in a field having been chased by security from a research center where he'd been busy copying their files. Unable to get away clean, he'd found himself in the open on a moonless night. Instead of running, he'd simply lain down at the meadow's edge. The three-person security team had stormed right past him, their feet miraculously missing him by inches in a fruitless search. Once they'd passed, he'd run off and never looked back.

Now, hidden, he had the advantage to take them down.

He raised himself up into a crouch, suppressing a groan of pain. The biker ahead was huge, perhaps eight inches taller than him and easily weighing another hundred pounds. Aiden had to take him down quickly. Two against one would leave him overwhelmed. He wouldn't get a second chance.

He aimed for the biker's legs and managed to wrap both arms around the man's knees as they collided and tumbled to the ground. The biker's shotgun slid away out of his grip as he tried to cry out, but Aiden pushed his face into the ground to muffle the sound. The biker struck out, a foot connecting with Aiden's side. Crying out in pain, Aiden's fingers found the biker's lost shotgun and he tried to get a shot off, but his aim was too wild.

The biker clambered to his feet. "Mother…" he said in a thick drawl before kicking Aiden and knocking him back. "Come here, you little fuck."

A hand grasped at Aiden's coat collar and yanked him up. "Mr Blake wants you dead, so dead you're gonna be." The biker flung Aiden onto the ground. Aiden landed with a crunch just as the second biker joined the first.

He'd barely managed to hang on to the shotgun. The idea of sitting up, leveling it, aiming, and then firing it was somewhere akin to putting a rocket into space fueled only by candy.

The second biker laughed at him. This one was as tall as the first but thinner and had grown a magnificent beard right down to his chest.

So much for killing Blake, thought Aiden again. This might be where I punch my ticket instead.

But the thought of leaving Scotty to deal with all this shit on his own lit a fire in Aiden's bruised guts. The kid didn't deserve that. He had a life to live – something that shouldn't be stained by revenge and hatred because of the cruelty of others. Aiden was going to live long enough to help Scotty get the revenge he deserved or steer the young man as far away from it as he could.

"I'm gonna beat him to death with my hands. Much more fun," the big biker said, cracking his knuckles.

Aiden groaned and scrabbled to get away, dragging the gun with him.

"Oh," said the biker as he approached, fists raised. "There's my gun. Thanks for that, but like I said, it will be a pleasure to punch your face in."

"No," said Aiden, trying to hold onto the weapon, but the biker grabbed the barrel and pulled. Aiden refused to let go and shifted, put his finger on the trigger. The blast was deafening, and the kickback rammed into his bicep, bruising him. The biker's arm blew off at the shoulder, minced and ruined. Blood sprayed in the dark. The man screamed.

As the other biker leveled his semi-automatic rifle and fired, screaming at Aiden, Aiden launched behind the first biker, using the man as a shield. The biker's friend was peppered with bullets.

The gunfire stopped, and the first biker collapsed unmoving. Aiden rolled over and got to his feet, fearful that the second biker would finish him off.

Instead, the shooter dropped his empty weapon and ran over to his very dead friend. He fell to his knees, begging him to still be alive.

Aiden steadied himself and grabbed the shotgun. Pumped it.

"I'm going to pull you to pieces and feed you to my dogs!" the biker screamed at him.

Only, Aiden wasn't listening. With a last burst of energy, he unloaded the final shell into the biker.

When he was done, he dropped the gun and fell to his knees, then onto his face as he lost his fight with consciousness.

CHAPTER FOURTEEN

His face was wet. Aiden touched his cheek. He tasted blood and sweat. The sky was lightening, but the sun hadn't broken the horizon yet. There were purples and oranges slung across the narrow crescent he could see through the field.

He turned to see the carnage. A raven pecked at one of the bikers and cawed at Aiden before going back to feasting, satisfied he was no threat to its breakfast.

Somehow, Aiden made it to his feet.

Shooing the bird away, Aiden checked their bodies, and found phones in their pockets that were switched off. He expected the entire gang had hacked the tracking and GPS functions to ensure they could call each other without anyone's satellite pinging their positions. But, with them off, that didn't matter.

The upside was none of the other bikers would know where their friends had gone.

His network managed to pull up some semblance of a connection and pinged weakly. He ambled toward the road, thankful the signal seemed to get stronger. He called Jordi.

"Fuck, you're still alive. I owe the kid twenty."

"I'm not entirely sure you'll have to pay out yet," said Aiden. "I'm in the middle of somewhere rural without any connection. Come and get me."

"Don't do anything stupid while you're waiting, city boy," said Jordi. "Don't start talking to scarecrows." He cut the call, leaving Aiden to amble down the road and brood. When Jordi arrived over an hour later, Aiden decided he never wanted to be lost in the wilderness again. If you could consider this the wilderness.

"I want to kill her," he said to Jordi after he'd climbed into the car.

"Nice to see you too," Jordi replied. "You look like shit, by the way. Did you wrestle a hog?"

"Sure," said Aiden, noting his clothes were a ragged mess and he'd lost his cap in the struggle. "Big metal one. I've had better days, Jordi."

"Haven't we all?"

Aiden explained what had happened, and with each revelation about Leech, the bikers, and Blake, Jordi whistled his disbelief.

"Gotta admire the audacity," said Jordi. "A senator stealing tech from his own government, using it to bolster his own white supremacist group, and still handing that tech out to constituents dying of one disease or another. That's one hell of a political stunt. And Leech? You sure she's not scamming both sides?"

"I think she might have stalled Blake to buy some time by considering his offer, and he took matters into his own hands. She might have weighed making the deal, until she found out he was a full-blown white supremacist."

"So our government agent has some good bones in her, after all. Not many. But some."

Aiden didn't respond. His only feeling about the situation involved several cans of gas and a box of matches.

"You sure she doesn't want us dead?" asked Jordi as they hit Washington's outer limits.

"She doesn't want us dead," said Aiden. "She wants Blake and Abraham dead."

"Woo. I'll cancel the ad for the surgery interns then?"

"Don't go that far." Aiden snorted. "She will still do anything to get the Wetware back. And, she still has a deal dangled by the senator if she really feels like she's in hot water. But it's not Leech I'm worried about. The real issue is we don't know what Blake's end game is. What does he want?"

"Blake sounds like he's invulnerable," said Jordi, saluting the absent senator.

"Exactly. So why go to all this trouble with the Stripes? Why authorize experimentation? He's already so popular, it's not like he's losing an election anytime soon. Something is missing. Speaking of… what did you do with Scotty?"

"He's a medic." Jordi shrugged. "I left him tinkering with his arms."

"Did they act up on their own?"

Jordi nodded. "Fucking glad he ain't got no ammo. I woke up to the sound of his firing mechanism clicking away all by itself. Kid's good people. Tells me he can fix his arms. Maybe remove the Wetware if he can figure out how it's integrated with his body."

"Good people don't ask to go on murdering rampages," said Aiden.

"Good people," said Jordi, "know when they need to take no more shit. Good people know when to fight back. He's good people."

"Careful now, you'll make it sound like we're good people." The idea of righteous vengeance appealed to Aiden. Burn the world down because it was the right thing to do. Start fresh. Start new. But even so, he felt protective over Scotty in a way he hadn't felt in a long time. He didn't want Scotty close to Leech or the senator and their machinations.

"I don't think anyone would mistake us for good," said Jordi, running a hand through his hair. "But a broken clock's right twice a day. As long as it isn't digital, then it's just shit all the time. Don't you get the wrong idea – Scotty's a resource. Don't think I didn't notice you hesitating to use him to get what we need."

Sometimes Aiden wanted to punch Jordi right in the face. Instead, he said, "I won't hesitate to end Blake. Does that make you feel better? And, while we do that, we're going to do the same for Abraham and his merry band of racist fucks."

"I like this plan," said Jordi. "By which I mean I'll get you your guns and you'll go and slay them until they're dead. Bonus being that the kid wants to put the barrel into Abraham's mouth and pull the trigger."

"He isn't a soldier," said Aiden as they pulled into DC proper. "Just like all the people at Senator Blake's private event weren't Stripes. Just because they have patriotic views doesn't slot them into the far right, you know? Some of them just wanted the augmentations to save their lives."

"Are you having a crisis, Aiden Pearce?" Jordi asked.

"You know what I mean."

"Think of it this way. Do the ends justify the means?" Jordi asked. "Do the ends of Blake handing out Wetware to those dying justify those hurt like Scotty? My bet is you're gonna say no."

"You're right on that account."

"So stop thinking so hard on it. Blake is a stain on the earth. Ergo, it's up to you, the Vigilante, to make him pay his dues. So, how you gonna find him?"

"I've got his GPS," said Aiden. "Fucker can't hide from me anywhere on the planet."

Jordi chewed at his lip. "And then what?"

"Leech," replied Aiden. "We get her the Wetware, but we launch that virus and render it all useless, so no one has to die."

"Good plan," Jordi said and pulled into the motel.

Scotty waited for them when they arrived, a nervous and excited look on his face that faltered when he saw Aiden. "Whoa. Are you all right?"

"Barely," Aiden said before going to clean himself up with a shower. When he was done, Jordi nudged them down to the bar, which was empty that early in the morning. Scotty covered his arms as much as possible, and the three of them each nursed a beer while filling Scotty in about the previous night.

Watching people walk away from others' suffering was something Aiden had experienced again and again, but it had always been personal. Seeing Leech act like she had, seeing how committed Abraham and Blake were to changing America to be more like them – whiter and openly hostile to anyone who wasn't… nothing new there. What was new was the Wetware.

Aiden could think of a hundred uses for the tech, and none of them were pretty.

"So you think Blake's going to control people with Wetware?" asked Jordi as they circled back around to Blake's plans.

"Don't think so," said Aiden slowly. "The more I puzzle it out, the more I think Blake's using it to do two things. Build a loyal base of those who'll look the other way when he does the really bad shit, and then empower those who'll actually do the really bad shit."

"What kind of bad shit does a senator need weaponized tech for?" asked Jordi.

"Wasn't just weapons," said Scotty. "I mean, some of them were weapons. Like mine, yeah? Others were like armor or enhanced strength, but I don't think they were meant to be used in the way the Stripes intended. You can't just give someone an arm that can rip a car in two – their shoulders can't take it. A fact of the human body. You have to integrate it in a way which allows the body to survive the stresses. Take my arms, right? A shotgun has a kick and gunpowder. There's a lot of force needed to make it shoot. My arms aren't able to handle that kind of stress, no matter if the weapon is integrated with my tendons and muscles and bones. At some point the tech needs to support the body's needs alongside what it gives the person using the Wetware."

"So someone jumping a couple of stories *could* work?" asked Aiden, wanting to establish a baseline for Gin's abilities.

"Yeah, or like, you know, ripping a car in half. But think of her joints. Even if she might be able to do it for a short time, the long-term damage on her human body would be catastrophic."

"But once they do figure out how to compensate for the human body, it could be like something out of a movie," said Jordi.

"All the more reason to kick the shit out of them before they get too far along," said Aiden.

"Well, something like that would be a far more advanced process that I don't think Leech intended. Even though she may be putting recovered soldiers back in the field, I think her goal is to recover them to the level of human, not ruin them for one battle or one mission by making them like a super soldier," Scotty said.

Aiden glanced at Jordi, who was busy throwing nuts into his mouth in a big arc. He knew Jordi had opinions that were usually hidden in his pointless chatter, but the man didn't venture them often. You could spend a month with Jordi and know nothing more about him at the end than you did at the beginning. But it was Jordi's choice to be a blank slate.

Thing was, Aiden was having trouble seeing Scotty as a resource, like Jordi suggested. He saw Scotty as an innocent, someone better than Aiden. He stared at Scotty, surprised when he realized the young man wasn't filled with the poisonous kind of anger he'd spent years cultivating.

When did you start caring? he thought.

He'd been here before. It was bizarre that it might fall to Aiden to make the difference, to stop the world from following a path that could only lead to hate and misery for untold numbers. He always took on that burden and he always failed to make the world a better place.

You don't have the best track record, he said to himself. Most of those you've tried to help have ended up disappointed or worse. There weren't many of them left alive to complain.

Scotty, though. He could do something about Scotty.

Which brought him back to creating a virus that rendered

the Wetware useless and using Scotty's arms as the first test subject to see if it worked. God, he hated having to do this, but he'd given Scotty time to think it over. Time to see if the young man felt the way he did before.

"You still want in?" he asked Scotty. "To use your arms as tests to see if we can immobilize the Wetware?"

"I'm still here, aren't I?" There was that defiance in his voice again. There wasn't any way of convincing him to do anything different.

"Fine. You need to accept that it might leave you with no arms."

"Jesus," said Jordi, throwing a nut at Aiden.

"He needs to know the risks," said Aiden, daring him to look away.

"I understand," said Scotty firmly. "This is bigger than me. You think the Stripes are going to take that tech and use it to plough fields and find orphans new homes?"

Aiden laughed. "No. I think they're going to kill a bunch of people and call it justice."

"I don't think you were listening to me earlier, Aiden," Scotty said, shifting forward. "My body isn't meant to deal with the impact of a firearm integrated into it. It's likely I will lose my arms either way. At this point, I choose the way it happens. So, tell me. When do we start?"

"Starting's not the problem," Aiden said, admiring Scotty's tenacity and strength. "Finishing is. You don't just whack out a virus like this in an afternoon. It's going to take a few days, at best. And I think the way your Wetware is already acting up is the perfect skeleton for me to mimic."

"You think we have that kind of time?" asked Jordi.

Aiden fixed him with a flat stare. "You got everything I asked for?"

Jordi shifted, embarrassed. "Look, you can't just order up… ah. Yeah. Sure. A few days sounds perfect."

"What do I do?" asked Scotty.

Aiden pointed at Scotty. "I need your arms for this. Think of it like sitting for a portrait in olden times."

CHAPTER FIFTEEN

Aside from letting them all shower, the hotel was no good for tinkering. Rather than waste more time, Aiden had Jordi find them a place where they could work undisturbed – an empty office suite on a strip mall off on the southern edge of the city.

It came with broken blinds, a couple of abandoned desks, and no chairs. The bonus? It smelled of stale smoke and fish, the latter of which Aiden knew meant bad wiring.

Aiden left Jordi ordering a delivery of guns, ammo, and a coffee machine and found Scotty loading a couple of cheap desks, half a dozen old-fashioned, second-hand holographic displays, and accessories to go with them into the office from the back of a truck. Aiden didn't want to know if it had all been stolen. After all, it was enough to give them the appropriate tools and space, and Jordi had done it inside of a day.

Aiden was itching to get to it, but he still needed a decent, and secure, deck from which he could begin work on Scotty's arms. It wasn't like he had nothing to do – he checked on Blake at least twenty times and tried, in his calmer moments, to sketch out in his head how the code he was going to stitch together would be structured.

Tellingly, Blake didn't move more than a hundred yards the whole time, ensconced over in the Capitol Building. By evening, Aiden wished for him to do something other than sit in his office. The whole thing made Aiden restless.

So he did what he always did when the world tried to tell him something was impossible – Aiden broke it down into small steps that he could manage, knowing that if he kept going, eventually he'd have the whole thing sorted out.

That was, until Jordi poked him in the shoulder and pointed at a couple of bags under one of the desks. "New clothes. Go get changed."

"What about everything else?" asked Aiden.

"When you're clean and don't smell like the food recycling trashcan in the back of a Wendy's, I'll take you on a tour of paradise."

Aiden sniffed at his top and wrinkled his nose. He took advantage of Jordi's kindness and found his new clothes were a carbon copy of what he'd been wearing before, right down to the gray baseball cap.

Never gets old, he thought with satisfaction as he stared at his reflection in the restroom mirror. *Unlike me.*

Jordi looked him up and down when he returned and nodded. "There's the man the government knows and hates."

"Give me the tour then," said Aiden, and they spent the next twenty minutes cataloging what Jordi had amassed. Seeing the deck waiting for him to access Scotty's Wetware filled Aiden with a glowing sense of purpose.

"Where's Scotty?" asked Aiden, ready to get started.

"Supplies, dude. Chill."

As if on cue the door to the office opened, showing Scotty carrying party size bags of chips, drinks, and candy.

Not a green option among them, thought Aiden.

"How are your arms?" he asked.

"Great," said Scotty.

"Let's get started then." Despite his eagerness, Aiden wasn't exactly sure where to start. Once he knew what he was aiming for, he could collect the scripts from which he'd build the virus construct. In his mind he had a couple of choices: he could brick people's prosthetics or he could try for something more complex like controlling them or using them to harm their owners. He didn't know yet if the Wetware sent data uploads to a corporation headquarters where updates were automatically distributed, nor if the Wetware responded to electromagnetic interference.

His answers hung on what he could discover in Scotty's arms.

He had Scotty sit and place his arms on one of the tables. Aiden studied where the prosthetics broke the skin, close enough to see how the skin had healed into a mesh that ran around the edge of the tech where it needed to be exposed to the air.

"How long ago did this happen?" he asked.

"About three weeks," said Scotty.

"You heal quick," said Aiden.

"It's the Wetware," said Scotty. "Something about it bypasses the normal risks of rejection." Seeing Aiden's expression, he coughed. "No, not like a super-charged ability, just what should take months takes weeks and what should take weeks takes days instead."

"Bruises disappear overnight?" asked Jordi from across the room where he was fiddling with their holographic projectors.

"No. It works around wounds, deals with the knitting of flesh and bones but minor stuff isn't touched."

"Right," said Aiden, using his phone and profiler to try to access the systems running Scotty's arm. He ran into the exact same interference as before but was ready for it this time. To his surprise, working calmly without pressure he could see it was the same kind of encryption Abraham had used, even if more complex. Settling in, he started to understand the Wetware beyond its simple appearance of a shotgun melded into a hand. He began to see it as a tool.

An hour later he was in.

The architecture impressed him – whoever had designed it was smart enough to build a blazingly smart learning algorithm, give it some clever instructions, and then let it teach itself how to deliver on them. The code he was looking at had an alien feel, the kind he'd come to recognize as developed by a machine and not a human. In one way, it was self-contained, yet in others, the skeleton of the tech controlling Scotty's arms was viral in nature – learning, adaptive, and with simple objectives.

The tech had a spine from which it farmed out all its various objectives. Aiden worked with it for another hour, following it up and down the design hierarchy until he found what he believed was a node through which a lot of decision making was routed by the tech whenever Scotty's nervous system told it to move or lift and the like.

"I'm going to try something," he told Scotty, who was busy doing nothing except yawning occasionally.

"Sure, be better than sitting here like a ragdoll waiting for you to finish," said Scotty.

Aiden did the equivalent of telling Scotty's arms to scratch his chin from the code downloaded onto his deck and phone.

Instead of rising up, the cartridge chamber clicked like it was processing a shell.

Aiden tutted, wondering what he'd done to send such a divergent message.

"That feels weird," said Scotty slowly, as his arms lifted up and then smashed back down and through the table like it was made of crepe paper.

"Shit," said Scotty as one hand grasped for Aiden, who shoved his chair back and jumped desperately to the side.

Scotty's arms swung through the air where Aiden's head had been moments before, then jerked the other way as if searching for something.

"You gotta get out," said Scotty, his voice terrified.

"What did you do?" shouted Jordi, who had his gun out.

"Put that thing away," shouted Aiden at Jordi.

Scotty's arms swung around, as if they'd sensed Aiden creep in, and smashed through the air in his direction. Scotty lurched after them, pulled by his own arms, passing Aiden by a hair's width as he ducked out of the way before crunching into the flimsy partition walls at Aiden's back.

Scotty's hands sank in up to his wrists before pulling out again in a shower of masonry and dust.

"How do we make it stop?" shouted Jordi.

Scotty yelled over the noise of his fists punching repeatedly into the wall. "Get out, get out. You can't do anything. If you come too close it'll go for you."

Aiden wasn't going anywhere. The office wasn't small, and even though Scotty was smashing his way through a wall, Aiden refused to leave him alone.

Would the customers in the other shops in the strip investigate the disturbance? Aiden feared discovery when the sudden noise of a twenty-four-hour news channel drowned out Scotty's convulsions.

"You need to see something," said Jordi from over his shoulder even as Scotty screamed in frustration as his arms smashed through the partition and he disappeared into the kitchen that was on the other side.

Is Jordi not fucking paying attention? thought Aiden.

Seeing his look, Jordi shrugged. "Just don't get close and his arms won't see you as a threat."

Aiden followed Scotty, wanting to make sure he was OK. Inside the kitchen he found the young man slowly crushing the metal heating plate the owner had left for them. Scotty was covered in sweat.

Scotty spoke through gritted teeth. "Don't come too close."

"You realize we're going to lose our deposit," said Aiden, hoping to make him smile, but Scotty was beyond such encouragements.

"I'm sorry. I didn't mean to do this," he said.

"Scotty…" said Aiden but Scotty's hands released their clamp on the balled-up heating plate and ripped the door off an elderly microwave.

"It'll be OK, nothing you can do." Scotty waved Aiden back.

How was Aiden going to hack into Scotty's arms if they kept going psychotic? Instead, he kept his worries to himself and said, "If you're not going to actually hurt yourself, I'll be in the other room when you're done." He backed slowly away.

The channel Jordi had brought up showed a cool looking Senator Blake denying something someone had asked off screen.

Jordi grunted and flipped to another channel. This time the president was on screen in the White House press room. She was answering questions.

"The vice president is unwell. No, I cannot say when he will return to his duties."

Someone asked if the vice president would resign their role rather than carry on as a lame duck.

"I don't think that's a fair characterization. He has worked tirelessly on behalf of the American people, and right now I'd ask you to have compassion for his entire family."

"I'd heard rumors about this on some of our favorite dark web forums," muttered Jordi. "Didn't think they were real."

"Of what?" asked Aiden.

"See what living under a rock gets you?" said Jordi. "People have been saying the Veep has advanced cancer, could be stomach cancer, bone cancer. Different calls each time I've heard it except it's always cancer."

"Bullshit," said Aiden. "Why isn't the Speaker objecting to this?"

"He's sick," said Jordi. "Hell, I object to cancer too, but it don't give a shit about my opinion. Same for the Speaker, I'd expect. This just means the president gets to nominate a new second-in-command. Although, it has to be approved by Congress."

On the screen they cut away from the president, and in the studio, the two anchors were discussing what would happen next with whatever two-cent expert they'd rustled up.

"Well, Karen," said the expert, a man with a beard but no hair.

"It seems likely the president will announce the vice president's departure at the State of the Union on Sunday."

"Who do you think will be announced to replace him?" asked Karen.

"Right now, there's three candidates. Senator Tom Branch-flower of Connecticut. Long-time supporter of the president, stumped with him for the nomination. Family friend. Seems likely.

"Then there's Senator Diane Reilstein, California representative since 2020. Party elder and hugely influential. As a woman she'd make the one, two of the nation's leadership female, which would be entirely unprecedented.

"Finally, and he's a bit of a dark horse, comes Senator Edward Blake."

"He's a Republican though. Tell us why people are mentioning his name."

"As you know, Karen, the Democrats lost both houses in the midterms, and this president campaigned on holding the middle ground and working with both sides. She was a true compromise candidate. That didn't translate to action in her first year though, and finding bipartisan support across both houses proved a huge challenge. Bringing in someone like Senator Blake, a rising star among the Republican base, would give the president a foot in both camps."

"How would this impact the issues?" asked Karen.

The expert shook his head. "I don't know about that. Some would see this as a power grab against a weakened incumbent. No one really believes this will bring the nation together, but it would cement Blake's position in his own party and potentially change the legislative agenda for the remainder of the president's term. That, and Blake would be well positioned to take the nomination come the campaign season – he's made it clear he intends to run for president."

"A lot to watch for then," said Karen, winding up the segment.

Aiden's stomach sank. Did the president know what she was doing? Did she have any idea about Blake and what lay behind his pleasant demeanor?

She must know, he thought. The intelligence agencies were solid, independent, and for all their flaws and biases, they remained unquestioningly loyal to the United States, having proved time and again that they would stand to one side of both Republicans and Democrats.

Jordi sucked at his teeth. "This isn't what we signed up for, Aiden. I think we just figured out what Blake is really after. He's doing it in all the right ways."

"He's got to be blackmailing someone," Aiden said, knowing he sounded desperate. "There's no way this would happen."

"But it's all legal," Jordi said. "Once he has power, and with the Stripes on his side, he can advance any kind of agenda he wants."

Aiden ignored him. "We've got work to do. It's Tuesday. We have until Saturday."

"You telling me you're going to strike at the Capitol?" asked Jordi, his tone flat and his mouth pressed thin.

"What I'm going to do is finish this. The stability of the government is on the line. What you have to do is get me there."

"Excuse me," said Jordi primly. "We're going to need more firepower." With that, he turned and slumped down into one of the office seats, his fingers swaying on a computer keyboard as he immediately set to work.

"We already have rifles, flash bangs, and grenades," Aiden said.

"And we need hand cannons and a backpack full of countermeasures," Jordi answered.

"What about drones? Static movement tracking sentry guns?"

"Now you're thinking," Jordi said. "What about your resource in there? The sounds of wreckage have stopped." Jordi thumbed at the kitchen.

"Scotty won't need any guns," said Aiden.

"That isn't what I mean, Aiden. He's got shotguns for arms. And don't think I haven't seen your heart peeking out from your sleeve. He isn't your family, Aiden, and even if he was, how do you think that would work out for him? You gotta put aside this strange new soft chewy center you've developed. Can you afford to take the risk that treating him with kid gloves is still the best solution?"

"Buy your guns, Chin," Aiden snarled and turned back to concentrate on the data he'd pulled from Scotty's Wetware. He hated being so open. Even though he'd learned a lot by looking at Scotty's arms, the outcome had been less than optimal. But time was of the essence, with not enough of it to perfect an optimal solution in time to take Blake down before the State of the Union.

Right then he wished he had access to a proper AI, someone who could help him infiltrate the Capitol's systems and wage true electronic warfare. Fanciful thinking, he knew, but the rumors were out there of real AI. London had advanced far beyond the capabilities of the United States.

He'd like, just for once, for them to be working for him.

Aiden steepled his fingers and ran over plans in his mind. He didn't want to smash his way into the Capitol Building. It wouldn't do him any good if Blake died in a hail of gunfire. That was the way martyrs were made.

Nor did dealing with Blake in such a manner address the problem of Abraham and the Stripes. Done wrong and they'd flee for cover, leaving him without a victory and them with Leech's tech and enough fury to use it in the open where others could get hurt. He had to neutralize Abraham and his fanatical fascists.

He considered abandoning Blake and dealing with Abraham, but there were two problems there. First, he had no idea where Abraham had gone, and without that knowledge he had no way of tracking him down and taking him out before Sunday... even if he could get the arms and armor.

No. Abraham would have to be done after Blake. With any luck, he could deal with them both at the same time. His gut told him that when he found Blake, Abraham wouldn't be far away.

The second reason to focus on Blake was that if he did manage to deal with Abraham but Blake ascended to the position of vice president, it wouldn't matter if Abraham's faction supported him or not. He'd be the second most powerful man in the world. If ordinary people thought their lives were crappy now, just wait until an unrepentant white supremacist was influencing policy decisions.

If the whole of the Stripes knew Blake was one of their own, his newfound power would only encourage them to murder their way across the country.

"Jordi. Find out what you can for me about Blake." Aiden

rubbed his forehead. There was a lot to do and little time to do it.

"Shoe size? Inside leg?" asked Jordi sarcastically.

"You really do have shit for brains. I want to know what the usual suspects think about his highness and the prospect of him becoming vice president. Also, find out what cop message boards think. Just how dangerous is he? We're missing something. He's about to become Veep, why does he need this goddamned tech so bad? Like you said, everything he's doing is legal. So find the shit he's trying to hide."

Jordi nodded, his sneering gone. "Sure thing."

Blake had to leave the Capitol Building. The senator didn't sleep there, and Aiden suspected there was no secure way of communicating with Abraham from inside, especially with intelligence services listening for talk of sedition and treason. Somehow, Aiden needed to get ahold of Blake's phone or communication software and find a way of rooting out Abraham.

A car crash was his easiest tactic – send Blake's car tumbling over and over, crushing the man to death inside. Like most of the Senate, and unlike the bikers he'd tangled with, Blake's official vehicles were electric. No gas tanks blowing up to seal the deal but plenty of computing power to hijack.

He felt good about it. As far as the kinds of people Aiden dealt with, putting a senator on the list of billionaire tech psychopaths, politicians, and murderers who fell before the Vigilante seemed like a nice addition.

CHAPTER SIXTEEN

"Tell me about yourself, Scotty," Aiden said, once Scotty's arms had calmed down enough that they could get back to work.

Scotty sat up straight and, for a moment, looked shy. Aiden flashed him an encouraging smile. He usually didn't do this kind of thing – he'd have hated it if someone did it to him – but he couldn't help himself. Like Jordi said, the heart on his sleeve was starting to show.

"Nothing remarkable about me," said Scotty. "I can't even shake my accent."

"Hadn't noticed," said Aiden, who'd clocked his Philly twang the first time he'd spoken down in the church basement. "You sound like you should have left it behind, though?"

Scotty sighed, resting his forearms on his knees palm up. "You'd think five years at college would have set me free. It's all about finding yourself, right?"

"I wouldn't know," said Aiden.

"What?" said Scotty, eyes wide open. Off to the side, head inside a box of electronics, Jordi snorted.

"Just I didn't do that kind of thing, so if you're saying it didn't work for you then you're welcome to join my club."

"Don't do it, kid," came Jordi's muffled comment.

"I'll decide on that," Scotty said with a small smile while Aiden carefully tried to decipher the code of his arm. "I went into medicine. My mom was a coder, dad a mechanic. I was always really proud of how she supported us when he was between jobs." He shrugged. "She earned more, and he was proud of her, too. My uncles thought he was a limp dick for letting his woman earn more, but they didn't have a clue.

"She wanted me to follow in her footsteps, but I wasn't interested in sitting at a screen writing code. I loved figuring out puzzles, but what got me really interested? Seeing medicine change people's lives. I said I was going to be a doctor from five years old. Got there eventually, with a lot of help and sacrifice from my family." He looked unsure then, as if he might wake from his dream of vengeance, but his mouth kept telling the story anyway.

"Finished university and discovered that my friends, my white friends, all walked into jobs. Sometimes we applied for the same place, and they'd get it and I'd not even get an interview, just a template rejection."

"Let me guess," came Jordi. "Your GPA was better."

Scotty nodded. "This one time two of us applied after an open day when the company rep said there were two roles, and they were struggling to find people who wanted to work emergency departments. He got a job. I didn't. After he started, he told me they were still searching for someone in the role and handed my resumé right to HR. I still didn't even get invited for interview."

Aiden listened, growing increasingly uncomfortable, a mix of anger and a need to fix what had happened roiling in his guts.

His feelings were made worse knowing he couldn't do anything to help Scotty.

"What happened?" he asked.

"Eventually a friend of the family – and it's always this way, right – that friend put my resumé on the desk of a head attending physician here in DC. They scrubbed my surname from it, and the next day I got an interview. I met the attending, and they were amazing, offered me a role right there in the interview.

"HR queried my status, my religious beliefs, whether I'd been in trouble with the police, but my new boss intervened and got them off my back. I've been working there now for three years." His eyes were fragile, like shattered glass, and Aiden couldn't see Scotty ever returning to such normal, everyday work.

"You'll get yourself back on that path," Aiden said.

"As long as Abraham and his get what's coming to them. What about you?"

"Oh, nothing much to say," said Aiden. He wasn't ready for Scotty to ask about his family. Or what remained of it.

"He's a loser, Scotty," Jordi piped up. "You don't want to learn about him except to figure out what not to do with your life."

"Says you," said Aiden, both irritated and relieved at the intervention.

"If your life is one of mistakes being made, mine's one of disasters not quite averted. Neither of us are role models for a fine upstanding young man like Scotty here."

Aiden grunted and figured talking would just lead to trouble and more questions, so he furrowed his brow and ran a series of diagnostics designed to see how easy it was to override the inbuilt motor functions and the software that ran them, being especially careful not to actually interfere with any of the systems. He thought he'd identified the trigger, or at least the spot where, if he messed around, the arms would try to kill him. There was a mass of something behind it, but there was no time to fix Scotty's arms, only to take what information Aiden needed.

It turned out to be harder than he'd thought. Leech's people had layered in security tight as a drum all throughout the various subroutines and objects on which they'd built the mechanisms for his arm movements. That security was responsible for the static that sprayed out each time he tried to hack it. He sat back, exhausted, and knew he hadn't even begun to analyze how the arm was articulated. Breaking in was only part of the job.

"The human arm's a complicated thing," he said at the end of the evening, slumping back in his seat and shutting down the various virtual realities he'd been working in.

"You ever wonder why it took so long for them to create drones that could walk by themselves?" asked Scotty. "Cause it's not as simple as just moving limbs. Humans walk by falling forward and moving their bodies so they don't hit the ground. When we walk, we decide to not fall over in a specific direction, and that takes us where we want to go. Capturing that mechanism isn't trivial, and fixing it's even harder. It is possible though. People who've had strokes can often learn to walk again."

Aiden looked at Scotty with a raised eyebrow.

"Studied it for my dissertation," Scotty said proudly.

"Can you help me?" asked Aiden.

"I can try," said Scotty. "Honestly, I was beginning to feel like I was just another tool for you to use, and it was grinding my gears."

"It's why you thought you could fix your arm," said Aiden, suddenly understanding.

Scotty held up his arms. "Turns out electronics is quite a lot different from biology." He smiled, embarrassed. "Who knew?"

"Medics," said Aiden. "Always think you know everything."

Scotty shrugged, but his face was light. He understood Aiden's joke.

"Can you code?" asked Aiden.

Scotty shook his head.

"Then this is all you can do. Don't feel like a burden. Your arms are your value. I hate to be harsh, kid, but your usefulness isn't based on what you can do. I'm done for tonight," said Aiden. Once upon a time he'd have gone on until the early hours, but his body still ached. His bruises from the car crash were only just coming out a deep purple, and each time he breathed deeply his chest felt like a buffalo had sat on him. Sleep was his best medicine.

Scotty didn't look happy, and when Aiden asked him if he wanted to go back to the hotel he declined.

Leaving Jordi and Scotty furiously watching television, he returned to the hotel where he slept like a slightly manhandled baby until his own mind whirred and woke him up, making him hop on his phone for research.

The next morning, he arrived at the office to find empty chip bags and soda cans strewn around the place like teenagers had thrown a party. Aiden kicked them away from his work desk and started back in on the code he was stitching together.

He'd found a series of scripts from groups in the Ukraine, Russia, Norway, and Myanmar as well as some stuff he'd been sent by a group of preteens out in Alabama who'd put their own bits together so they could spoof online roleplaying games and make their avatars super powerful. Between the different pieces of code, he felt like he had a working skeleton of how to control Scotty's arm without either triggering whatever fault the kid had been trying to fix or permanently damaging the base software his hack was going to infiltrate.

The trick was making them compatible with whatever was controlling Scotty's arm. Fortunately, Leech's Wetware had used a language Aiden knew, but some algorithm had done much of the coding, and he found unraveling its design decisions slow going, as if one of the things it had done was deliberately make it hard for someone to understand its process.

The problem for Aiden was Scotty's software linked directly to his flesh and blood arms. Scotty had said repeatedly he was prepared to sacrifice his arms for the sake of stopping the Stripes, but Aiden was determined to find any possible solution that avoided the young man losing his limbs, or worse. After what had been done to him, to then take his arms away was a mail order package full of shit Aiden didn't want to deliver.

About lunchtime he'd had enough of banging his head against the various layers of security in the Wetware and blinked blearily to locate Blake's schedule.

Having forty-eight hours of tracking logged, he was surprised to notice Blake had not been out of the Capitol Building the whole time.

Aiden put his head down and did the first thing he always did when he encountered something which didn't make sense – he double checked his own assumptions and tools.

It took a couple of hours of huffing and sighing and muttering to himself before he sat back in disgust and cussed at the world in general.

"Can't get your favorite oat milk?" asked Jordi from a computer screen, seemingly deep in some forum that was speculating about the Veep exchange.

"Come look at this," said Aiden, and both Scotty and Jordi sauntered over to stand behind him as he flicked from his VR into the real world via a set of projectors Jordi had set up.

"He isn't moving," said Jordi. "You being spoofed? Worse yet, you think he's dead?"

Aiden shook his head. "He hasn't found my hitchhiking virus, or I'd have lost him completely, and there's no sign they're spoofing me in return."

Jordi nodded. "Teddy Blake is really living inside the Capitol Building then."

"Seems like it," said Aiden.

"He's planning something," said Scotty. "Like he's holing up, terrified something might happen on the outside to him if he leaves. Thinks he fears for his life?"

"Fuck," said Aiden, stiffening. "The State of the Union."

Scotty screwed his face up. "You think he's going to kill the president?"

Aiden wanted to throttle everyone involved. "I'm no fan of the way this country works but this? Once he's chosen as Veep, succession falls to him, even if he's responsible for the president's death. By the time they sort it out he'll be established in the Oval Office, and he can blame the president's demise on some of the crazy white supremacist Stripes that, by the way, are probably loyal to him to a fault. He can usurp power easily, but there's one hitch in his plan. Congress must confirm him as Veep after the president nominates him, and that could take months. Then, what if all his associations with the Stripes come to light during that time?" Aiden paused. "No wonder he wants the Wetware. He's building an army of voters who'll back him no matter what because he saved their lives, and an actual army of bastards to help him get away with it on Sunday. Right now, he's creating an alibi. No communication with the Stripes if they attack on Sunday."

It fit perfectly. No matter what Blake's intentions, or how his plan rolled out, the president's life would be in jeopardy come Sunday. Blake would be the nominated official, and with a strong backing, be ushered through by Congress... especially if he had something like the Wetware to help persuade the reluctant Congressional members to help them make their decisions *faster*.

The next question struck him like lightning – how was Blake planning on smuggling Abraham and the Stripes into the building?

Aiden's breath came in short gulps. Not for the first time, he thought about running, about finding somewhere safe and waiting to see what would happen, but he couldn't let something like this happen on his watch. He was the Fox, and if someone was going to do something it would be him.

Scotty looked at him as if this whole thing had suddenly become much larger than he'd realized.

"We're gonna ruin them, Scotty," Aiden said. "This is all noise, right? When you design a system, you build in tolerances without knowing precisely what may end up testing them. This is that."

"What if we don't get them?" asked Jordi. "What if he has

leverage on Congress that makes them push the decision through quickly? You know, get Blake confirmed in record time?"

"Then we make sure he's the shortest-lived president in history."

"You're talking about assassinating the president."

"A fake, blackmailing, good-for-nothing president wanting to turn the tides of history and ruin this country."

"That's a big ask, Aiden."

"Not for you and me."

Jordi didn't say anything, but stepped back, turned, and walked from the office. Aiden let him go – he'd be back when he'd processed what they were going to do.

Scotty's voice was clear in the quiet of the office. "If Senator Blake is still there and he's trying to establish an alibi, that makes sense. But it also indicates he knows we're coming for him. He's planning in the event we do attack. He's also trying to stay safe. We're the thing he fears. If he's in the Capitol already, taking advantage of the security protocols there, then he's not worried that whatever plan he's concocted is going to fail – he must have that completely figured out by now. We're his last point of failure."

"All the more reason to get this virus in place," Aiden said and then suddenly asked, "Have you ever fought? Been in a fight?"

"No, not really," Scotty said, trying to look brave. "Not like this."

"I'm not judging you, Scotty. I just want us all to know what we can do. There's no point in asking you to shoot people if you don't know how to strip a gun down and rebuild it."

Scotty laughed and lifted his arms. "Really?"

Aiden burst out laughing. "I accept your terms. Shotguns for arms aside, Scotty, I've been doing this a long time. I was trained for it, or I fell into it by mistake. It's a shitshow from morning to night, but it's who I am. You come from a good place, and you should get to go back to them – your family, your job, anyone who is most likely worried about your disappearance. You don't have to let Abraham and the assholes around him shape you."

"I'm not," said Scotty severely. "Don't try to talk me out of this. I'm choosing this because if I don't then who will? If I don't then who'll die because I didn't act? This isn't them *making* me, Aiden. I'm doing this because it's who I am, because my mom and pop taught me what was right and wrong."

Aiden nodded. "Sorry to talk about it again, but I want to make sure you're going into this with your eyes open."

Scotty saluted. "I'm in, Aiden. One hundred percent. Are you ready to let me? Can you trust *me*?"

Aiden felt that particular jab. "You're not coming with me, Scotty."

"You're not even letting me help now," said Scotty. He turned away, slapping his hands against his waist. "I'm just sitting here while you work. I can do more. I want to do more. Don't deny me this chance."

"Listen, I'm struggling with this software as it is, and I know it's not your thing, but where it falls apart for me is in how all this code" – here he threw some of the key routines into the air around them – "basically translates into motor functions for your arm. It's so smooth it's almost unbelievable. It makes those dancing robots and spider drones look like fairground sideshows."

"I've been thinking about this," said Scotty, expression

brightening. "I have an idea, comes from why my arms kept glitching."

"Go on," Aiden said, desperate for any lead that wouldn't leave Scotty's arms flailing and trying to shoot their way out of the office.

"Seems to me the best way to hack this isn't to break it but to amend the protocols for how my motor functions operate. We need to think about how viruses work in the human body, not in computer systems."

"Aren't they basically the same?" he asked.

"Now who thinks he knows how everything works?" asked Scotty.

"Enlighten me," said Aiden.

"Actual viruses don't seek specific functions to damage, they mutate and adapt and seek control only insofar as they need to in order to replicate. They don't overly care if they kill the host if they can just propagate themselves in the meantime."

Aiden admitted it was different from how he built digital viruses – their main point of being was to co-opt a parent system and create a specific outcome. That outcome could be control or access or even closing a system down, but self-perpetuation wasn't even a feature he'd considered.

He thought through how the difference could help if he wanted to brick Leech's tech.

"Can we use this idea to break it? Overwhelm it via replication?" Ideas popped into his mind, a slew of possibilities. "Yeah, there's a bandwidth limit, right? The total amount of processing power available to control the arm? We could jam it up, stop it working until it keels over," said Aiden, following the idea through. "Yeah, that could work. I can do that."

"What defenses will the system throw at you?" asked Scotty, frowning. "Human bodies have defense systems, designed to stop this kind of attack. It's why we don't die from any old virus that comes along." He started talking about biological arms races and how different viruses and bodies came to strange agreements where one would allow the other as long as it wasn't deadly to the host. Like the common cold.

Aiden listened intently, soaking it all up like a sponge. All of it fed into why Scotty's arms might resist him if he tried to set free a virus like that on the system. His best hope was they'd be just as overwhelmed as the rest of the system. Hell, it might even fix the glitch, but then mimic it to interfere with the Stripes' Wetware.

The library of scripts Aiden had downloaded were quietly shuffled off to one side as he worked on understanding Scotty's tech from this new angle. By the time Jordi arrived, Aiden's stomach was gurgling. He noted Jordi was empty handed.

"You could have brought something to eat," said Aiden.

Jordi's expression was like thunder. "I'm being followed," he spat.

"And you brought them back here?" asked Aiden, adrenaline spiking through his chest.

Jordi didn't answer, reaching instead into one of the boxes that had piled up in the room. He pulled out a black hard case that was then laid carefully on the ground. From within Jordi pulled an FN SCAR assault rifle with a modified long barrel.

Aiden stopped the argument he was about to start and moved to where Jordi stood, checking the mechanism on the rifle.

"How many of them?" he asked.

"Six that I could identify. Their movement pattern was suggestive of another two operating as coordination."

"Fixers?"

Jordi nodded.

Which was better and worse than having been found by Abraham's people. At least he could predict how the fixers would come at them and if they'd been found they wouldn't have let Abraham's people know the location.

The problem was they were fixers. Their enemy knew what they were doing, would be heavily armed, and wouldn't hesitate. Fixers were hired mercenaries, and they could be here to kill both Aiden and Jordi, and recover any data Aiden had stolen or created. Jordi counted among their ranks, but fixers didn't have loyalty to each other – only the job they were paid to do.

"They know who we are?" he asked Jordi.

"Does it matter?"

"Guess not," said Aiden, who picked through the boxes and found a Desert Eagle and a .45 caliber UMP machine gun.

"What about me?" asked Scotty.

Jordi threw him a box of shotgun shells. "Your arms still work?" he asked.

Scotty looked at Aiden who shrugged. "You tell us," he said.

Scotty looked at the box of ammo as if it might give him the answer he was looking for. "Yeah, all good."

"Right then," said Aiden. "How long before they get here?"

"Now?" said Jordi. "They were tailing me pretty close, like they wanted me to know they were there."

"Dicks," said Aiden. "Which means they're overconfident, and that's our first advantage. Second, if they're coming in hot, they won't have electronic countermeasures in place, and that makes them stupid fucking meat. Scotty, you take the back of the office. Shoot anyone who tries to come through that door. Better still, start packing up the gear you and I have been using because whatever happens this place is burned and we're going to need to get the fuck out of dodge once we've dealt with this mess."

"How'd they find us?" asked Scotty, moving to the back door and locking it.

"Someone talked," said Jordi. "Or they were tracking us. Our circle of friends is shrinking, Aiden. People don't like what's coming, and they don't like us being involved."

"I'm supposed to be dead," said Aiden.

"You're Lazarus, walking around and upsetting people who thought you should have stayed down," Jordi corrected. "And Leech wouldn't have burned her link to us. Fact is, there are new fixers out there with a bright future ahead of them. And they just cornered some great prey."

Teeth grinding, Aiden focused on their immediate problem. Shit like this made finishing the virus in time an uphill challenge.

Jordi pulled up another box with a grunt of effort and, slicing through the tape sealing it shut, pulled out a plastic wrapped package, which he threw at Aiden. Catching it awkwardly, Aiden saw it was an armored vest.

"Got anything for my legs?" he asked as Jordi stuck an earpiece into his ear and tapped it. At least they'd be able to communicate that way.

"Best I could do in the time. People are fleeing like rats from a ship. At least, that's the chatter. Getting this was a victory I didn't expect to have to fight for."

"They think Blake's going to succeed?"

Jordi's expression darkened, but before he could answer, the large window facing the highway splintered as a canister flew through, bouncing into the room and spinning to a halt under one of the desks.

"Down," shouted Aiden, closing his eyes and putting the armored vest over his head.

The air whumped like the world's biggest drum had been sounded, then washed over his body in a wave of heat. Aiden crouched, pushing all his weight down into the floor, and rocked with the power of the blast. Squinting, he yanked the armor down and over his head fully, tightening the straps.

He grabbed the machine gun and aimed for the door while tapping his phone to pinpoint all the electronic signatures in the vicinity. On the other side of the room Scotty groaned and twitched on the floor, his arms jerking unsteadily.

Aiden hoped he hadn't loaded them – he wasn't ready to be shot in the back by his own side. He hoped Scotty wasn't simply being brave when he said his arms were fine to use.

Jordi was slowly climbing to his feet, slipping his own vest on, and aiming the SCAR assault rifle at the door.

A fraction later, gunfire ripped through the room at waist height, shattered the monitors and electrical equipment, and tore up the walls.

It was a weekday, early evening, so most of the other businesses would be shut, but Aiden worried someone would be caught in the crossfire. He willed the fuckers on the other side of the broken windows to come into the building so they could finish them off.

He signaled to Jordi to wait. If they counter-attacked too

soon, whoever remained outside would be able to target them with impunity and wouldn't be lured instead. Aiden didn't want this to be a siege – his goal was to get out as fast as they could.

Jordi flattened himself against the inside wall, rifle raised, eyes on the entrance and body tensed for movement. Aiden, still behind a desk, crouched, hoping the fixers would enter the building en masse. They'd want to clear the place quickly per standard operating procedure.

Unable to see the front door because of the smoke canister, he heard glass and metal grind over one another as the door burst open. He pinged the people around him, accounted for Jordi and Scotty, which left the others as foes. He tracked them across his VR as they approached. Footsteps, no voices, and then absolute quiet as the fixers entered fast but stopped when no one shot at them.

They'd move quickly to clear the office now.

Aiden's heart pounded, urging him to shoot before someone spotted him. Instead, he hunkered down, breathing slow through his mouth, and gripped his machine gun while he watched the dot that was the nearest of them slowly creep forward.

In times like these his discipline was to remember how to hold his weapon, to ensure it wasn't too tight. Hard grips led to wild swings of the weapon, to forgetting the nature of the tool in his hands and instead, in a blaze of fear and desperation, to treating it like it was some kind of wildfire. He scrolled down his phone, frantically wondering if he could hack into any systems they were currently using and take them down, but again, time wasn't on his side.

Glass crinkled underfoot. He counted one, then two sets of

footsteps and mapped them to his GPS. He tagged another two of them hanging around by the entrance, possibly even on the outside looking in but close enough he'd be able to see them if he stood up.

He assumed the final two would be coming for them through the back of the building.

Whoever was out there would be able to see Scotty lying prone. That they hadn't shot him suggested they had images of specific targets they were there to kill, and Scotty wasn't on that list.

Just me and Jordi then, thought Aiden. That, at least, was good news. It meant that whoever had hired them – be it Blake or the Stripes or Leech – still didn't know of Scotty's identity or that he'd gotten away.

Aiden wanted to find the command and control pair, but that would have to wait until they'd survived the six who had them surrounded.

Given Jordi's position, once the fixers started firing the two of them would set up a field of fire that would hopefully disorient their attackers long enough to take three, if not all four of them down.

Problem was Scotty was down and they had guns to their backs.

We have to wait for them to come further in, but if we wait too long the bastards will surge through the back door and we'll be toast, he thought.

The footsteps crept closer. He could hear each shard of glass crunch as they advanced. Across from him, in the shadows, Jordi signaled. One man, the other side of the desk. The man's ping was so close to him they merged into one on his GPS.

Aiden held his breath, staying still, feeling like the world would collapse down into speed and fire, instinct and action.

A breath let out slowly, and then Aiden spun around the edge of the desk, gun up, and opened fire. The first barrage of rounds powered into the legs of the man on the other side. With a shout, the enemy stumbled back, gun firing at the ceiling as he fell.

Aiden heard the distinctive sound of the FN SCAR as it spat rounds out of the office and into bodies.

Coming up into a standing crouch, Aiden sighted the second of his targets, and as the man looked back at him with shock, Aiden fired, his finger held down as the UMP sprayed the man down.

Two down.

Risking a swift glance around the room, he saw Jordi had taken down one of the two beyond the building. With a swift pointing of fingers, he turned to the back door and left Jordi to finish off the remaining fixer out front. Scotty was coming to, rolling onto his front and trying to climb to his knees.

As if planned, the lock was shot out on the back door by the blast of a shotgun and a figure came charging through only to have Aiden pepper them with a dozen rounds. Aiden moved quickly, knowing they were still alive, but they were also in no state to threaten him while he focused on the second of the two, who he expected to come through the door.

A shotgun blast made a soccer ball-sized hole in the rear wall. Aiden threw himself to the floor to avoid scatter and aimed at the door.

Another blast, then a shadow at the door. Aiden fired but missed. The figure ducked back.

Shots flew over his head from behind, toward the front of the office, and he heard Jordi cursing. "There's more of them!"

Aiden risked a look over his shoulder but couldn't see who Jordi was shooting at. He had to deal with the shotgun wielder now then back Jordi up, try to even the odds.

Scotty had crawled toward the back door with determination. Everything would be for nothing if Scotty died.

Aiden reached the door as a flash bang came through and bounced off his chest. Eyes wide, he watched it drop, and then without thinking kicked it back out and leapt to one side before the explosion came.

A shout from outside, then a huge bang. The walls of the office sheltered them from the worst of it, and before his head had stopped spinning, Aiden launched out through the door, machine gun raised.

His eyes met those of the fixer holding a gun. Aiden shot her center mass and as she fell, followed up with a shot to the head. The back now covered, he ran around to the front, desperate to locate any other forces waiting in the wings.

There were three units before he got to the public parking lot. His GPS led him to a single woman using an SUV as cover trading fire with Jordi. Aiden came around the side and splattered her with gunfire, taking her in the leg and arm. The fixer screamed and went down.

"The other two," said Jordi.

Aiden was already on it. Pinging the area, he had half a dozen return handshakes. Two were new ctOS hubs, and two others were in a car driving a block over at the edge of range.

The last two were together about a hundred yards away. Which meant the other end of the shopping strip. Aiden checked the surroundings and, seeing nothing, stepped out from the car cover to run to the other end. The last two fixers weren't going to get away.

As he did so, a sound cracked right next to him. The windshield of the car he'd used to hide behind shattered.

Aiden threw himself to the ground, grunting with pain from his already bruised ribs. Frantically, he tried to work out where the shot had come from.

"They've got a sharpshooter," said Jordi.

Helpful, thought Aiden.

He broke into a camera security system across the road and pulled the view up. From the camera's angle, he could see the sharpshooter wasn't perched that high up. As if to confirm, another shot struck the car above the wheel arch, telling Aiden whoever it was didn't have the height to strike at him while he was hugging concrete.

"They're in the parking lot, other end of the mall," he replied.

"Circling around," said Jordi. "Tell Scotty to stay with you."

Aiden frowned. "He isn't with me."

"Ah shit," said Jordi.

Aiden crawled away from the car. With each movement, he expected a bullet to take him out, but no shots came from the sharpshooter. Finally, he crawled to the wall of the office and risked standing up.

"Any sign?" he asked Jordi, but the bastard didn't bother answering.

Aiden tried pinging Scotty through his arms, as if he could communicate with the Wetware, since he knew Scotty didn't have a phone.

I need to fix that, thought Aiden, unwilling to contemplate the possibility Scotty was already dead.

A shot and then another in quick succession. "I'm pinned down," said Jordi.

"I'm coming," said Aiden. "On my mark, give me a distraction and we'll see what we can do." He checked his load out and saw he had half a dozen rounds left in the magazine. He wasn't going to get much of a chance.

"Oh shit," came Jordi. Shotgun blasts.

"Jordi? Jordi!" Aiden sprang out from behind the wall and burst from the corner of the mall, the overhanging roof offering no cover, to find Scotty standing over the ruined carnage of the sharpshooter.

He turned to face Aiden. "Didn't see me coming," he said, his face triumphant and shaky at the same time.

Seeing the body at Scotty's feet, Aiden turned to scope out alternate hiding places for the last of the coordinators. They had to be close – the ping put them at this end of the parking lot. Jordi was climbing to his feet when Aiden caught his eye.

Aiden signaled there was one left, and Jordi's eyes went wide. He checked the security camera again and spotted them – a small figure hiding two cars over and armed with what looked like a high-powered rifle. The kind that would happily shoot through a car one side to the other.

He needed a diversion. Aiden profiled them and to his surprise found they weren't as secure as they'd hoped. He found a bank account with a decent wedge of cash, overrode the authentication requirements, and sent it direct to a children's cancer charity. He couldn't help but smile as he sent a message telling them what he'd done.

There was a shout of outrage from the car where they were hidden, but he was already moving, Jordi coming along the other side.

The fixer made it easy for him, standing up to take a shot and leaving his back open. Aiden swept forward and planted two shots between his shoulder blades.

He scanned the area one more time, but the fixers were done.

"Get as much as you can carry," he shouted across to Scotty. "We've got to go."

"What about you?" asked Scotty, and Aiden could see he was shaking, the aftermath of what he'd done starting to hit.

"I've got answers to get."

He left Scotty, knowing the man wouldn't freeze, and made for where he'd left the female fixer he'd surprised against the car.

She'd crawled about fifteen feet, leaving a trail of blood in her wake. Aiden walked up and put a boot on the back of her mangled thigh.

"You know how this ends." He pushed his boot in further as a warning.

To her credit she didn't struggle, waiting for him to put two in the back of her head.

"I've got questions," he said.

She laughed. Fair enough, he thought. He'd have done the same were the situations reversed.

"I'll make you an offer. I'm no fixer. Not like you. I'm not doing this for money."

She was silent but he could tell she was listening. He refused to get his hopes up – she'd lost a lot of blood, and it might be too late to make good on his offer even if she accepted.

"I'll get you somewhere safe, get you medical attention, if you tell me who hired you."

She coughed, and it sounded like her lungs were full of liquid.

"It's your only option," he said.

"You know who hired us," she said.

"Humor me," he replied. "Imagine I've upset a lot of people over the years."

"They won't let you kill the president," she replied.

Aiden turned her words over. "Blake sent you," he said eventually. "He indicated we were going to take out the president?"

"You think the police could handle this?" she asked. "This is what fixers do."

Aiden didn't need to look around at the wreckage to answer her question. Except, he believed the security services would fuck him up before breakfast if they truly thought him a threat. Having said that, how many times had they missed the most obvious red flags only to blame it on data overload or poor protocols?

He didn't know. Regardless, he did know that Blake wouldn't risk bringing in people who might stumble upon the bigger picture, who might ask awkward questions. Way too dangerous given what he was planning.

"Right," he said and grabbed her under the arms. She was heavier than expected and, when he rolled her over, she was dead. So much for medical help.

"Stop molesting the helpless," said Jordi's voice over his shoulder.

"You all packed up?"

"Always ready to leave town," confirmed Jordi. "Got a place on the north side of DC. Far from here."

"How long till we can go?"

"Ten minutes," said Jordi. "Eight if you stop harassing the dead and help."

They found Scotty packing things into the few boxes that hadn't been shredded by gunfire. He wasn't going about it with any sense of order, just mechanically throwing things into boxes until they were full. Aiden could see his face was blank.

It was all he could do not to shake his head and tell Scotty it wouldn't get any better. Kid deserved better than his condescension.

Jordi triumphantly showed them how he'd used the reinforced gun boxes to shield some of the electronics. It meant that despite the mess, most of what they had in the building was in one piece.

The work they'd been doing on Scotty's arm was intact – saved as it was in a secure online space Aiden had created many years before. Within minutes, they were packed and loaded into a swanky German estate car Jordi had stashed. No other fixers showed to interrupt their evacuation.

As they were doing a final check, a woman emerged from the building at the far end of the mall. She looked terrified, her tight curly hair swept back behind her head, but there was fire in her eyes when she approached Aiden. She had the tiniest pistol in her hand.

Just typical to get a gut shot when the danger is supposedly passed, he thought.

"You going?" she said, looking past him at the car where the other two were looking back at her. The pistol shook as she raised it. "I called the police."

"We are."

"Good," she said.

"You should too. This mall isn't safe."

"This is my place," she said.

"I get it," he replied, although he had no idea how it felt to belong to somewhere enough to fight for it like she was promising to do.

"Don't y'all come back though," she said, keeping the pistol aimed at them. "Enough trouble in this world as it is."

"You got it," Aiden said, knowing this was one civilian who had only been living her life before he walked in and destroyed it.

CHAPTER SEVENTEEN

Jordi's place was nothing more than a storage unit at a rusty, rundown facility on the north side of the city opposite the Rock Creek Golf Park in the shadow of multi-story apartment blocks.

Aiden was surprised at how the phrase "the wrong side of the tracks" applied to the bright green fields to the west of a long wide road and what appeared to be once prosperous homes slowly decaying to the east.

They unloaded their scavenged supplies from the car, and Jordi drove off to get rid of it on the basis that if fixers had tracked them to the office, then as long as they ditched everything they'd had at that point, anyone else trying to find them would have to start again from scratch.

"The city's small," said Aiden to Scotty while Jordi was gone. "They know we're tied here. If they don't find us again before we hit Blake, then it's possible they'll be waiting for us when we try for him." He wasn't entirely sure Blake would risk having fixers interfere with his plan – but he knew he didn't want the Stripes to draw any attention before Sunday.

"Does that mean we can't do it?" asked Scotty, looking concerned. "Take Blake out?"

Aiden shook his head. "Just makes it more interesting." He thought their encounter with the fixers might have changed Scotty's mind, but he was as resolute as ever.

"But it never gets easier," said Scotty after they'd discovered the storage unit had only one power socket, a single light, and no connection to any network worth shit.

"Killing?" asked Aiden. "It is what it is. Best thing to do is not to think about it. Reason they send young men off to war is because they're too young to look at the other team and realize they're all just as human as the rest of us. You wonder why mooks on television shows are always faceless and indistinguishable from each other? It's because they can then be mowed down without anyone caring that actual people are dying. So, no, it doesn't get easier, you just learn to stop thinking about the lives behind the faces."

Scotty swallowed and looked away.

"It's not a good thing to find this normal," said Aiden, while his mind reeled with how they were going to be ready in time for the State of the Union. They'd made a breakthrough thanks to Scotty's lesson on organic viruses, but he was still miles off from being done.

I haven't even tested it yet, he thought. *Not really.*

"We should keep going," said Scotty, gesturing at his arms.

Aiden pushed away from the wall. "We've got system access," he said, firing up the hardware they'd saved from the office.

"You worried anyone going through what we left behind would be able to figure out what we've been doing?" Scotty asked as Aiden tried, unsuccessfully, to bring up a network connection.

"The kit we left behind was destroyed. Sure, any fixer with a nose for hacking and data and forensics will catch on to us, but I'm not worried about that."

"How can that not worry you?" asked Scotty, standing up straight and massaging his lower back. Aiden could see he was angry.

"We simply haven't got time," Aiden said, and it felt weird to tell someone what was worrying him. He spent so much time alone that saying it out loud was bizarrely unreal. "I'm at the bottom of the mountain," he finished and tapped Scotty's arms. "The peak is a long way up. I want to work directly in your arms. They have their own, degraded, version of the operating system. I can link to them and finish up that way."

Scotty sat on the concrete floor and rested his forearms on his raised knees. "What happens when you're done?" he asked, offering up his Wetware.

"Let's focus on finishing first," said Aiden, unwilling to be drawn into Scotty's frustration. Or his worry about losing his arms.

Aiden perched cross legged beside him and logged into Scotty's arms. The operating system was a sparse version of the full thing, designed to give enough of a platform for Scotty's arms to work but no more. Aiden navigated through it, testing what was there, and what was simply inactive and what pieces of code were outright missing.

It took a couple of hours, and just as he was wondering where Jordi could be, the fixer returned. His face looked grim.

"We've got to get out of here," he said to them both from the doorway.

"Why?" asked Aiden. "Is this place compromised?"

"Not what I mean. This is not what I signed up for, Aiden.

We're not the people to stop an assassination of the president by her own potential vice president. We won't get within a hundred yards of either of them to pull a stunt like this off."

"You're in it whether you like it or not," said Aiden. He didn't need Jordi flaking on him just when they might have found their chance at getting it done.

"The House Speaker is in on it, Aiden. I dug into it further. He's being blackmailed into letting the president force the existing Veep into retirement and supporting Blake as a replacement. Word is they'll kill one or both of them if they resist. Then, the Veep might be in line to get Blake's updated Wetware to survive. There are rumors on more blackmail hitting certain recalcitrant members of Congress, but nothing concrete I can use. Blake is setting it all up to push his confirmation through without a hitch after the president is gone."

"Is the president in on it too?" asked Aiden, a chill going through his bones.

Jordi looked gray and tired in the wan light of the lock up's single bulb. "I don't know. The read I get on it from the chatter, which is all over the place by the way, is the president doesn't like Blake and doesn't like that Blake's coming up, but with the Speaker refusing to side with her and a lack of base support to resist him, she's fucked. People in her own party want Blake in that role."

Aiden remembered Abraham's comment about the Stripes having friends everywhere. He should have expected that to mean people on both sides of the divide no matter how partisan the nation had become.

"Everyone's so focused on just how powerless she is that they're not looking at Blake hard enough," Jordi continued.

"No one's giving Blake anything in terms of assessment except he's another right wing conservative happy to talk dog whistles but who's really only interested in power."

"Why don't white folks ever believe in actual racism?" asked Scotty angrily. "They'll get themselves in a twist over certain things, but they look at laws designed to restrict voting and protect police unions that consistently shield racist officers and tell me they see nothing wrong, that it's just an accident or a few bad apples."

Aiden felt so uncomfortable his mouth had gone dry.

"Nothing ever changes," said Jordi. "Everything's dragged from their hands, like giving other people the same chances they have will kill them and see the world fall into darkness."

Scotty's arms shook. They couldn't afford another glitch, and Aiden watched carefully, just in case something triggered them to go berserk again.

"Can't you go any faster?" Scotty stared right at Aiden, his face a direct challenge.

Jordi sighed. "Don't look at him to solve your problems. Nor me because I don't care, Scotty. I've had the life I choose, made it my own. There've been assholes at every turn, but this is me."

"So what?" asked Scotty, his voice rising. "You think that because you're here you've got no obligations to others? You're pulling the ladder up behind you and telling me to build my own?"

"Fuck off," said Jordi but his tone was friendly enough. "This isn't about getting your kid into the right school. This is about the president getting murdered. We are in way over our heads."

"So what?" said Scotty.

"I'm not getting into it. It's too much. Too far. You think, even if we succeeded and emerged with Blake losing the Veep selection that they'll let us walk away? Leech used us because we're disposable. I'm committed to not getting a bullet in the back of my head." He eyed Scotty. "You should be too. You've got family. You think they won't come after them, too?"

"I'm going to stop them – Blake, the Stripes – from making everything worse," seethed Scotty. "Nothing ever changes except when we drag their bullshit beliefs screaming from their grasping hands, but you? You're running away – how you gonna explain that to your family?"

"I don't have a family," said Jordi flatly. He looked at Aiden as if expecting support.

Aiden shook his head "Don't look at me, Jordi. I'm with Scotty. We take them down here and now, or the world plunges into shit."

"And you care because they're racists? You're full of crap, Pearce."

The truth was, the Stripes were bastards with a tech that gave them an advantage over everyone. Anyone who thought they could slip away from justice because of standing or power needed a hard lesson that Aiden was more than happy to provide.

Jordi sneered at him. "You want Leech, you want Blake, you want to take them out because they made you look like a fool. Admit it."

Aiden shrugged. "Does it matter, Jordi? I'm in until the end."

"It doesn't matter," said Scotty. "I've seen enough of my friends and family suffer to take my allies where I can find them."

"This isn't about you," said Jordi. "We're the ones who were detained, threatened, and sent off to die."

Aiden winced at his words, thoughts of how he'd found Scotty crouching in the kennel large in his mind.

Scotty didn't shout this time. "You do you and screw the rest of us. At some point, they'll come for you."

"And I'll greet them with a grenade," countered Jordi.

"How courageous of you," said Scotty.

"Jordi," warned Aiden. All he could see from the discussion between Scotty and the old fixer was a hardening of lines, a confirmation there were no bridges that could be crossed. "Stay. What can you win by leaving? We can do this, but I need you. There's countless people out there who need you."

Jordi swept the hair from his forehead, looked at Aiden askance. "We can get out of this, Aiden, get away. Don't you see what's happening here? I have a way out for us both. New identity. Leave the country. Fresh start."

He's genuinely frightened, thought Aiden, and reflected he probably should be too. "It matters," he replied. "We've always operated in a space hidden from people. These jokers come to power and that all changes. You think they'll let us keep playing while they're busy rounding up anyone who disagrees, who teaches the wrong thing or believes in the wrong thing? There's a road here and we're about to cartwheel off it. Everything we do needs us to keep the car on the road."

"You want to maintain the status quo," said Jordi drily. "As if that hasn't been against us forever already by this point."

"Fuck it, yes. What else? Walk away and let the shitshow we do have descend even further?"

Scotty shook his head. "This is how bad it is, Jordi."

"If what you're saying about the Speaker is true then Blake isn't coming out of the Capitol until this is done," said Aiden.

"I'm going to have to infiltrate the place, take him out, and leave again without getting caught up in whatever security nets they have in place to catch assholes like me. I can't do that without you."

Jordi slouched down and collapsed into a sitting position on the floor, his arms flopping by his side.

"I hate this, Aiden," he said.

"Worse than Atlanta?" asked Aiden.

Jordi's snarl turned into a grin. "You douche. This is worse than Canada."

"Probably," agreed Aiden.

"You're going to stay then?" asked Scotty and ruined the mood. Jordi tensed but didn't respond.

He doesn't like being put on the spot, Aiden thought. Just like me.

"You're both going to stay," said Aiden.

"I'm not babysitting anyone," said Jordi at the same time as Scotty protested.

"You think I can take you into the Capitol with me? In case you hadn't noticed, we don't yet have a virus nor a way to deliver it. Even if I get that working, you're a liability, Scotty. I'll kill when I have to. I can hack and slip in unseen."

"So I sit in a storage unit and wait for the feds to come get me after they shoot you dead?"

"I need plans, to reconnoiter the buildings, work out patrols, security features, what's hackable and what I'll have to do old school."

Jordi nodded. "I've still got some friends out there, ones who haven't yet decided to sell us out. I suppose I could do some recon for you."

"Is there no loyalty?" asked Scotty, incredulous.

"This is it," said Aiden, looking at Jordi who, oddly, he knew was as good as his word. At least right now, at this moment.

"This is the life," said Jordi and it was the most philosophical he'd been in all the years Aiden had known him.

"What the fuck happened to us?" he asked.

"Something about years and mileage," said Jordi wearily. "Your order still the same as before?"

"Drones, spiders, birds, pistols? Yeah. Oh, and a stun baton. I don't feel right without my baton."

Jordi nodded. "Better get to it then."

"I won't stop you from leaving, Jordi," said Aiden.

"As if you could," said Jordi flatly, but he nodded his respect for Aiden's understanding.

"I need to know the lay of the land. I need to know how many people are working security, what drones they have in place. You know the score."

Jordi pursed his lips then nodded. "I'm on it. Just remember. Fresh identity just one confirmation away."

"Thanks," said Aiden.

Jordi didn't reply as he stepped past Scotty and out of the storage unit.

"Don't forget coffee this time," said Aiden to his back, and Jordi gave him the bird over his shoulder.

CHAPTER EIGHTEEN

Aiden didn't expect Jordi back for the rest of the day. The first thing the fixer would do was check who exactly would sell to them without burning them at the same time. Plenty of their suppliers would take his money and then rake in any bounties on their names the moment the call was ended.

He put it out of his mind. Jordi knew what he was doing. Without him, they'd be dead twice over at this point.

Completing the virus was the goal now. This was new ground, and the stakes were high enough that he worried about unforced errors and stress-induced delays. It was Friday now, and the State of the Union was Sunday evening. He needed to be inside the Capitol before dawn broke on Sunday – the building would be locked down tight.

Aiden wished the people and their representatives would object to what was happening, but he was pretty certain a sizeable minority would simply cheer at the overriding of democracy and law, would see it as their right to overturn the constitution if it had the temerity to deny them what they believed was theirs by right, anyway.

What frustrated him more was how useless those who should oppose them were.

So much for checks and balances, he thought. Aiden had fought every kind of enemy, and the one lesson he'd learned, the only rule he followed, was that if you wanted to survive a fight to the death you did whatever it took to win.

There was no right or wrong, just survival. The way he saw it, Blake's natural enemies never recognized that if they lost, they wouldn't survive. It was like the police robbing your house and then you asking them to investigate while they offered to sell your things back to you. Finally, though, he managed to craft a skeleton outline of a virus based on the schematics of Scotty's Wetware. For the moment, he didn't need to be hooked up to Scotty's arms. But the young man was chomping at the bit for purpose.

"Give me something to do. I'm going out of my mind here, Aiden."

He was so sincere, so reasonable that Aiden found it hard not to apologize and utter a hundred thank-yous to him. After all, even though Scotty most likely felt like he was sitting around, he was providing what Aiden needed to take out the Stripes. Without Scotty, Blake's plan would most likely succeed.

"Find me floor plans for the Capitol," he said. "And for the Russell Senate Office Building."

"Seriously?"

"You want to help?"

Scotty nodded and turned away to one of the computers. Aiden hoped it would keep him busy for a while.

The virus was coming together. He had built a virtual copy of Scotty's arms and was getting ready to test on that. He wasn't going to risk Scotty again if he could manage it – not least because they couldn't afford him going haywire inside the storage unit.

Once the testing started, he'd need a couple of hours before the virus was ready – if there were no glitches. Which would mean he would have to be inside the Capitol Building when the virus would be ready to deploy.

He'd need Scotty then to send it to him. Be close enough for such a virus to be downloaded into his phone with enough of a connection to make that happen. He didn't trust that Jordi wouldn't throw in the towel or flake out on him at a crucial moment.

Ideally, he'd be able to get Scotty to safety then, too. They hadn't talked about the killing in the parking lot since it happened, and Aiden wasn't about to open up that topic, but he could see it was weighing on Scotty. The young man barely slept.

Scotty was on the cusp of becoming like Aiden and Jordi, but he wasn't there yet. He might still go home. Have the chance to recover some semblance of his former life.

Once Scotty was done with the floorplans – which were frighteningly easy to find – Aiden had him watch the news channels for anything on the State of the Union. When Jordi reappeared, he looked troubled. "I need to talk," he said quietly to Aiden, his eyes sliding over to Scotty.

The two of them wandered out of the storage unit and down one of the many corridors that formed the storage facility.

"What is it?" asked Aiden when they were suitably far away.

"You really don't want out?" said Jordi.

"We've talked about this," said Aiden.

"I'm not storming the Capitol Building. This is too big for us. If you're smart, you'll do the same. I know you like the kid, I like him too, but he's a liability and we're just two people against an army."

"What have you heard?" asked Aiden.

"Abraham's Stripes are great in number. The dark web is silent on Leech's Wetware, but either the Stripes or someone else is leaking that there will be a drastic change in government by the end of Sunday."

"And these people are just going to stand back?" asked Aiden. "They aren't alerting anyone?"

"We're fixers, Aiden, not paladins. You should remember that. Security is the lightest I've ever seen it. Intelligence and the local police department have had all leave approved. You hear me? Approved. They're deployed elsewhere. All they've got left are automated drone patrols, those few who, for whatever reason, couldn't or wouldn't take leave, and the president's own security detail. Once you're inside I doubt anyone will check your credentials at all. I'm assuming you know how you're getting inside."

"I do," said Aiden.

"Good, then you don't need me."

"I need someone to spot me, Jordi. To do your job. To warn me of drones or patrols or chatter. I need someone to deliver me arms once I'm inside, and I need someone to send me the virus when it's compiled."

Jordi nodded his head in the direction of the storage unit. "I'm pretty sure Scotty can press enter when it's ready."

"Fine," said Aiden, accepting that his original assumption about Jordi was right. "Stay outside. But don't leave, Jordi. Not yet. Help me get inside and then do whatever seems right to you."

Jordi chewed at his lip then nodded. "Look, I'm not just bailing. I've got aliases for all of us, Aiden. We could go now."

"Give it to Scotty," said Aiden. "Get him out of this life, if you're so determined."

Jordi sighed. "From now on I'm going to remind you of your sudden conscience whenever I see fit. And I'm not babysitting him."

It was a small price to pay to keep Jordi on the job, thought Aiden. He knew that no kind of argument would persuade Jordi once he'd made up his mind.

But I had to try, he thought. Besides, he now had Jordi until he was inside.

"We better get on with it."

They returned to the storage unit to find Scotty still watching the news.

"You two kiss and make up?" he asked as they walked in.

Jordi snorted. "We have a plan, at least."

Scotty pulled the screwdriver from the depths of his arm, straightened up and looked at them both. "Come on then, let's hear it."

"Who died and made you the boss?" asked Jordi.

"Security is pared back, drone patrols, all the standard stuff, nothing additional," Aiden reported.

"Stinks," said Jordi. "Someone is setting up for this to happen."

Aiden ignored him, no need to confirm the obvious. "Getting in is the issue, and tomorrow I'll square that away. However, once I'm inside I'll be going for Blake first. Assuming I can reach him. Then once I've got his network connection, I'll be able to locate the Stripes and deal with them."

"Blake will be using his hideaway for this," said Jordi.

"What's that?" asked Scotty.

"Most Senators and even a few members of Congress have a hideaway in the building. They're not on maps and can only be found by knowing the number of your room and the route to it. Last time the Capitol was stormed, people hid in them when they couldn't get out safely. Most of them don't look any different from a storage closet from the outside."

"What's on the inside?"

"Depends," said Jordi. "You can find the occasional article with pictures. Some are lavish and huge; others really are just storage rooms. They made a few more of them in the basement a while back, but if they've made more since then no one really knows. They used to be famous for senators wanting to stash their mistresses somewhere or to handle delicate negotiations, you know, before it all became so partisan."

"So the maps we have are useless," said Scotty, looking at Aiden in despair.

"Nope," said Aiden. "It's pretty easy to look at those maps and work out which party stashes its people where and then examine the spaces between rooms and on staircases. Wherever you see a gap? That's where they've put their hideaways. None of them were in the original plans, they've all been added, so they're injected into existing spots, spaces, storage rooms under stairs. There are a lot of unknowns and always will be."

Jordi threw him a glance as if to say this was why he wanted out.

Scotty processed the information. "That's not your plan though," he said.

Kid can keep to the point, thought Aiden, impressed again. Maybe he did have it in him to be a fixer.

"I don't know when Blake is going to stage his attack. I'm not even sure if he will be behind the attack or if he'll make it seem as if he's innocent in everything. Whatever move he makes, it will most likely take place after the State of the Union when succession is indicated to fall to him, but who knows. I don't know how many people he has and how many of them have Leech's Wetware. I don't know how local law enforcement are going to respond. The area's pretty safe from individuals, but we've seen that a crowd can overwhelm the building's defenses pretty easily."

"So?" asked Scotty.

"So, I get in, I use the drones Jordi's been sourcing for me as a distraction to draw away law enforcement and move as quickly as I can."

"What about me?" asked Scotty.

"You're going to be here," said Aiden.

"Like fuck I am," responded Scotty without raising his voice.

"You're not coming with me," said Aiden. "You don't know your way around a gun, something to be admired by the way. You don't know how to fight empty handed; you don't have experience of spoofing your way into secured environments, and I'm willing to bet you haven't ever hacked security systems on the fly while doing all of the above."

He thought Scotty was going to argue, but instead his shoulders slumped. "What do I do while the two of you go and save the world?" he asked despondently.

"You're going to send me the virus," Aiden said. "The most important part."

"What about him?" asked Scotty, thumbing at Jordi.

"I'm going to monitor," said Jordi. "Make the drones smarter than their AI, if I can. Besides, most of the time my job's done by the time the chosen one here gets to work, isn't that right?"

"There's a decided lack of guns here," said Aiden. "Not sure your job is really done."

"They're coming. Patience is a virtue," answered Jordi. "Look, tomorrow you'll be too hyped to relax, and I'll be busy trying to deliver everything you've asked for without also getting ganked by our suppliers. Why don't we go get dinner, get drunk, and set the world to rights?"

Aiden winced but Scotty smiled.

"Sure thing, Jordi. You can start by telling us over wings why you're bailing when you should be doubling down," said Scotty.

CHAPTER NINETEEN

They ended up in a fried chicken place that did huge milkshakes and burgers up to the same thirty-two-ounce size.

None of them were so ambitious, although Scotty ordered a bourbon-soaked caramel milkshake, which was so sweet that when he tried it, Aiden went straight back to his beer to clear the sickly taste from his mouth.

They'd driven out of town to find the place, east into the poorer districts of the city not yet overtaken by gentrification. In other words, they wound up hanging out in a fried chicken shack on the edge of Kingman Park.

"Being in a relationship doesn't work for a lot of people," Scotty said when Aiden tried to get to know Scotty better and learned a partner wasn't out there, worried for him. "But I'm happy enough on my own most of the time. Anyway, being a medic isn't really a relationship gig. Not at my age."

"When I was your age, my dick was doing all the talking," said Jordi.

Aiden couldn't tell if he should be embarrassed for the fixer or if Jordi was simply stating facts.

"Different world now," said Scotty and slid into talking about the neighborhood lawn mowing business he'd had as a kid. "The mower broke down once a week and there wasn't anyone else to fix it, but I had sneakers to buy and games I wanted to play."

Aiden let Scotty's conversation roll over him, giving him insight into the support system Scotty had. It tore Aiden up inside to learn that Scotty's family was most likely worried sick over him, but it was obvious that Scotty's need for revenge usurped everything else. Hearing Scotty talk about his family, about how they were still close, was a stone in the pool of his emotions. Aiden thought about what family he had left. They weren't even on the same continent. He thought about those who he'd lost, had been responsible for losing, and wished harder than ever for Scotty to live a different life from the one he'd ended up choosing.

"What about you?" asked Scotty.

"People like us don't have families," said Jordi, flipping a drinking mat off the edge of the table and catching it in his hands as it spun in the air. "They've either disowned us, died, or we didn't have them in the first place. That's the bullshit about fantasy stories – there's no humble loner who turns out to be the chosen one. We're all just assholes who shouldn't be given power."

Scotty looked incredulous and turned to Aiden for confirmation.

"He won't talk about it," said Jordi but didn't elaborate, which was all that saved him from getting punched in the face.

"He's right," Aiden managed, fighting to stop from being overwhelmed by feelings he thought he'd extinguished long ago. He thought about the stories he heard from other fixers when they got together and they were empty, focused on who had killed who and how. Was it a spoon or a fork, a knife or a gun, in the kitchen or the restroom?

We're nothing but dust, he thought. "Let's talk about something else."

Aside from family, they also avoided talking about Sunday. Aiden could feel it crawling around the edge of their conversations, pushing them to talk about what they'd be doing in five years, about their dream holiday destination and the kind of place they would live if money wasn't a problem. Nothing but looking forward.

Jordi necked back half a dozen beers then started in on the vodka. Aiden couldn't follow. He couldn't let go like that.

"You still look like shit," said Jordi, as if reading his mind.

"When I was his age," he replied, waggling his eyebrows in Scotty's direction, "I'd be up and about the day after. Then my body decided it was in charge and it had concerns about how I'd been treating it for the last thirty years."

"You and me both," said Jordi, slinging back another shot.

Between them Scotty was steadily putting away the beers but declined Jordi's invitation to see who could drink the most vodka without puking.

"They sent more fixers for us," said Jordi as the waitress stacked chairs on tables and grumbled none too subtly about them hanging around when she wanted to close up.

The nape of Aiden's neck prickled, a sharp tingle running down between his shoulder blades. Despite sitting with his back to the wall he had the sudden urge to get out and drive away before trouble found them again. The shadows outside, pooling around the sparse streetlights, took on a menacing feel, as if the darkness hid guns waiting just for them.

"And?" he asked when Jordi glazed over.

Like a stuck motor jerking to life Jordi continued, "They have no idea where we are, been trawling the north of the city looking for us. Some anonymous commentators have been telling them we're out west as of an hour before we got here. By anonymous I mean me."

"Huh," said Aiden. "How many?"

"I dunno. All of them? As many as were within a hundred miles. Someone's paying a lot of money to have us taken down before tomorrow."

"How many of them are pointing at the Capitol Building?"

"Funny that," said Jordi, waving at the waitress for more vodka. She ignored him and with a shrug he turned back to Aiden and Scotty. "None of them. Not that anyone's gone out of their way to divert them and not that they've been hired because someone suggested we were gunning for POTUS. The order's just to burn us, no context given. If it were me, I'd be asking why I've been sent after a big fat goose. But I'm experienced in that way."

"Except that goose killed half a dozen of them yesterday," said Aiden.

"Geese are seriously mean motherfuckers," said Scotty with a grin.

Jordi lifted an empty shot glass, frowning at it as if he'd no idea how it had got that way.

"Time to go," said Aiden. "Big day tomorrow." Despite Jordi's assurances that he'd diverted any further fixer trouble, he didn't feel safe out in the open. Already, he dreaded sleeping on the concrete floor of the storage unit, and checked his phone again, which showed a progress bar for the virus. Not even halfway. It had a long way to go.

Aiden just hoped it would be ready in time.

CHAPTER TWENTY

The morning brought rain and an unseasonable mildness to the air. Aiden stood outside gazing up at the sky as if willing it to bring the sun out from behind the heavy gray clouds, which were slowly traipsing their way from one side of the world to the other.

Jordi joined him, loading up a large Japanese minivan.

"Off shopping," said Jordi. "Should be back in an hour."

"You are coming back, right?" asked Aiden.

"You got foot in mouth disease today?" asked Jordi. "'Cause questions like that are not the way to keep people."

Aiden left him to it, returning to find Scotty sitting staring at a screen floating in the air, code all over it.

"I'm lost, man," said Scotty. "This isn't my shit. Give me the tendons in a wrist and I can do it."

Aiden stepped in close and ran his gaze down the lines of code Scotty was looking at. "What were you looking for?" he asked.

"I thought I could help," said Scotty.

"I'll have it working," Aiden said as reassurance. "Get some breakfast. Let me work."

Sitting down, Aiden relished coding again, losing himself in the lines instead of thinking about what the day would bring. With the other two out, he had space to think through his plans, what might happen if he got it wrong and how, exactly, he might face the world if, against all the odds, he survived past Sunday night.

Aiden didn't expect to live. He never did. He found it was best to make his peace before he went in on a mission, hacking with abandon. Between drones, racists, law enforcement, and the Secret Service, he expected someone to put a bullet in him. Behind it all was Leech, who'd fucked up so monumentally she was witnessing her Wetware being used to overthrow the government. He wanted her to pay but, realistically, no one was going to benefit by exposing her mistakes for the public to see – it would all be swept quietly under the carpet.

Enough, he thought, flexing his fingers like he was about to play a recital, and he went to work on the code.

Aiden successfully compiled the code and started bug hunting just as Scotty got back.

"Where we at?" asked Scotty. A chair scraped across the floor, and the two of them sat together while Aiden talked Scotty through what he'd done.

Aiden spent the rest of the day working through the errors in the code he'd scraped together, weaving their different scripts into a coherent whole, but by the evening, when Jordi arrived all cheery, they were still going.

He had Scotty learning to pilot the different types of drones Jordi was supposed to be bringing back. If the young man wanted to help out so badly, Aiden figured helping out with the drones would keep him safe without asking for anything requiring finesse, but Aiden also needed to know that if he asked for a drone to be somewhere specific it was going to be there.

Scotty had piloted small drones before, but this was something new, and the VR simulations witnessed a large number of messy crashes before he got his head around piloting them.

Aiden looked at his to-do list. It was only half satisfied. While it was nothing to be ashamed of, he had to deal with misplaced variables due to errors in basic logic, leaving the code looped and completely stalled. A long night beckoned.

"I can see you two are getting married," said Jordi. "But y'all want to come see this, I promise."

Happy for an excuse to have a proper break, Aiden stood, stretched out his aching back, took some painkillers, and followed Jordi to the parking lot at the side of the storage facility.

In the trunk were bags. On the two rows of back seats, there were bags. The front passenger seat was the same. They carried everything to the storage unit before opening the first.

Many of the bags held guns, but most of the volume was taken up by the boxes inside the bags, which were full of drones.

"I got four of the combats, two spiders and many, many flying critters," said Jordi.

Scotty was elbow deep in the boxes before Aiden had taken it all in. "Three different classes of interdictors," he breathed in awe, holding one up for Aiden to see.

Jordi had gotten Aiden everything he'd asked for and more. *How much of this over achievement is guilt?* he wondered, expecting Jordi to up and leave now that this, the most important of his tasks, was complete.

"What's this?" asked Scotty, as Aiden picked over the different drones, slowly unpacking them from the foam and plastic wrapping in which they'd arrived.

Scotty held up what looked like a piece of slim, shiny tech in the shape of a half-diamond.

"Ah, now I'm a little bit proud of this one," said Jordi. "It's an AR cloak. Basically anyone using augmented reality tools will be spoofed to make it seem like you're not there."

Aiden took the piece and flipped it over with his fingers. He found a small square in one corner that, when pressed, tried to link up with his phone and earpiece. "Just connects and gets on with it?" he asked.

"Plug and play, baby," said Jordi. "Oh, best remember it's not going to hide you from shit if they're not using AR. It's augmented reality, not actual invisibility. Something smuggled in from London, if you can believe it."

"It's not the UK," said Aiden. "Not everyone's going to be using augmented reality."

"You think there's a fixer or law enforcement official not using it?" asked Jordi. "And drones will see precisely nothing when looking at you."

"Good point," said Aiden. Perhaps there'd be a use for it after all.

The last item to come in from the car was a small box about the size of a large rucksack. Jordi treated it very carefully, and when he opened the case, Scotty took a sharp intake of breath.

Together the two of them set up the 3D printer while Aiden looked on.

"It can print metal as well as ceramics and plastics," said Jordi, sounding proud of himself.

"What're we going to make?" asked Scotty.

"Passes for the Capitol Building," said Aiden, understanding at last.

"Ye of little imagination," said Jordi. "I mean, yes, but what we're actually going to do is make you some ablative armor, which should hold up against getting punched by the likes of Scotty here."

Aiden cocked his head. "You can do that?"

"Sure as shit can't buy the armor without half the city's intelligence services coming to knock on the door."

Just how much they still had to do pressed itself against the back of Aiden's mind. "OK. We'd better get moving."

Scotty looked torn, but Aiden let him help Jordi before going back to practicing piloting the actual drones while he returned to the code and started the painstaking work of debugging it.

It was about three in the morning when Aiden's eyes refused to stay open any longer.

Scotty leaned against one wall, mouth open and breathing heavily as he slept. Jordi worked by the light of two flashlights perched on boxes as he finished up yet another palm sized plate.

"What do we attach them to?" asked Aiden, picking one up and feeling its strangely flat surface under his fingers.

"I've got a jacket for you. Plus some thigh guards." Jordi pointed over to a duffel bag, half unzipped under a pile of other bits and pieces. The thigh guards were anything but discreet, looking like those worn by football players.

"I'll look like a jock on steroids if I wear these," said Aiden.

"I was assuming you'd put them on once you were inside."

"Ha, yeah," said Aiden. "You going to get some sleep?"

"I'm outta here tomorrow, Aiden. You need all this done

before that happens. Scotty can monitor the drones. He'll be your guy monitoring everything tomorrow."

Aiden couldn't hide his disappointment. Sure, he and Jordi had fought in the past. Hell, they'd even tried to kill each other back in the day, but for the old bastard to be walking away now?

Aiden realized he'd kept hoping Jordi would stay to the end of it.

He grabbed painkillers, checked his body for acute pains, and satisfied he'd last through the first fight he came to, if not the second, put his head down and tried to sleep.

CHAPTER TWENTY-ONE

Aiden woke to find Jordi slumped over the printer. A stack of ceramic plates sat on one side with another inside the machine.

"We nearly there?" Scotty asked, yawning and stretching.

"More than we'll ever be," said Aiden blearily. His body ached. He'd managed about seven hours of sleep in fits and starts, and although there was no sunshine reaching them inside the storage unit, it was very definitely midmorning on Sunday.

Aiden wanted to be at the Capitol already, checking on the buildup in preparation for the president's speech. Instead, he fought the urge to yawn while Scotty tapped at the screen flowing in the air above him.

Jordi rolled his head and groaned.

"What time did you call it?" asked Aiden, tying his laces.

Jordi blew a raspberry. "I said hello to Lady Dawn then collapsed."

Aiden, feeling awake now, ran his fingers down the stack of armor plates. "You all done on these?"

Jordi stared at them as if seeing them for the first time before counting them off. "Got two more to make. I'd have liked to make you a helmet, but there won't be time."

"We've got all day," said Scotty.

"Jordi's right," said Aiden. "I'll be gone by early afternoon. There's too much to do."

"Will the virus be ready?" said Scotty, fear on his face.

"You'll send it to me when it's time. We will just have to wait and see."

The sense of responsibility clearly unnerved Scotty, whose hands slumped to his side.

Aiden grabbed him gently by the arms. "You got this. Like you say, we're really close, but this isn't something I can wait for here. Besides, now I'm giving you a job and you're going to back out on me? After all your grousing?"

Scotty swallowed and nodded, a flash of a reluctant grin on his features. "Sure thing."

"How are you going to deliver it?" asked Jordi.

"Short range blast. Too many innocents caught otherwise."

"Shit, Aiden. You're going to go around and tag each and every one?" Jordi looked a mix of disgusted and shocked.

"Abraham and his lot will all be there, Jordi."

Jordi nodded. "You don't like making it easy, do you?"

"What about the passes?" Aiden asked, ignoring Jordi.

"Shouldn't take long if you can provide me with images and specifications for the data strips."

"Right," said Aiden, feeling the pressure. "On it."

The remainder of the morning passed in a snap of the fingers, and Aiden looked up to see the other two working hard, the hiss and grind of the printer working nonstop.

He'd successfully run down the badges he needed to give to

Jordi. A couple of local firms who covered cleaning, a caterer, and then on one intelligence forum, a picture of a guard with his badge who had been easily coaxed into talking about his interview and the forms he'd filled in for security clearance.

With those in hand Aiden set Jordi to work. He didn't know if he'd need one, two or all three, but best to have them all just in case.

Aiden then turned his mind to the drones. He'd activated them one by one, linked them each to a private network to which he gave Jordi, Scotty, and himself access then asked the kid to test them. Scotty had abandoned one of the smaller bug drones – faulty right out of the box – but he reported the rest were good.

It was about two when Jordi handed the badges over, together with the armored coat.

Aiden tried it on. The jacket wasn't quite his style – too synthetic for his tastes, but the gray was acceptable, and the profile gave no hint of the articulated armor on the inside. It weighed about as much as a decent leather jacket.

Jordi handed him his baseball cap. "Was the best I could do at short notice," he said. "Thought you'd feel at home."

"You could almost forget how old I am," said Aiden. The thigh guards were stuffed into a bag along with bandages and a flask full of water.

He didn't need anything else. His baton was broken up and inserted into the lining of his coat, and he was going to have one of the larger drones drop off his pistols inside the Capitol grounds once he was in. Each of the combat drones carried an assault rifle, but Aiden didn't expect to ever get his hands on them. His power resided in his phone.

"I overdid it with the guns," said Jordi.

Aiden stared at the stash and grinned. "I'm sure we'll get to use them sometime."

"You better get going, Aiden," said Jordi.

"Right," he replied. The two men shared a long look. Aiden wanted to argue with Jordi one last time, but what could he say that hadn't already been said? He set his jaw and shook Jordi's hand.

"What is it about your generation? Why can't you just talk to one another?" asked Scotty from off to the side.

"You got what you need?" Aiden asked him. "You know the plan for the drones, right?"

Scotty nodded. "Keep people busy with them. Keep people away from the Capitol. I wish…"

"You're better staying here or as far from the Capitol as possible where we can still communicate," said Aiden firmly. "And leaving when Jordi does. Right?"

"I know," said Scotty, but his expression told a different story.

At least he has a job to keep him busy, thought Aiden.

"See you on the other side," he said and left them to it.

He made for Union Station, better to avoid scrutiny and the traffic control measures in place closer to the Capitol itself. From there he walked down toward the Russell Senate Office Building, on Constitution Avenue.

There was no way he could walk straight into the Capitol. Not on the day of the State of the Union. The brick laid plaza and stone steps made for grand architecture and wonderful television but were not the doors through which staff entered.

He circled the building counterclockwise once, looking for a likely candidate to hack. As he was coming back around the north side of the block, he saw the right target. A man who'd been working the six in the morning shift had finished up and was leaving for the day.

His profiler listed him as Pedro Modovar. Mexican immigrant, forty-eight, three kids and one ex-wife. Lived over in the east, like so many of those who kept the city running. He wouldn't be back on shift until Tuesday.

Aiden wasn't stealing his identity – passing as an overweight, overtired man with tan skin wasn't something that would work. Instead, he pored through Pedro's account until he found the link to his access pass and copied the basic security protocols with which it was programmed.

From there he created his own identity, similar to Pedro's, but fictionalized to match a man fitting Aiden's description and age. Nothing to stand out but the kind of background job that would get him most places in the building without anyone remarking, or likely, even noticing him.

In other words, he created himself a pass as a cleaner.

Done, Aiden took a breath and without slowing his pace ducked into the Russell Senate building. The entrance was open, guarded by just two officers armed with high-powered rifles. They gave every impression of ignoring him as he made his way in.

Once inside, the white stone exterior gave way to that mix of wood paneling and out of date materials so common in government offices. Transparent screens blocked the entry point with X-ray machines and guards patting people down – even those they knew by name.

Aiden waited in line until called forward, put his bag on the conveyor belt, and stepped through the metal detector. He came up clean and said a little prayer of thanks to Jordi that the armor hadn't brought him unwelcome attention at the very first hurdle.

His bag was handed back to him, his badge scanned, and then he was inside.

The halls were high and wide. A renovation a few years back had done the opposite of normal and actually squeezed junior senators out into a building a block north. This meant the inside became slightly more opulent once Aiden was past the tatty entrance.

He wasn't interested in how things looked or even where Blake's office was because he assumed none of the Stripes would be here yet. Blake's GPS continued to show him inside the Capitol as it had done for almost the entire last week.

The point of using the Russell Senate Office Building was that it connected directly to the Capitol via an underground metro station and walkway.

There'd be checks, but Aiden was banking on them being less stringent than trying to enter the Capitol directly. Everyone inside the Russell building had already passed pretty much the same tests they'd apply at the Senate. He'd have to go through some version of them again, but he wasn't worried.

They'd bring him into the basement of the building, but it had long since been converted into a visitors' center, which would allow Aiden to move through to the first floor without encountering much in the way of any kind of security.

"Scotty here," came over his earpiece.

Aiden didn't answer except to click his tongue.

"Loud and clear," said Scotty. "Bugs are reporting the level of security is precisely as Jordi reported it yesterday. Seems sus, Aiden."

"It's not a trap for us," said Aiden. "They're hunting the president. How far away is the equipment? I'm about to go under, so you'll lose me for roughly fifteen minutes."

"It'll be there, balcony on the north side of the Senate wing as agreed."

"Tight," said Aiden. "Speak shortly."

The underground station was surprisingly old fashioned, as if no one had bothered to update it since it had been originally built back at the dawn of time. Fittings were brass and green and wood as much as they were the white stone of the bones of the building.

A soldier checked his ID, still the cleaner, as he got on the subway car and waited as others climbed on board. When it was about two-thirds full, the train pulled out for the two-minute journey under the parkland surrounding the Capitol Building. Aiden stared at the darkness and contemplated what was to come.

Like nothing I've done before, he thought. They should give me a fucking medal after this. He smirked at his reflection in the window. The train passed small white lights in the tunnel and on the tenth they were there, pulling in quickly and stopping with a judder.

Aiden let the other passengers get off first then followed, keeping a couple of feet back from a young man in a very expensive suit and small backpack as they were processed a second time by another soldier.

The second soldier eyed his ID then asked which firm he worked for. Aiden told him the name of Pedro's employer and waited as the soldier checked it out. A moment later he handed Aiden back his pass but didn't move to let him go.

"You're late," he said.

"I know," said Aiden unapologetically.

The soldier waited as if he was due an explanation. He's not going to get one, thought Aiden. Sometimes you gave people exactly what they wanted when you were fooling them, other times you treated them like this, because people tended to believe that no one trying to deceive them would risk irritating them. Thing was, Aiden knew that ordinary people irritated others without even knowing it or just because they could. A soldier like this would be watching for newcomers with too smooth a story and attitude.

The soldier kept on staring and Aiden looked away. "Fine," said the soldier and stepped to the side. "They're gonna have your hide. You know what night it is."

"Thanks, bud, won't be the first time," said Aiden as he walked off, holding his breath that the soldier wouldn't call him back.

He climbed the stairs and walked through the single exit from the station where he entered the Senate proper. A long central corridor ran the length of the original building, and the thick stone walls forming the foundations made it seem cramped, not helped by strip lighting in cold white.

Aiden found an elevator, but before he could get in, he heard an instantly recognizable sound coming from down the hall. That familiar tone of Gin Whitmore.

Feeling entirely exposed standing waiting for the elevator, Aiden turned and walked as swiftly as he could get away with, head down, in the opposite direction from the sound of Gin's voice. He reached a corner, turned, and pushed his back against the wall. He thought about activating the AR cloak, but there was no time and no guarantee it would even work.

Cold sweat beaded on his upper lip. Gin's voice grew louder, followed by a raucous laugh from someone else.

"Use the fucking elevator," said the other person.

"I like walking," replied Gin.

"Whatever," said the first. Aiden heard Gin stomp off down the corridor, away from him.

The elevator door pinged, and coming around the corner, Aiden smiled at the man who'd been walking with Gin. Together they entered the elevator. The man offered him a thin smile as a greeting.

"Busy night, huh?" asked Aiden as the doors closed.

"You work here?" asked the man, as if he wanted to wipe Aiden from his shoes like so much dog crap.

"Not if I can help it," said Aiden and elbowed the man hard in the temple. The man fell sideways, landing heavily against the side of the elevator cabin, and Aiden followed up with a hard punch to the man's nose, hearing it crunch under his fist.

Blood splattered out across the man's face and his eyes. He tried to put his hands to his face to staunch the blood, but the first blow had left him disoriented. Aiden stomped on his exposed stomach, which pushed him, breathless, to the floor.

The doors opened, and a woman stood there reading something on a pad. Their eyes met ever so slowly.

Aiden stooped to pick the man up from the floor and, looking embarrassed, said, "He's got a terrible nosebleed. Where's the nearest first aid station?"

For a moment he thought she'd scream, but instead, trembling, she pointed down the hallway.

Spouting whatever effusive bullshit and thanks he could think of, Aiden dragged the groaning man down the corridor in the direction she'd pointed until he heard the elevator doors close. The moment they were alone, he pushed the man up against the wall.

"How many of you fucks are here?"

The man's eyes focused on him and seeing defiance there, Aiden kneed him hard in the groin, holding him up as he tried to neatly fold over.

"Am I going to have to ask again?" he hissed. Aiden dragged him through the top of the building toward the balcony where Scotty should have deposited his kit bag. The fresh air hit him like a blast, the wind suddenly coming cold and hard from a northerly direction.

Wasting no time, Aiden lifted the man up onto his tiptoes and hefted him against the safety railing. "We're several stories up. At best you'll need some of that Wetware you're putting into others."

The man started begging for his life. "I didn't... I didn't... please don't, don't!"

"How many of you are there?" He ground his thumbs into the man's cheek, pushing towards his eyes.

"Thirty," screamed the man.

Aiden almost choked. Thirty? Fuck.

He spotted a bug drone the size of his thumb hovering just the other side of the railing. The drone quickly dropped down inside the railing and hovered above a small package.

Grabbing the man's belt, Aiden punched him twice more and, as the man was spluttering in pain, used it to tie him to the railing. Then he grabbed his bag, found the plastic ties, and secured the man properly.

"Abraham? Is he here?"

The man nodded miserably, his wrists and ankles tight against each other.

"What's the plan?"

The man laughed. Surprised, Aiden stood back and looked at him. "What's so funny?" he asked.

The man shook his head and, with the first ounce of defiance, stared right back. "Fuck you. Tonight is promised to be a night that changes the tide for us! Abraham told us so."

Aiden pulled out his baton and slowly, piece by piece, put it together without saying a word.

When it was assembled, he gave it a couple of exploratory swings through the air before finishing with a third right across the man's face, snapping his head to the side with a gout of blood slicing across the stonework.

"I hate punching people," said Aiden conversationally. "It leaves my knuckles broken and bruised. It was fine when I was thirty – a few days later you'd never know. Now? I'm old and my body hates repairing me after I've gotten fucked up." He poked the man hard in the middle of his chest. "This lets me go for hours."

He smiled as coldly as he could manage.

"Now, I'll ask you again. What's the plan?"

The man hocked up blood and phlegm, spitting in a glob to the side.

Aiden drew his arm back to hit him again. As he did the door opened onto the balcony and Gin came charging out.

She launched through the air, feet first, and Aiden scrambled to the side as she swept past, landing on her feet just the other side of his captive.

"You!" she seethed and lunged for him.

Aiden stepped back, wary of her legs and the power she had at her disposal. Her first punch was short. Aiden leaned back to avoid it. The second was wild, powerful enough to knock him down, but he diverted it. Her punch whistled past his ear.

She was no fighter. A brawler maybe, but no fighter.

Aiden set his feet and brought his hands up, his baton at the ready. Those legs were no joke, but he could manage Gin.

"Abraham's gonna shit his pants when he realizes we got you too." Gin grinned.

Which was news to him. Gin launched a kick at his head. He dove to the side, twisting to get out of the way. Her foot smashed into the stonework and sank in like it was made of gelatin.

Before she could pull her foot free, Aiden punched her in the thigh, hoping to deaden her leg. Instead, Gin stopped as if stunned then started laughing.

"That's what you got, little man?" She pulled her leg free and swept it around too quick for him to avoid. Aiden was flung away, clattering into the safety railing. He grabbed it and hauled himself back to his feet.

A sharp smile of cruelty slashed across her face. She came at him again, another kick bending the rail out of shape when it missed his arm by an inch.

"You have to avoid me every time," she said. "I only have to get you once."

Aiden pulled back, keeping his back to the railing. "Please," he said lightly. "You're all legs and still can't dance."

She snarled and came again. Up against the railing, Aiden waited for the right moment. When she kicked at him, he grabbed her foot and pulled. Off balance, Gin came barreling forward, completely out of control, and with a quick shift of his hands to her shoulders, Aiden hefted her up and over the barrier.

She screamed as she fell.

There was no clump of her body on the ground below. Leaning over to see what had happened, Aiden felt a chill go through him as he saw Gin had landed on her feet and was looking up at him with her expression all kinds of murder.

Another thing those legs are good for, he thought grimly, but Scotty's analysis filled his mind. Such antics from her wouldn't last.

She ran for the building, making it clear it was time he needed to be elsewhere.

The man he'd tied up made the mistake of saying, "She'll come for you."

"I was going to leave you there," said Aiden. "Despite you being a racist piece of shit. How did she know you were here? Can your Wetware communicate?"

The man sneered at him, and Aiden checked his phone, trying to hack into anything the man had available, but there was nothing. The virus still wasn't ready. There was only one thing left to do. He pulled his pistol from the kit bag, wrapped the barrel in the man's winter jacket as he struggled, and shot him in the heart.

"On second thought I'm going to take Scotty's word for it and kill every single one of you."

Aiden checked if he'd been noticed, but no lights shone his way. No drones pounced down from the roof or clambered their way up from underneath the balcony. He couldn't do this kind of thing – barreling through looking for a fight. Bloodshed never served him well. He needed to get back to his basics and infiltrate in a stealthy way. The only problem was Gin would have told the other Stripes he was here.

Aiden let himself back into the building and hurried for shelter, looking for the hidden offices used by senators. A quick glance at his phone indicated the virus still wasn't ready.

A scan of the State of the Union's attendee list told him that one of the senators from Washington State was still at home, meaning his offices were empty. Aiden found a room number, H.334, associated with the senator's name. Aiden started searching. The numbers on the floor were out of sequence, but there wasn't anything approaching the address he sought in the Senate wing. With one eye repeatedly glancing over his shoulder, he rushed down a series of winding corridors into the main hall. H.333 was next to H.326, because of course it was.

However, the map he'd downloaded, from about twenty years prior, showed that he could get to the office he wanted through H.333. Aiden tried the door and found it was locked the old-fashioned way – with an actual key.

It took him about thirty seconds to pick it – the lock wasn't designed to provide more than a barrier to prevent being disturbed.

Once inside he ignored the desks, chairs, and bookcases as he crossed the room to the only other door and, turning the handle, let himself in.

The room smelled of furniture polish and dust. Despite the sense of neglect, the furniture was antique and expensive. His gaze landed on a glass-fronted drinks cabinet with whiskeys, bourbons, and brandies that cost more than Jordi had spent on all the drones put together. The senator from Washington State liked hardwood and harder drink.

Buried within the heart of the Capitol Building, the office had no windows. A digital screen on one side blinked into life with a view of a cold northern beach. Given the view, Aiden guessed it was somewhere in the Puget Sound.

"Thank you, senator," Aiden whispered to himself as he used the network connection to introduce himself to the Capitol's network.

Creating himself a super user engineer's access, Aiden brought up news feeds, and with those in the background, he went searching for the building's security camera network.

It took him longer than he wanted, but about twenty minutes later he had access to the system and was scrolling through footage. He wiped any evidence of himself from the footage being uploaded into a cloud server, and then shifted the cameras so that they no longer focused on the dead Stripe. From there, he found the record of after he'd tipped Gin over the balcony and scanned for her presence.

There she was. He'd hoped she hadn't been able to get into the building once she was outside. Except, to his horror, he watched as she waited by one of the smaller access doors for a few minutes and then two men dressed as Secret Service opened the door from the inside and beckoned her in. That answered the question of how Blake had got thirty people into the building.

The three of them moved inside, and Aiden was forced to tag the agents' own hardware using his profiler to keep track of them. Now that he knew where they were, he needed to find them and disable their communications in the event the Secret Service was pivotal in enacting the Stripes' plan.

Can't live forever, he thought, as he left the room, knowing the fuse was lit. Whatever happened now, he was in the endgame. The camera feed played silently on his phone.

The agents, together with Gin, had come up to the third floor and were on the move. Aiden assumed the other Stripes were there, too. If it were him, he'd have gone straight to Abraham or Blake to inform them about Aiden being on site, but he couldn't rule out Gin doing something stupid like gunning for him instead of sharing her intelligence.

Working on the assumption she was competent, Aiden closed in on the agents who seemed to be meandering but were more than likely waiting for other Stripes to usher into the House Chamber.

He finally came upon them in the gallery level of the Statuary Hall, which opened via a large hallway directly into the House Chamber. At some point in the next few hours the president herself would walk this way and on into the House Chamber to make her speech.

Aiden assumed the plan was to assassinate her in public after Blake was selected as Veep but still before Congressional confirmation. If the Stripes had selected Secret Service agents on their side, the scope for what they could achieve was so much worse than if they tried an armed insurrection – no matter how well prepared they were, they'd still be fighting the government. If there were allies among the Secret Services, then they'd only need to hold the House long enough to enact whatever else they wanted to do.

Which was the big question.

If the president was dead and Blake could be pinpointed for her murder, would he still be able to ascend to the presidency?

The answer was no, but Aiden knew it wouldn't slow Blake

down. The man was a capable speaker, and the president lived on the other side of the political divide. Hundreds of thousands, if not millions, of Americans would stand up for him no matter what he did – even if he decided to enact a coup here and now. If Abraham killed the president, then Blake would insist his grievances were reasonable and needed to be listened to, using certain Stripes as willing sacrifices to set up their personal agenda. He might even condemn Abraham to capitalize on what had happened.

There were few circumstances that Aiden could see in which Blake was served justice.

Well, he would do his best.

The agents, a thickset man and an extremely tall woman, were bent over, looking down into the hall.

"Excuse me," said Aiden, approaching them.

They turned around, looked him up and down.

"Sorry to bother you," he said, trying to look nervous, biting his lip and wringing his hands.

"What is it?" asked the woman with a flat Midwest accent.

"I was in the central building and saw one of the other cleaners picking a lock. I think? It looked suspicious. Should I call ICE?"

The two agents stood up straight, their bodies suddenly stiff and ready for action. "Where were they?"

"Follow me," said Aiden.

"No," said the woman, putting a hand on his shoulder. "We'll handle it."

"They're over near H.333," Aiden said.

The agents exchanged glances, and Aiden gave them a few moments head start, then followed. He was already in their headsets and could hear their chatter; inane, procedural, damning. These two had let in Gin and who knew how many other Stripes, yet carried on as if they were a legitimate and trusted resource. If he hadn't seen it all before, Aiden might have been incensed. As they approached the room, guns out but pointed at the floor, Aiden couldn't even muster the effort to be disappointed as he cut their link to the Capitol's network. There'd be no calling for help.

The woman, Harris, crouched at the door and he heard her say to her partner, "Someone's picked the lock."

"Supposed to be empty, yeah?"

"One of ours?"

"Everyone of importance is already in place."

They opened the door in a flash of movement, pushing into the room as if expecting to find half a dozen armed intruders. Aiden got near enough to follow them inside and then close the door behind him.

"There's no one here…" the male Secret Service agent said.

Aiden slammed the side of the man's head with his baton, releasing the electric charge in a sizzle of air. The man jerked and fell sideways.

The woman managed to turn halfway around, her eyes wide, before Aiden kicked her in the back, sending her sprawling against the liquor cabinet. The bottles rattled.

She tried to turn back around and fire at him. Aiden leapt through the air, smashing the hand holding her gun and knocking it across the floor.

"You won't get away with this," she said as he clubbed her in the face and discharged the second of his six stun charges right into her nose. Harris juddered and stopped moving.

It wouldn't keep them down long, but they'd feel like three-day old shit when they woke. He checked the time and realized that it would be two hours before the speech kicked off. He hoped they wouldn't be recovered by then to start searching for him.

He stripped every piece of tech off them, crushing it underfoot. None of it would be helpful to him. He dragged them both into the corner of the room, then bound and gagged them.

"Scotty," he said through his earpiece. "You there?"

"You got the kit bag?"

"Easy," said Aiden.

"Looked like you had to scramble for it from where I was watching," replied Scotty. "Sure you don't need me down there?"

"Hold back on the distraction until I say – things aren't quite what I thought they'd be," Aiden said, ignoring Scotty's request.

"What changed?" said Scotty.

"There're thirty of Abraham's Stripes here, but these two Secret Service agents are legit, and I caught them helping Gin in after I showed her the door the first time."

After a pause, Jordi's voice cut into the communication. "You can still get out. No shame in not wanting to go up against thirty tech-enhanced humans."

"What, and miss working out who the racist traitors are?"

Blake's GPS started moving.

"Crap," said Aiden. "Gotta go. Our favorite senator's on the move."

The idea that Blake would slip beyond his reach when he'd come so close clutched at Aiden's heart.

He ran across the main hall and into the House wing to try to catch Blake, but he was too late. The dot representing Blake strode across the second floor, out of the Statuary Hall and into the House Chamber on the far side.

But Blake wasn't in the grand auditorium itself. Members of Congress were already seated, while aides, secretaries, and assistants scuttled around in preparation in case anyone required anything. Aiden watched as Blake went to the balcony above the main area.

Aiden rushed through, slinking low to the ground in the event he was seen, but holding his security service pass tightly in his hand in case anyone challenged him. He had to be careful not to be seen.

Aiden dipped his cap to hide his face better and hugged the blue papered walls that ran along the outside of the chamber's balcony. There were doors every seven or eight seats, but handrails meant he couldn't slip along without walking down and then going back up the short flights of stairs which gave access to the banked rows of seats.

Besides, the balcony was half full of people – some coming and going, others sitting in small huddles talking in whispered conversation. Blake greeted some of them, shook hands, and spoke in hushed tones to certain individuals.

Aiden couldn't see anything except potential supporters for Blake, but he anticipated that Blake's colleagues weren't in on what was coming beyond the need-to-know basis. Conspiracies worked when the circle of trust was small.

He was certain Blake's supporters from the fundraiser had no idea what he really had planned. The only ones who knew? The Stripes – Blake, Abraham, Gin, and their cohort waiting no more than a hundred feet away from where he now stood. Blake nodded his head to them. Gin scanned the balcony, as if searching for him.

Aiden ducked further down behind the chairs and checked his phone, sure the virus would be live by now. But no such luck. He gritted his teeth, looking for what he could do next.

He used his phone to zoom in and spotted that Blake, Gin, and Abraham each wore lapel pins with the Stripes logo on it. So close to the official flag most people wouldn't even see the difference, but Aiden knew what he was looking for.

Armed with that knowledge, he used his profiler to set up a scan of the entire room and found fifteen other pins. Some were on aides and others on suits working on the chamber floor, but eight of them were up in the balcony, on the other side to him and around the pronged end of the horseshoe-shaped edge, where Blake stood. It left as many again unaccounted for. Had they all been let into the building or were they still outside?

Aiden hunkered down and logged back into the security cameras covering the outside of the Capitol Building. He ran the same code he'd used inside the hideaway room, but the results came back negative – no additional pins or logos identified.

"Scotty?" he whispered.

"I'm here," came the response.

"I need control of the flying bugs."

"What's going on?"

"Do it now," said Aiden, glancing around the room.

Scotty didn't say anything, but the bugs blinked into Aiden's VR, small dots overlaid on a larger top-down map of the area. Aiden fed them the code he was using and sent them on a hunt and detect mission to locate the others wearing the pins. It was entirely possible they were inside, but his gut told him the other fifteen guests were waiting outside to intercept anyone who might come to help when events started to go down.

Thirty people with Leech's Wetware was more than enough to secure the Capitol long enough for Blake to take control. Now, Aiden was absolutely convinced Abraham would be the one doing the killing – allowing Blake to claim he was an innocent, perhaps even heroic, bystander as his own people took down the president. After all, Abraham had sent out the livestream, garnering his flock of gatherers. No better way to make a martyr.

There was a tap on his arm. It was a larger woman with sharp eyes and a friendly expression.

"I'm sorry, I think that's my seat?" She gestured where he was huddled.

Of course the seats were all allocated. The president was making the biggest political speech of the year.

"So sorry," he said with a smile and gave way for her. She settled down in the seat, pulled a thermos from her tote bag and glanced in his direction. "I always bring supplies. There's no way I could hold on until the end. Don't forget to take your hat off. Out of respect."

He tapped his brim. "Thank you for the reminder." Then, he slunk back into the shadows to plan his attack.

CHAPTER TWENTY-TWO

There was a lot of pomp and ceremony before the president arrived.

No one disturbed Aiden. Being in the Hall gave him a kind of permission no one bothered to challenge, and he found dozens of others did the same, standing in the spaces between banks of seats, sitting on stairs, leaning on railings, all with the intent of seeing the speech live. For all the formal dress, the security, the sense they were at the heart of things, the place was buzzing with excitement.

The Hall's blue carpet was hidden by the sheer number of bodies on the floor of the chamber. Four hundred and thirty-five representatives. A hundred senators. That was without counting the aides and other officials.

For Aiden it was useful even if also a nightmare. If the Stripes acted there was no way he could reach them to intervene – the crowd would take minutes to thread through the exits under normal circumstances. The range to deploy the virus was no more than fifteen feet. If the civilians in the room were panicked all bets were off.

The room grew warm and humid as the bodies crowded in. It was clear the woman with the thermos wasn't the only person to have prepared for a long wait, and Aiden slowly grew as hungry as he was nervous.

His injuries from the car crash were mostly on the mend. His ribs still ached, but he'd gotten away with severe bruising. Still, as his sore feet reminded him, standing for several hours was not his idea of fun.

Aiden wiped beads of sweat from his brow. A similarly solitary man off to his right offered him a chocolate cookie which he took with awkward thanks.

"No hats," said the man. "It's the tradition. Disrespectful to wear a hat inside."

Aiden eyed him. "Second time I've been told that."

"First time?" the man asked.

"For so much," said Aiden and checked his phone. "I didn't expect all these people."

"Oh, it gets unbearable," said the man. "You think it's hot now? Wait until the president arrives. It'll be like Texas in July."

The drinks people had made a lot more sense now.

Aiden considered his options. The balcony was built like a theater. He could dart out one of the many doors and go around the outside if he needed to get closer to Abraham quickly, but each door now had security guarding it. The risk of being unable to get back inside was too high. He still needed to get fifteen feet away from the Stripes without being detected. He maneuvered through the crowd as best he could.

Half an hour from when the president was due to arrive, Abraham's people shifted. As he watched he realized he was looking at the two agents he'd secured earlier. They were accompanied by a couple of others and were talking urgently to Abraham.

Aiden slipped into VR and activated his profiler; the entire room was a sea of IDs as nearly everyone networked phones. He slowly tagged each of the agents talking to Abraham as well as each of the Stripes he'd previously identified. He started profiling them, but it was a litany of mundane cruelty and violence, so he concentrated on slowly shunting each of them off the network and into a bridge where he controlled their access to the internet.

He used the time to take stock of their upgrades. Half a dozen of them had prosthetic arms and legs. A couple chest plates. And yet, their Wetware was nothing like Scotty's. He scanned Senator Blake and was surprised to discover the senator had his own augmented additions: an upgraded skeletal frame along with a bulletproof plate across his chest, arms, and legs. It seemed like he was now a veritable tank. None of them were close enough to push the virus out to… not that he'd had the all-clear it was ready to go yet anyway. One of the Secret Service agents nudged his elbow, and he began to move into the hallway, and out of the balcony.

Abraham remained a blank slate, his encryption the best of anyone else in the room. Aiden couldn't see any sign of prosthetics, but it was highly likely the man just had excellent shielding from detection.

Aiden sent a chaser to Scotty who said the virus was very nearly done. After that he inserted a trigger in the Stripes' network connections to allow him to cut them off when he felt the time was right.

He watched as the agents retreated and slowly began to make

their way through the crowd, checking people's IDs. They had to be searching for him.

The rest of the Stripes slowly filtered across both the balcony and the chamber until they were spread in groups of ones and twos. Aiden was stiff with tension. He had good cover now, but it wouldn't last long.

Suddenly, the room hushed as if the attendants had agreed ahead of time to all go quiet together. Aiden perked up from where he'd been scanning the locations of the Stripes and the agents when the president arrived from behind the podium and the members of the House greeted her, welcomed her to the chamber, and then officially gave her the floor for her speech.

Aiden's hand tightened around his baton, slung against his coat so no one could see. The Stripes and agents stopped moving. The room fell so quiet he could hear his own breathing.

Hundreds of people strained to listen, and standing before them, holding their attention, smiled the president.

She began to talk, and despite decades of ignoring everything that happened in this room, on this hill, Aiden found he wanted to listen. She spoke of the Union, of the country, and the challenges it faced. She spoke of how she wanted to make the world a better place. The room cheered and clapped as she continued, and then as if moments had passed rather than thirty minutes, she finished by saying, "You're all aware of the turmoil we have faced across both chambers, across the executive and throughout the expanding of the Supreme Court. To that end, and as a sign this country is built on something greater than partisanship, I welcome the new vice president to the chamber. Senator Blake has agreed to join me and work toward a new America, one which, rooted in its history, will look to the future. We look forward to Congress confirming this decision and ushering us into a new era."

The room clapped, and Aiden thought, for the first time, he detected a reluctance in the audience. Numerous pools of people sat stony faced, hands in their laps while others cheered and whooped. The Stripes remained still, but Blake sauntered towards the podium with what looked like a microphone in his hand.

He stopped short of joining the president and turned to face the room no more than fifteen feet directly below Aiden.

"I am humbled," he said with a bright smile. His voice became a drone in the background as Aiden watched the Stripes spreading apart like pollen blown on the breeze. Some filtered down, closer to the edge of the balcony. Others seemed to move around those seated at the bottom of the theater. Meanwhile, Abraham remained on the balcony with Gin.

Aiden's heart crashed against his chest. He wanted to shout, but if he was wrong, he would simply be branded as an enemy. The Stripes would get a free chance in the confusion. His fist clenched tight. He checked his phone. No sign of the virus from Scotty.

"I am humbled and blessed by this chamber," said Blake. "Like the president, I believe in the history of this great nation, this greatest of nations. We have a long, proud heritage, a culture going back to the founding fathers. We have strayed from it too often, but now, with the president herself inviting us up and into partnership, we will restore what has been lost even as we shape this great people and give them back their strength." He lifted the mic over his head as the room applauded him.

Aiden's earpiece pinged. "One virus ready for use," said a happy sounding Scotty.

"Where's Jordi?" he asked even as he brought his phone up and watched it download to him.

"Thanks to you, too," said Scotty. "He's gone, Aiden. Left about half an hour ago."

Aiden sighed, his eyes on the room. "You were supposed to go with him," he said.

"Your virus wasn't done compiling. What was I supposed to do?"

Blake was still speaking. Aiden could see the president looking down at him, her expression frozen, blankly smiling while her eyes were full of trouble.

This wasn't the script, he thought. Blake should be up there next to her, meekly accepting her magnanimity. Perhaps Blake's original plan wasn't going to work out the way he'd thought. Jordi had confirmed the Speaker was being blackmailed, but it might be possible whatever Congress members were getting the same treatment fought back. It seemed that Blake was going in a different direction, one that stripped off the gloves and took power no matter what the cost. The senator was committed now and there was no going back.

Whatever shadow of flame and violence was coming stood at the edge of the stage ready to make its entrance.

Blake lowered his microphone back to his mouth. "I do not come alone. There's a reason I stand here today and not the Old Guard of the party. I represent the future, the dispossessed, those too scared to speak their minds for fear of discrimination or losing their jobs or being hounded out of roles they've stewarded faithfully for all their lives. I speak for police officers, for rank-and-file soldiers. I speak for teachers fed up with abiding by forced curriculum standards, for doctors forced to treat those who've truly put themselves beyond deserving medical care. I speak for those of us who think the country can be run better. The question is …" he continued.

Behind him, Aiden saw panic in people's faces. Someone had tried to cut his amplification, but Blake wasn't relying on them for his mic.

He's prepared for this, has been preparing for this for a long time, thought Aiden. Blake wasn't going to play by the rules. Maybe he never planned to in the first place. The virus was still downloading and almost complete. Hurry, he urged it.

He connected back to the building's network and cut the amplification at source, denying Blake access to the systems that delivered the speakers as well as cutting him off from streaming his speech directly to viewers or those using earpieces to listen in.

Blake kept speaking even as his voice dropped away to nothing. He looked at his mic, frowning before tapping it with his free hand then glancing right up at Abraham and Gin for an explanation.

Aiden cut their connection just as the Stripes began to frantically work out what was going on. Seeing their panic felt fantastic.

Throwing the mic onto the ground Blake raised his arms and shouted, "Since you mean to stop me taking my rightful place, we shall begin this and continue as we were meant to."

Aiden squeezed past the person in front of him and headed for the rail. He brought the speakers back online as dozens of people around the room stepped forward, donning Stripe masks. "They're going to kill the president," he projected into the theater. "Everyone get out now!"

Fear and panic exploded just as Stripes across the Hall lifted weapons into sight.

The president was grabbed by three agents and pulled to the ground. A gunshot punched through the air where she'd been standing a fraction of a second before. Whoever was firing tried a second and third time, hitting one of the agents shielding the president. They returned fire.

"Step aside," Blake shouted at the agents, ignoring the people tearing for the doors. Aiden withstood the people barging past him. Blake was too far from him, and he pushed to get closer to Abraham to release the virus.

"Scotty," he said.

"It's time. I'm watching it live."

"Good," said Aiden, glancing around to see where the cameras might be. At least now they could see the Stripes for what they were, but it still put Aiden's own identity at risk.

Baton it was then. Aiden put his cap on, located the nearest Stripe to him and found one not ten feet away on the balcony. He moved forward and deployed the virus, but if the Stripe had any kind of specific Wetware, it didn't hamper him much. Aiden grimaced and struck the man behind the knees with the baton. The man shrieked and finally seized up, collapsing to the floor.

A nearby man screamed. Aiden ignored him until the spectator tried to tackle him and Aiden was forced to flip the man onto his back using his own weight against him. Aiden realized that all anyone would see was a man in a cap attacking people. They might even assume he was working with the Stripes.

Watch Dogs

If he didn't move fast, they'd overwhelm him. His chance to save the president would be gone. He looked to his phone, hoping the virus would do more damage against those like Gin and Abraham. From a quick diagnostic, the Stripe he'd attacked only had a chest plate. Not much that would stop him, unless Aiden was hitting it directly with the baton.

Looking up, Aiden cursed. He'd lost sight of Gin and Abraham. A scattering of agents on the ground were returning fire and heading towards those who had Stripes' masks on, but they were outnumbered. One of the Stripes threw people around like they were dolls. Another jumped down from the balcony, landing like they were taking a stroll, and punched right into one of the president's security detail, sending them sprawling.

Aiden pushed to the edge of the balcony and saw Blake holding a pistol in his hands. Ahead of the other Stripes, he strode towards the same door through which the agents were bundling the president.

"Help me!" Blake cried out and an agent ran for him. The senator allowed himself to be pulled towards the president as if he too were being rescued.

"Scotty, send the drones in now. Have them engage with those Stripes who remained outside as well as any security forces inbound now the alarm's been raised. We can't have them interfering," said Aiden, leaning over the balcony, trying to get a clear view of Blake.

Blake got near the president, but then one of the agents saw his pistol and tried to stop him. Blake moved quicker than any normal human, surging forward and grabbing the agent before flinging them through the air.

As he did so he shouted about protecting the president. The cameras watching would only see him fighting to protect the president, not kill her.

A second agent raised their gun, but Blake spun around and snatched the gun from their grasp.

Aiden watched, momentarily stunned. He needed to get down to the ground floor and now. He was too far away to deploy the virus. Aiden pushed through the thinning crowd and ran back to the stairs, the sounds of melee and gunshots rattling in his ears. He emerged onto the ground floor of the chamber, darting between clusters of people fighting for their lives. The moment he was within range, he located Blake's ID and spiked his augments with the virus.

Please work, he thought, thinking of the man with the chest plate. Please don't fail me.

Nothing happened.

"It's not working," said Aiden, despair and terror lancing through him.

The newly minted so-called vice president saw Aiden and gave him an award-winning smile. There was no one left between him and the president.

The president looked terrified even as an aide fumbled unsuccessfully with the door to get her to safety. No other agents arrived to help.

But then, as Blake approached her, he stumbled.

"The drones have engaged," said Scotty suddenly in Aiden's ear, sending Aiden a link to a livestream. Aiden minimized both it and the comms chatter to better concentrate. He reached for his baton. If he had to, he'd take Blake out like this.

Blake stepped forward like a wind-up toy whose spring had unwound.

Hope sprang in Aiden's chest. Was it working? He hoped the virus would brick Blake's whole system, leaving him immobilized until a confession could be extracted from him.

Blake's body shuddered and then jerked. Aiden pulled up the diagnostics on his phone, scanning the senator and seeing the upgraded skeletal frame being attacked with Aiden's designed virus – bricking the skeleton's motions and interfering with its communication with the blood and bone organic material. Aiden detected that Blake was fighting back – perhaps with some software from Abraham – yet it was nowhere as advanced as Aiden's virus.

"Scotty, what's happening here?" Aiden asked and quickly described what he was seeing.

"The communication between Wetware and organic seemed to be overloading both. It sounds like the senator is going into organ failure due to excitotoxicity – a buildup of chemicals turning toxic in the muscles and bloodstream, making his neurotransmitters lead to cell and nerve death," Scotty replied.

"The virus is inadvertently killing him," Aiden said. He'd wanted Blake to pay for everything that he'd done… hell, he'd made it a mission to take Blake out himself at one point. But if Blake died, it might have drastic effects for the innocents who used the Wetware. Plus, it wouldn't give the public understanding of everything that Blake had done and how much of a traitor he was. They might need Blake to confess. He couldn't become a martyr, either.

Aiden started shuffling subroutines around to have it shut down all non-essential prosthetics quickly and leave everything else alone. But it seemed that he'd unleashed a beast that could not be contained. Blake fell to his knees, his body twitching and spasming. He tried to stop whatever countermeasures Blake had launched against the virus, but the two seemed to be competing, with the virus overriding any other systems. The augmentation began to shut down, which Aiden knew was integrally tied to the senator's lungs and heart and bloodstream.

"Scotty, how fast does this... internal poisoning take effect?" Aiden asked, his voice panicked. "He's seizing. I can't get the virus to stop. He has a countermeasure that's fighting back."

"There's nothing you can do," Scotty said, sounding firm. "Like I said, the Wetware doesn't take into account what it does to the body's natural systems."

Senator Blake crashed to the floor, motionless.

CHAPTER TWENTY-THREE

The sound of automatic gunfire shattered Aiden's shock at watching the senator pass. He now understood the limits of his virus – if the Wetware was integrated in a life-changing way, it could very well mean the death of those he used it against. He'd have to be careful.

Three of the Stripes had managed to get to the front of the balcony with assault rifles and from there were firing indiscriminately down into the chamber. Most of the members of Congress and their aides had fled, and it seemed that this was a distraction more than anything.

Aiden had lost sight of Gin and Abraham entirely.

Raising a pistol lost on the floor, he shot the first of the Stripes. The other two tried ducking.

Bad news for you, thought Aiden. He ran for the stairs ahead of them. He could either direct his virus and hope they didn't have a countermeasure installed like Blake, or he could fire on them. He deployed the virus and watched the remaining two stumble to the ground, their legs locked as if suddenly made of wood.

His earpiece pinged as another Stripe's tag moved toward

him. The balcony was largely deserted now, which meant Aiden could fight freely without others getting hurt, but he wasn't eager to go up against someone with Leech's Wetware in their bones.

A quick scan showed him this was the last Stripe on the balcony. Abraham and Gin must have fled the moment it went sideways. It seemed many of the Stripes had abandoned their posts.

I need to catch them, he thought, before focusing again on the approaching Stripe.

Overlapping the approaching Stripe's progress to a map of the room, Aiden realized he had the drop on them. He stood up and deployed the virus, watching as the Stripe fell down and didn't get back up again.

Aiden scanned for any other Stripes, but nothing else pinged beyond motionless shapes. He widened his scope, seeing a couple of those tagged running outside the main chamber and nearing the exit. He hoped it was Abraham or Gin, but Aiden knew he had to stop the Stripes once and for all. The tag didn't indicate any sort of augmentation, so Aiden assumed it had to be Abraham.

Aiden would have loved to believe that without Blake, Abraham was no longer a danger. But even were it true, he wasn't letting the bastard escape. After all, there were at least fifteen of his augmented followers as well. Aiden hoped that with the Stripes' attempted coup streamed live to the nation, hundreds of other racist militia groups wouldn't take the initiative and be busy making havoc in their own small parts of the world.

He needed and wanted to take Abraham down now.

"Scotty. Any drones you can spare. I'm going to send you what I believe is Abraham's location. Stop him if you can. Then get out of there like you should have done an hour ago. It's going to get really hairy soon."

"The drones are already gone," said Scotty.

And agents loyal to the United States were, at last, establishing control. Aiden could get out and pursue the rest of the Stripes before they caused more havoc and chaos. He burst out of the chamber following the tags for the Stripes, which were scattered, except for a clump of them heading west.

He was buried in his phone when he ran into a woman with her face streaked with tears. "Did you see what happened? Is the president still alive?" she demanded.

"She's alive," he told the woman, and the relief in her face was everything.

"I saw where those people with the striped masks went," she said, pointing down the hallway. "I think they said they were headed for the Lincoln Memorial."

"Thank you," he said and started running.

"I'll make sure people know you helped us!" the woman shouted from behind him. "Keep your cap on!"

"Watch out for those hiding in plain sight," he shouted back.

He burst outside. In the sky overhead helicopters and dozens of drones hovered over the Capitol Building. He wondered if the city had been put in lockdown.

He tried pinging for his own drone network, but there was no response from any of the flying bugs. The Secret Service was beginning to secure the area, and the first part of that was locking down the airspace around the Capitol. He was on his own.

Aiden came around the south side of the Capitol Building and ran for the Garfield Monument. He accessed a motorcycle and leapt on it, rushing ahead toward the Lincoln Memorial.

The first couple of Stripes' tags pinged just ahead. The tag he thought was Abraham was already at Union Square. Instead of engaging them, he slowed and got close enough to fire the virus in their direction. He watched with satisfaction as the two of them, both men, slowed to a halt, one of them screaming about his arm, the other simply falling to the ground convulsing. Two more who were done for, and they'd be picked up by very angry intelligence agents soon enough.

Lucky, Aiden thought, balancing back on the bike. Something like that wouldn't happen again.

Other tags had formed a line up ahead. They'd arranged themselves into an inverted V-shape, defensive, like they knew he was coming.

Aiden kept rattling through his options to keep Abraham from getting further ahead. The soft pad of rubber came alongside him, and he saw one of the combat drones keeping pace. Its side opened up, and out came a snub-nosed machine gun.

"Thought you could use the help," said Scotty into his earpiece.

"I thought you'd gone," said Aiden.

"I'm well and clear," came the response.

Aiden grabbed the offering and stopped the bike. If he wanted to use the virus on these, he wanted to ensure he was the right distance away and in no danger of crashing. The drone ran ahead and leapt right into the middle of the five Stripes waiting for him. Bodies tumbled but not as quickly as he'd hoped, and although two of the five were suddenly very concerned about the drone the other three detached from the melee and came to meet him.

The first of them swung for his head, and Aiden ducked underneath, letting the virus hop onto each of them, and then he struck his first attacker, a huge man with an equally huge beard, around the back of the knees.

Stepping past the sprawling man, Aiden was in turn hit hard on the shoulder, spinning him around and leaving him scrabbling to stay on his feet.

A second punch nearly smashed his face in, but he ducked back just in time. The third of the Stripes had metal hands and determined eyes. Aiden was sure they'd crush his skull if they could.

Aiden ducked back from the first attack, ready to deploy the virus, but the metal-handed attacker was too fast and grabbed Aiden around the throat. His phone slipped from his grasp and landed on the ground. But the grip didn't squeeze. It was as if his hands were frozen. The second attacker was frozen, too, whatever Wetware was inside him bricked. Aiden pushed the metal hands off him, grabbed the bike, and started to speed away, watching the tags pass the National Gallery of Art and then down past the Washington Monument. Two miles felt like a lifetime.

At one point, he saw police officers wrestling and fighting with Stripes. The Stripes were beating the crap out of them, taking on three or four each, but they were heavily outnumbered. He paused and deployed the virus, watching as one of the Stripes seized up while the other one was taken out by the other forces.

He tried to pass around them but ran into two drones coming

the other way. The first of them had a camera mounted on its back and a voice said, "Stop and identify yourself."

Aiden pushed his baton onto one of them and discharged the stun round. The drone shuddered then collapsed. The other scuttled back and zoomed away into the air.

In the distance, Abraham's tag continued moving, but Aiden realized that one of the police officers that he'd helped had spotted him. The officer held his hands up and out as if making peace. "You're him, right? The Vigilante?"

How did the officer know that? He expected to be arrested, and his eyes looked not at the police officer but the direction in which Abraham was escaping.

"Go," said the officer, bending down to pick up Aiden's phone and hand it to him. "We've had a bulletin. You won't be stopped. Not tonight."

Aiden forced a lungful of air into his body and started his bike up again. Could it have been Leech? She was the only one who would know he was there, hunting down the Wetware and the Stripes.

He zipped alongside the reflecting pool. The sounds of sirens and helicopters filled the night air. Ahead, Abraham's crew was just half a dozen now. Most of the others had escaped in different directions or were currently involved in running battles with what remained of the Capitol's loyal law enforcement units.

With the Memorial in sight, Aiden slowed as he realized Abraham's tag had stopped. Aiden killed the bike and jumped off it, running up the steps. Abraham Lincoln's face stared the Stripe leader down from behind.

"You just won't give up, will you?" said Abraham from the stairs.

"Not until you're fucking dead," said Aiden, raising his gun.

Abraham laughed. "Me?" He waved a hand dismissively in Aiden's direction, and all the remaining Stripes came down the steps.

One of them raised an assault rifle. Aiden dove to one side but he couldn't move faster than a high velocity round, and he was punched backward as shots slammed into his torso. His machine gun went flying across the floor.

Light and dark spun in Aiden's vision as he fell. He couldn't breathe. Immediately, he wondered if his phone was broken, and the virus gone for good. The sounds of approaching Stripes slowed as if they were trying to work out just how badly he was injured.

To Aiden's surprise, he wasn't dead. Better still, although his lungs hurt like he'd just been run over by a rhinoceros, Jordi's armor had held up.

He rolled over, expecting to get shot again the very next moment. His hands clawed for his phone, dragging the black square over to him. With clumsy fingers, he punched at the phone's menu. The Stripes were close enough to him. He could take them out, if only his vision would stop spinning.

As things finally came into focus, he saw that the Stripes had him surrounded. It was then he saw Gin, one hand bunched up in a fist smacking into her other, open hand.

"He's mine," she said, and the others backed away.

Abraham watched from the steps with eyes glittering in the dark.

Aiden dusted himself down and got to his knees. "You want my head, is that it?" His chest really hurt, and his left eye wanted to close up and not open again.

"I want to hold your head in my hands and have everyone remember you are nothing except some woke cuck who got what they deserved," she replied.

"Go woke, go broke!" someone in the ring shouted.

Gin grinned like she was going to bite a chunk out of him and came forward.

Aiden ripped out his baton and met her charge point on, pressing the baton right into the nape of her neck and discharging it for the final time.

Gin ignored his attack like he'd hit her with a cotton ball and, grabbing him by the front of his jacket, headbutted him hard. His nose cracked. Blood burst across his face.

Gin threw him to the ground. Aiden groaned, his hands still scrambling for his phone and protecting the device from being shattered or destroyed.

"You ruined everything, you know? And even with it all up in flames, we're still going to win," she said.

"Miss Whitmore, if you'll please hurry it up," called Abraham from beyond the ring of legs surrounding Aiden.

Aiden got to one knee and looked for her next attack. If she kicked him in the head, he was done for.

Thing is, he thought blearily at her, I have weapons you don't know about yet. He used his AR overlay to select as many of the Stripes as he could and hit the deployment. The moment he took to send the virus was enough for Gin to pick him up in a bear hug and start squeezing.

"You killed my friends," she said. "They deserved to live a hundred times more than you."

He felt the air squeeze out of his lungs as his ribs ground together in his chest. The indicator on his VR turned green as the virus uploaded to each of those around him, including Gin.

Suddenly, the pressure eased off around him. "What are you doing?" she hissed.

He smiled and spat in her face.

She dropped him to the ground, her arms suddenly slack at her side. Around him, the ring of Stripes jerked and stuttered as if controlled by an electrocuted puppet master.

Aiden rolled away from her reach and, finding his machine gun on the floor, pulled it up and shot her in the chest. She collapsed on the ground.

Spitting blood onto the slabs of the Memorial, he looked for Abraham as one by one the Stripes slowed to a stop like robots whose batteries had run out.

Abraham ran down the other side of the Memorial, his feet slapping against the stone.

Aiden had had quite enough of all this and blasted the virus at Abraham as he struggled to keep up. Yet, somehow, either Abraham reached the limits the virus could deploy, or he had some other kind of countermeasure. Aiden grimaced and ran after him. He hit the deployment again, but nothing happened.

Abraham had none of Leech's Wetware in his body. And he'd left his gun back behind him with Gin's body.

The sound of heavy bikes roared around him, making Abraham stop and turn, folding his arms as bright lights covered the Memorial.

"It's too late," Abraham crowed. "You've done me harm, and you've done this nation harm."

Aiden pointed at him. "I'd say the same about you."

"You know the difference between us?" asked Abraham.

"No, but I'm sure you're going to tell me," said Aiden, stalling for time.

"The difference is I have friends, family. You? You're all alone."

Which is a good point, thought Aiden, looking at the dozen or so bikers waiting on either side of Abraham, armed with their own firepower. Some of them dismounted and started walking toward Aiden.

"Scotty, if you're listening, get the hell out, OK?" Aiden said into his earpiece. "I'm not going to make it. You deserve better than the life I've had." He stared at the bikers and hoped he said his last words to silence, and that Scotty had gotten away. "It's too lonely. We're not built for it. In the end, it brings us down. Family doesn't survive what we do."

"Kneel," said one of the bikers.

"Never," said Aiden.

"Fine by me," said the biker and, as he got to about six feet away, raised his military grade repeating shotgun so it was level with Aiden's head. "Not so full of it now, are you?"

Aiden refused to close his eyes, determined to look his killer in the face. He recounted his sins, but also his accomplishments. The president was alive. Blake was dead. It wasn't everything he wanted, but it was going to have to do. His nephew drifted into his mind, and he wondered if his final words to Scotty should have been to him instead.

"Look to your right," came Jordi's voice from his earpiece. Aiden dodged without thinking, and the biker's head popped like a grape.

A surge of adrenaline and hope filled Aiden. Another gunshot took out a Stripe further back. Somewhere, Jordi was sharpshooting. Aiden spotted the last of the flying drones divebomb the ground to his side. In the wreckage was a handgun.

He grabbed it as the bikers retreated, trying to locate where the sniper was situated.

Another shot. Another body hitting the ground. The bikers ran and roared away on their bikes, their goal to kill Aiden all but forgotten.

Opening his phone, Aiden deployed the virus to as many targets as he could. Some of them seized and fell. Others managed to get away, too far out of range for success. He focused on the tags on his GPS when a punch to his cheek changed everything. Abraham hit him, and Aiden, blindsided as he'd tried to kill his nearest enemies, hit the ground one more time.

Groaning, blood in his mouth, he tried to level the gun between them.

A foot stomped down on his hand. A spike of fire burned through his fingers as they broke. The gun dropped uselessly.

"Oh, no," said Abraham, yanking Aiden closer to the pillars and seeking cover from Jordi as much as focusing on Aiden lying prone at his feet. "You've ruined everything. It's traitors like you who'll see us destroyed by our enemies."

"Your enemies are on the side of the angels," said Aiden.

"You? On the side of the angels? The Vigilante who's killed countless people just tonight?"

"Never cross a good man," cackled Aiden. "Jordi…" he started, but Abraham kicked him under the chin. Abraham bent over and scooped up Aiden's phone. A gunshot sounded, taking out a chunk of white stone near Abraham's head, but too far away for any damage. Aiden could imagine Jordi cursing.

"We're done here, Pearce. Clever what you've done though. Some kind of locking mechanism that takes out augmentations. I should have figured you'd do something of this kind. Stealth has always been more your style rather than violence." Abraham used Aiden's broken fingers to unlock the phone. "Our time will come, but you won't get to see it. Goodbye." He held a pistol in his other hand and aimed it down at Aiden.

"Freeze," came a voice. It was Scotty, far out of Aiden's field of view. Aiden opened his mouth to scream at Scotty to get away, to run.

Abraham looked up, revulsion on his face. "You're not going to stop me," he said, and with a ghastly smile, raised the phone in Scotty's direction. His thumb pressed on the screen even as the pistol aimed at Scotty simultaneously.

Scotty fired both his arms, and Abraham's face disintegrated. Aiden whipped his head around to see if the virus had enough reach to infect Scotty. Scotty's arms fell slack to his side, and he fell the ground, his thigh darkening with his own blood.

Cracks of Jordi's sniper rifle continued to sound, taking out enemies that Aiden couldn't see.

Finding a reserve of strength, Aiden lifted himself up and scrambled to Scotty's side. Blood welled from his left thigh, and his arms were limp and useless.

"I told you…" he started but couldn't finish.

He scrambled for his phone from the wreckage that had once been Abraham and called Jordi. "We need a safe place. Scotty's been hit by a bullet. I can't tell if the virus got him."

"I'll send you directions. You need to move now," Jordi responded in his ear. "This place is going to be swarmed by government agents in moments."

Aiden did his best to help Scotty up. The two of them stumbled away from the Memorial, following Jordi's directions. Above them, drones and helicopters shone lights on Abraham Lincoln's face and the scattered wreckage of the Stripes' running battle all the way down from the Capitol.

"I feel like my mom running from the rain at a picnic," said Scotty through pained breaths.

"Keep talking," said Aiden, hoping the young man wasn't falling to shock.

"Easier said than done," said Scotty as more gunfire lit up the Memorial. Aiden knew he hadn't gotten all the Stripes, but he hoped the rest of the government agents might.

They made it about half a mile up 23rd St NW when Scotty stumbled.

Aiden tried to lift him up, but Scotty's legs were like soggy noodles. No strength remained in his arms. "I can't manage it," said the younger man. "They're really cold, Aiden, but I feel all hot and tired."

"Let's sit down a moment," said Aiden and the two of them found the pavement in a tangle of indignity. He opened his phone, desperate to run diagnostics to see if the virus was going to do damage to Scotty, and he was briefly thankful he didn't have the time to run a test on Scotty's arms – he had relied on the young man more than once during the battle of the day.

"Jordi, the kid's hurt bad. Reckon the paramedics might be able to come pick us up?"

"Do you want to be that exposed?" Jordi shot back in his earpiece. "He might be considered a Stripe if the authorities see him with the Wetware."

"We have to do something," Aiden hissed as Scotty slumped into him.

"I'll see what I can do, Aiden, but someone shot up the Capitol, if you haven't heard. All eyes are there right now."

"Stay with me, Scotty," Aiden said, but Scotty just let out a soft mumble. His arms were still slack at his sides. Aiden grabbed his phone, determined to do what he could, when a dark SUV came crawling down the street and pulled up right in front of them.

The window rolled down. The vehicle had only one passenger. Leech.

"You should let him go," she said, getting out of the car. "He's dead either way."

Aiden didn't speak.

"Cat got your tongue?" she laughed.

Aiden took his arm from where it had been around Scotty's shoulders to prop him up and said, "Hang in there, kid. This won't take long."

"All I want is the arms," she said as Aiden stood up. "They're government property."

"You can't have them," said Aiden. "We've done what you wanted. We've cleaned up your mess."

"Cleaned it up?" she sneered at him. "A dead senator frozen in place as my Wetware, my above top-secret tech, goes haywire? Dozens more dead, dozens of them with the same tech? You think this is cleaning up? What happens at home, you make an explosion in the microwave then dump it on the floor and call it dinner?"

"That's on you," said Aiden, watching her thumb the pistol at her waist carefully. "You've got the power to clean it all up. You can get back some of your precious Wetware. Hell, harvest it from the senator! Then convene a congressional committee to find out what happened and how Blake got that to begin with. You don't have to worry about being seen as the villain, Leech. After everything that's happened, you don't have to take Scotty. You have enough as it is."

"Questions will be asked," she hissed.

"Cry me a river," said Aiden, talking through the pain of his injured tongue. "Now get out of here before I decide I'll be one of the people answering them."

"You?" she said, and she flashed him a cruel grin. "You'll be wanted for questioning all right. I told you, Mr Pearce, I needed all Wetware returned to me, no matter where it came from."

"You're not taking Scotty," said Aiden.

She raised the gun in his direction. "OK."

"Duck and cover," said Jordi in his ear.

Aiden dropped like a stone. Leech jerked, her face looking surprised. She staggered backward, hitting the car, and looked down at her chest which blossomed red. Aiden looked behind him and saw a red laser sight blink twice in the distance.

"Take her car," said Jordi. "I'll send you coordinates. In spite of everything, Aiden, it's been fun working together again. Even if you have gone soft."

"If I don't hear from you for another three years, that'll be fine," said Aiden and hung up.

CHAPTER TWENTY-FOUR

There was no sign of Jordi at the coordinates he'd sent to Aiden. Aiden pulled into a small townhouse in the west of the city, painted white with large windows and a huge backyard. They were met by a private ambulance with two staff, a lanky southeast Asian lady and a woman who sounded like her ancestors had stepped off the boat from Norway.

They bandaged Scotty up without a word, gave him enough drugs to sedate a horse, and then turned their attention to Aiden.

Full of distrust, Aiden nevertheless let them treat him – his hand had swollen up to the size of a melon. Between tuts, they set the bones, put it in a cast, and warned him to take it easy.

When they were done, they waved away any semblance of payment, and Aiden knew this was another part of Jordi's apology for trying to bail on him.

The two of them hunkered down, during which time Aiden worked on reversing the damage caused to Scotty's arms by his own virus. The only upside being that whatever damage it had done seemed to have destroyed the glitch and the Wetware completely. Now, it just seemed like he had metal attached inside his arms. He expected the police to charge up to the front door at all hours of the day, but no one materialized. No new Leech. No Secret Service. No Stripes.

Nor was there any communication from Jordi.

Soon enough, Aiden got Scotty's arms working again. Scotty cried and hugged Aiden, declaring he wanted to go home.

Aiden couldn't have agreed more. Scotty had saved his life, and without his help, the operation against the Stripes would have been a complete failure. But they needed to stay put until things calmed down. Footage on the news channels continuously showed Aiden's covered face, the cap pulled low over his head, and announced the Vigilante had returned from the dead. Aiden didn't like having such scrutiny back on him. He wondered if he could bargain with Jordi for that passport out of the country, now that everything was over.

Even if he couldn't take down the Stripes completely, he spent his restless nights delving through any information he could find until he pinpointed Abraham's accounts and stole every single cent of his money. The feds had locked most of it down, but investment bank anti-money-laundering functions had been a joke for as long as dirty money had existed, so it wasn't hard to get in and take what he wanted.

By the end of two weeks, Aiden decided they were good to go.

He transferred the money to Scotty, something to keep the young hero comfortable for the foreseeable future, a fact he hoped Scotty wouldn't discover until they'd properly parted company. He didn't want to have to argue about whether it was the right thing to do and, having listened to Scotty talk for days straight, he knew that would be the exact first moral Scotty would question given the opportunity.

When Aiden told him it was time to go Scotty didn't argue. "Thank you," he said to Aiden.

"I was worried you were going to stay," he replied. "Become a fixer. Want to wipe the Stripes from all existence."

Scotty looked uncomfortable. "I think you were right. If I don't go now, I'll lose them. My family. My friends. My whole life. Would be a stupid thing to happen, yeah?"

"I think so," Aiden agreed and handed him a discreet number to call of some fixer contacts they could trust far from DC. "They might be able to fix your arms and remove the Wetware," he said. "No promises. But it's worth a shot."

"Thanks," Scotty said, taking the card. "Take me to the bus?"

Aiden nodded and dropped him off at the station. Just before he pulled away in Leech's SUV, he said, "Keep your head down, kid. Love your family and all that. Christ, Jordi was right. I am getting old."

Scotty smiled and shook his head, pulling his sleeves down and heading into the station.

Aiden tagged the kid, just so he could keep track of him, but hoped, with something approaching what he might have called his heart, never to hear from him.

If they never crossed paths again Aiden would feel like he had, at least in part, repaid Scotty for all he'd done.

FIVE MONTHS LATER

Aiden was asleep in the front seat of his car, cap down to keep the glare from the passing traffic out of his eyes.

A buzzing sound roused him. With a groan, he sat up. His phone showed it was Jordi.

What the hell does Jordi want? he thought with a big sigh. Whatever it was, he'd better pick up.

"Phone's burnt, make it quick," he said.

"Ah, I'm like your one friend, Aiden. You should be nicer to me," said Jordi.

"Great," said Aiden. "I'm hanging up now."

"It's a job, shithead. Fixer gig. I… can't take it. Travel restrictions."

"I told you, I'm not doing that hired gun work anymore," replied Aiden. Was this all Jordi wanted? Why waste his time?

"Oh, come on, it's corporate espionage – scumbags screwing scumbags. No bystanders, huge payday."

"Mmm," said Aiden. "What's the catch?"

"It's in… London. Which is not the easiest place to get to these days."

As Jordi spoke, Aiden glanced at an old picture of his family he'd kept.

"London… that's where Jackson lives." His eyes lingered on the picture, woefully out of date. Jackson had to be an adult now.

"Yeah, why do you think I called you, dipshit?"

"OK, I gotta go," said Aiden. He hung up, ditched the SIM, and started the car.

ACKNOWLEDGMENTS

Gwendolyn Nix is the first person I have to thank. She guided this project from the start and has been supportive and diligent the whole way. She is the definition of a stellar editor. Without Stewart Hotston, this book might have never existed. He really deserves most of the credit. I couldn't have asked for a better coauthor, who just so happens to be represented by the same amazing literary agent, John Jarrold. John, thanks for always being so cheerful and proactive. Paul Simpson has edited most of my published books, and it was so great to have him back to edit *Stars & Stripes*. He knows how to make characters and sentences shine like no other. Marc Gascoigne continues to prove that he's a joy to work with, and I want to thank Nick Tyler and all the other wonderful folx at Aconyte who do some of the best work in publishing. Thanks to Ubisoft for making a great game and trusting me with the direction I took with Aiden Pearce. Everything really is connected...

   – *Sean*

ABOUT THE CO-AUTHORS

SEAN GRIGSBY is the author of the Smoke Eaters series, as well as *Daughters of Forgotten Light*, short fiction printed in places like *Black Library* and *Amazing Stories*, and articles featured on Tor.com. He lives in Arkansas with his wife, Lisa, and their wild but wonderful children.

seangrigsby.com // twitter.com/seangrigsby

STEWART HOTSTON lives in Reading, UK. After completing a PhD in theoretical physics, Stewart now spends his days working in high finance. He has had numerous short stories published as well as three novels, including the political thriller *Tangle's Game*. When not writing or working, Stewart is a senior instructor at the School of the Sword and Team GB member in the HEMA categories of Rapier and Rapier & Dagger.

stewarthotston.com // twitter.com/stewhotston

WORLD EXPANDING FICTION

Have you read them all?

ASSASSIN'S CREED®
- ☐ *The Ming Storm* by Yan Leisheng
- ☐ *The Desert Threat* by Yan Leisheng *(coming soon)*
- ☐ *The Magus Conspiracy* by Kate Heartfield *(coming soon)*

ASSASSIN'S CREED® VALHALLA
- ☐ *Geirmund's Saga* by Matthew J Kirby
- ☐ *Sword of the White Horse* by Elsa Sjunneson

TOM CLANCY'S THE DIVISION®
- ☐ *Recruited* by Thomas Parrott

TOM CLANCY'S SPLINTER CELL®
- ☐ *Firewall* by James Swallow

WATCH DOGS®
- ☑ *Stars & Stripes* by Sean Grigsby & Stewart Hotston

WATCH DOGS® LEGION
- ☐ *Day Zero* by James Swallow & Josh Reynolds
- ☐ *Daybreak Legacy* by Stewart Hotston *(coming soon)*